TOMORROW NEVER COMES

Wings Press, Inc.

Vera Berry Burrows

Tomorrow Never Comes

He had to get away. If he were to prove his worth in this world, he would do it on his own without his mother looking over his shoulder. He would stay at Ben's tonight and start his quest tomorrow. Then he smiled to himself ironically. He recalled what his mother had said about tomorrows, but told himself, "My tomorrow will come. Just you wait and see."

Nell was beside herself. When Joel came downstairs with his rucksack and his guitar strung over his shoulder, a look of complete defiance in his eyes, she pleaded with him to reconsider. She grabbed hold of her little boy and begged him not to go.

"Where will you go? What will you do?" she implored until the tears prevented her from presenting a logical argument for him to stay.

"I'll go to Ben's tonight," he told her. He owed her that at least. "And then I'll decide what I am going to do in my own time."

"But—"

"No buts, Mother." He knew she hated that formal title, but he felt so estranged from her at that moment that any words of endearment would diminish the depth of his true feelings. She had to know he was determined to stand alone on this, and if it meant hurting her feelings in the process, then so be it. He was not falling for the guilt trip thing again. "You have to accept that I am no longer a child," he told her. "I have to demand that you respect my decision this time. I can't stand all this interference and the sooner you realise that, the better." They were strong words aimed at having an impact that should not be taken lightly and Nell felt the full force of his onslaught.

"You're being too sensitive, Joel. You are just like your father—"

"Don't you dare use my dad to make me feel guilty! That's typical of you, Mother. Never your fault. You're always right and woe betide anybody who disagrees with your decision."

When the door slammed in his wake, she dropped to her knees and sobbed. She ought to go after him, but he needed time to calm down, to see the error of his ways. Maybe tomorrow, he'd come back with his tail between his legs, realising she had been right all along. But what had she said about tomorrows?

"Oh God, what have I done?"

Tomorrow Never Comes

He had to get away. If he were to prove his worth in this world, he would do it on his own without his mother looking over his shoulder. He would stay at Ben's tonight and start his quest tomorrow. Then he smiled to himself ironically. He recalled what his mother had said about tomorrows, but told himself, "My tomorrow will come. Just you wait and see."

Nell was beside herself. When Joel came downstairs with his rucksack and his guitar strung over his shoulder, a look of complete defiance in his eyes, she pleaded with him to reconsider. She grabbed hold of her little boy and begged him not to go.

"Where will you go? What will you do?" she implored until the tears prevented her from presenting a logical argument for him to stay.

"I'll go to Ben's tonight," he told her. He owed her that at least. "And then I'll decide what I am going to do in my own time."

"But—"

"No buts, Mother." He knew she hated that formal title, but he felt so estranged from her at that moment that any words of endearment would diminish the depth of his true feelings. She had to know he was determined to stand alone on this, and if it meant hurting her feelings in the process, then so be it. He was not falling for the guilt trip thing again. "You have to accept that I am no longer a child," he told her. "I have to demand that you respect my decision this time. I can't stand all this interference and the sooner you realise that, the better." They were strong words aimed at having an impact that should not be taken lightly and Nell felt the full force of his onslaught.

"You're being too sensitive, Joel. You are just like your father—"

"Don't you dare use my dad to make me feel guilty! That's typical of you, Mother. Never your fault. You're always right and woe betide anybody who disagrees with your decision."

When the door slammed in his wake, she dropped to her knees and sobbed. She ought to go after him, but he needed time to calm down, to see the error of his ways. Maybe tomorrow, he'd come back with his tail between his legs, realising she had been right all along. But what had she said about tomorrows?

"Oh God, what have I done?"

TOMORROW NEVER COMES

Vera Berry Burrows

A Wings ePress, Inc.
Historical Novel

Wings ePress, Inc.

Edited by: Jeanne Smith
Copy Edited by: Karen Babcock
Senior Editor: Pat Evans
Executive Editor: Marilyn Kapp
Cover Artist: Trisha FitzGerald

All rights reserved

Wings ePress Books
https://www.wingsepress.com

Copyright © 2010 by Vera Berry Burrows
ISBN 978-1-59705-560-4

Published In the United States Of America

Wings ePress Inc.
3000 N. Rock Roaqd
Newton, KS 67114

Dedication

This is for my father, William (Billy) Berry, whose untimely death prevented him from sharing all the good things in my life.

One

1970

"Get up, Mother! What a disgusting mess! How long is it since you took a shower?"

Joel regarded her with nothing less than sickening repulsion. He found it difficult to accept that the unkempt, unwashed bundle of rags that was lying on the floor like a mangy dog was his mother, the woman he had long regarded as the self-righteous, supercilious Nell Winston, but just look at her now...

~ * ~

1947

Nell's mind was in turmoil. *Tom had no right to leave me, he had no right,* she thought angrily. *How dare he leave me on my own to bring up our child? I hate it, absolutely hate it.* She burst into tears frequently, sometimes in sorrow, but more often in frustration that she felt weak and hopeless. At first, she went from minute to minute in a daze. She had little interest in anything except her baby. Something from deep inside her soul kept her caring for the child. She couldn't have cared less about anybody else.

Margaret Benson watched her daughter change from a vibrant young woman to a listless individual who no longer had any desire to do all the things she had done before Tom's death. Margaret's efforts to help often fell on deaf ears. After weeks of trying unsuccessfully to guess Nell's mood, she took a deep breath and looked directly into her daughter's eyes. "We could go shopping, or to the theatre," she suggested brightly. "How about we go to Wales or The Lakes for a few days?"

"Mother?" she said unnecessarily harshly. "Those were *our* places, mine and Tom's. How dare you suggest I go there without him? You go if it's so important to you!"

Margaret was momentarily stunned into silence. As Nell's mother, she realised it was going to take a lot of patience and understanding on both their parts. Nell was headstrong, not to mention overtly difficult at times. Margaret understood very clearly that they would have to tread very carefully along the road to recovery. The period of mourning had to take its time.

Nell seemed to exist rather than live. For a while, she didn't feel the need to talk to anybody, and her only words were to comfort Joel when he cried for his feed or for a nappy change. In that respect, she never wavered. Joel was her world, and Margaret uncomfortably observed the very real danger of Nell becoming obsessed with the child. She dared to divert her daughter's attention.

"Nell, dear," she said quietly, "Don't you think you need a little break from the baby? Let me look after him for a little while and you could walk to the shop to buy something nice for tea."

"He's my baby, not yours, Mother, and I'll thank you to stop interfering. I'll look after him and I don't want anybody else to do that for me. What sort of a mother would I be if I handed him over to somebody else every time I wanted to go to the shop?" she asked a shocked Margaret.

"But I'm your mother, Nell, and Joel's granny, not just 'somebody else.' You allowed me to look after Joel when you went to Wales with Tom…"

"Oh, how perceptive of you, Mother," Nell said scornfully. "Trust you to throw that at me. How could you be so thoughtless? You of all people…"

"I'm not being thoughtless, Nell. I'm trying to be helpful. Please think about taking a little break. I promise it will do you good." Margaret's voice was gentle.

"Don't make promises you can't keep, Mother. Nothing will 'do me good,' as you put it. The only thing that will do me good is to have Tom back…" She paused consciously and then continued caustically "…and we all know that's impossible, don't we?"

Frustrated, Margaret stared through her tears. "I don't recognise you anymore, Nell. I don't know you at all." Initially, she had stayed with Nell to help her through her grief, but Nell had donned this unfathomable cloak of bitterness towards her mother and had frequently used her as a verbal punch bag when her anger spilled over. At the same time, she had also used her mother as a pillow when she needed comfort, and most of all, she had used her mother as a crutch to help her take those first faltering steps when her broken life needed to be supported in order to become meaningful again.

"Don't make promises you can't keep," she repeated and pointedly walked out of the room without another word. In her bedroom, she had looked at her medication and sometimes wondered if she dared take the lot, but then the smallest whimper from the cot beside her bed was enough to bring her back to reality.

It must have been a couple of months after Tom's funeral, Nell recalled, when something happened which had to be considered remarkable in the whole scheme of things. She had lain awake for most of the night, staring into the darkness, her eyes heavy through lack of sleep, but she had been unable to shut out her thoughts. At seven months old, Joel had been sleeping in his own room for a week or so, and Nell stretched out her arm to her right, half expecting to feel Tom sleeping by her side. She felt the coolness of the sheets and the emptiness that encapsulated her life. She smoothed the mattress with her hand and turned to face the pillow where Tom's head had rested.

"Tom," she whispered timidly. "Tom?" She sat bolt upright, breathing heavily, but instantly she realised her foolishness. She stopped abruptly, inwardly questioning her own feelings. *You're an idiot, Nell Winston. Why are you calling Tom's name?* she thought. She was incongruously calm. "Just get on with what you have to do," she said audibly and with a determination in her voice that emphasised the seriousness of her quest. "Tom can't hear you. He's gone and you're on your own now. Sort yourself out. You have to do this alone. Tom's gone." She told herself over and over again, "You can do it, Nell. You can do it. Too bloody true you can!"

~ * ~

When she appeared in the kitchen the following morning, she greeted Margaret with an uncharacteristic, modest smile. "Well," Margaret managed to say, fighting back tears of relief, "you'll never know how good it makes me feel to see you smile again."

"I've come to a decision," Nell said pointedly, "I think it's time you went home to Dad. I really can't explain why I should suddenly feel as I do, but I have to get back to normal, well what will pass as normal from now on." Her eyes were set with steely resolve.

Margaret looked at her only daughter, whose face was fixed in cold defiance, and decided instantly that this really wasn't the right time for her to go back to the Wirral. "If you can't explain how you feel, how can you make such a decision? I'll stay a little longer, love, just until you're absolutely certain you can cope on your own."

"No, Mum, don't. I'm determined..."

"Oh, you're certainly that," Margaret interjected light-heartedly.

"Don't interrupt, Mother," Nell continued undeterred. "I'm determined to stand on my own two feet. I need to sort out my life and Joel's." Her tone was confident, but when she noticed her mother's somewhat bemused expression, she suddenly displayed a rare hint of remorse. "I appreciate what you have done for me..."

"Do you, Nell? Do you really appreciate what I have done for you?" Margaret asked with unusual bluntness.

Nell eyed her mother questioningly.

"I'm not sure you appreciate that *my* life has been on hold for the past few months," Margaret stated.

"Don't start, Mother. Everybody knows that you and Dad lead very humdrum lives, so there was never anything that wouldn't keep," Nell told her coldly.

"Thanks for that, Nell. I appreciate your honesty, but your father and I are happy with our dull lives, dull that is, according to your blinkered view, so please try not to interrupt us too often in future, will you?" Margaret said with deliberate sarcasm. "It's about time you thought about other people instead of being so selfish. I'm tired of pussyfooting around you for fear of upsetting you. You might like to consider that, Nell." Her manner was unusually passionate. "I'll just get my things together and then I'll be off."

They bade each other a very cool farewell.

"I'll call you at the weekend," Nell said cheerily in an effort not to part on bad terms. "And thanks for everything," she said, showing Margaret that she still had the basic good manners instilled in her as a child. "I need to plan for the future on my own. My life, Joel's life, *my way*." Her voice rose with authoritative control.

Margaret smiled and nodded knowingly, gave her daughter an obligatory hug and drove off without another word.

Two

Two long, tedious years passed and Nell fluctuated between dogged determination and fragile uncertainty until she established herself as a single mother. She tried to make sense of her situation.

"How could I go from being blissfully happy one minute, to being completely desolate and alone the next?" she asked herself. As the three-year-old Joel took his nap, she sat staring at a room that often felt empty and cold. "Tom and I chose this furniture," she mused wistfully. "It doesn't give me joy anymore." She wandered round the room, pensively dragging her fingers across the back of the sofa, the sofa upon which they had made love as soon as the deliverymen had left. She smiled at the thought, but felt an odd sense of resignation. She made herself comfortable in what had become her favourite chair, its big, comfortable squashy cushions seemingly enveloping her, protecting her from the looming ills she imagined were lurking outside everywhere, waiting to pounce. "What have I done to deserve this life?" she asked herself, momentarily displaying much less of the unyielding, fierce determination and bravado she had shown when she sent her mother home. She never allowed such moments of vulnerability and weakness to surface for more than a few seconds, and she purposefully took a deep breath in order to regain her self-control. She lay back and closed her eyes, her mind readily harking back to the time before Joel was born ...

~ * ~

When they married, Nell and Tom had moved away from her parents in Liverpool to the Lancashire town of Bolton.

"My goodness, what boring lives they lead," Nell commented to Tom as her parents left after their weekly visit to the young couple's new home. "Dad's looking after other people's children all week and, apart from that, they just seem to mosey along day after day with nothing more than a morning's grocery shopping, or an afternoon at the bowling green at weekends to stop the rot from setting in. God forbid we should ever get to that state."

"That's a bit judgmental, darling," Tom told her. "They seem happy enough to me."

"What does happy mean, Tom?" she asked. "If boring is happy for middle-aged people, then I'm staying young for the rest of my life. I will never allow that to happen to us, not ever."

Tom remained quiet and allowed his wife to prattle on as usual. He knew her too well to contradict when she got on her high horse, but he also knew there were times when she was displaying bravado to cover her self-doubt.

"Darling Nell," Tom whispered as he held her tenderly after their love had been passionately satisfied, "you are the love of my life. Don't ever change."

"Why would I change? There is nothing that would make me wish for anything different," Nell told him, smiling cheekily at the man she loved with all her heart. "I know how lucky I am and, in my own opinionated way, I do wonder how I managed to end up with a husband as gentle and tolerant as you, but I would never do anything you'd disapprove of, well, not deliberately anyway."

Tom grinned. "Opinionated? So that's what you call it, is it? I'll remind you of that next time you accuse me of forgetting our anniversary," he told her.

~ * ~

Nell smiled amidst her reverie, even now feeling guilty and embarrassed as she recalled her disappointment, her unreasonable anger and her intense hurt when she didn't receive a card on the morning of their first anniversary. She had sulked belligerently during the whole journey to town thinking that Tom was merely taking her out to dinner to placate her, because he'd forgotten to buy a gift. She sighed audibly. *How could I have been so naive?* she thought. She rested her head on the back of the chair, closed her eyes and easily drifted back in time again.

~ * ~

"Touché, Mr. Winston," she conceded. "Much as I hate to admit it, I did act like a spoilt brat that day, but your anniversary surprise left me completely dumbstruck, to say the least. How was I to know you'd booked the honeymoon suite at The Pack Horse, the most exclusive hotel in Bolton? And not only that, the room was filled with roses—red roses! You are wonderful, darling, and I don't deserve you, but I do love you. Don't ever forget that."

"And I love you too, warts an' all!" Tom joked. He truly did love her and thought he was the one person on this earth who knew how vulnerable she was underneath that over-confident exterior.

"I'll tell you a secret," Nell informed him happily. "My present to you for our second anniversary is already ordered."

"Blimey! It won't be a secret, though, will it, if you tell me? It must be something special to order it ten months in advance."

Nell grinned. "Very special," she told him, "but you'll get it a couple of months early. Your first anniversary present reaped benefits! We're going to have a baby!"

~ * ~

She shifted in the chair to make herself more comfortable and smiled gently at the memories of her life with Tom, memories that were sweet and yet still very painful if she allowed them to be.

~ * ~

Tom was ecstatic when Nell told him about the baby, but just recently, he had looked tired and drawn. "I'm exhausted," he replied when Nell asked him what was wrong. "I need to do the overtime so we won't struggle when you finish work. Don't worry. It's nothing that a good night's sleep won't put right." He kissed her and affectionately patted her bulging midriff.

"Look, Tom, as long as there's a roof over our heads and food on the table, that's all that matters," she said sensibly in an effort to reassure him, "and anyway, we aren't exactly poverty stricken, so stop worrying."

She sailed through her pregnancy with the minimum of fuss. "I can't wait to give birth," she told Tom as she lay on her back one Sunday morning, her swollen belly rising from under the luxurious white silk eiderdown. "It has be one of the best feelings a woman could ever have. I'm going to be the best mother who ever walked this earth."

"Tall order, Mrs. Winston, but I know you'll try," Tom told her. "If nothing else, you're determined enough to do anything you want. Persistent at best." He paused and smiled as he thought, *Blatantly obstinate at worst*, before he bravely continued. "I could call it stubbornness, but I won't."

Nell looked questioningly at her husband. "Man speaks with forked tongue, I see. I think there's a backhanded compliment in there somewhere so I guess I'll accept it graciously," she said, "But I'll show you, just see if I don't." She slid out of bed and left the room, her head held haughtily as she forced herself not to slam the door.

Tom grinned knowingly to himself. *Ever the self-assured Nell,* he thought. *She's priceless.*

~ * ~

Nell opened her eyes and looked around the room again. This was the room they refurbished first, and she savoured the thought of the time when gradually it became a cosy and comfortable home, a home awaiting its first child.

~ * ~

Tom observed his wife quietly as nine months passed and then more days of frustration. In typically Nell fashion, she became increasingly intolerant of Nature's insistence on making her hold on to her child way past her due date. She snapped at and bickered with anybody who tried to humour her.

"Good gracious, Nell," he pointedly told her, his manner unusually brusque. "I wish you would just relax and be patient."

"Don't you start, Tom. I have enough with everybody else expressing their unwanted opinions when they see me still here in all my glory."

Tom looked resignedly at his wife and shook his head slowly. "Motherhood might just mellow her," he mused, completely unconvinced. He was very tired; too tired even to contemplate what her moods might be when she was overtaken by everything that comes with being a new mother.

When the day came, Margaret Benson, Nell's mother, was already ensconced in the spare room; she had been for the past week. "Your dad is capable of looking after himself while I'm here with you. He'll probably wallow in self-indulgence and gloat about it when I get back," she said with a knowing smile, "but I wouldn't miss this for the world."

Nell grudgingly appreciated her mother being around. Much as she loved Tom, she secretly depended on her mother's support. When the pains became really bad, her mother would help just by being there so long as she didn't fuss. Mothers do tend to fuss unnecessarily. Nell shrugged. "I'll be a mother soon. I wonder if I'll fuss." She smiled quietly to herself. "Of course I won't."

"You go to work," she told Tom when eventually her pains started. "Mum's here. She'll telephone when I need to go to hospital."

But childbirth has its own agenda. "For goodness sake, Nell, relax," her mother urged as Nell paced around the house and irritably watched the clock ticking on the wall.

"I can't relax," Nell snapped. "Just keep quiet, Mother. I don't need you to be telling me what to do."

Margaret looked pointedly at her wilful daughter. "You're not the first woman to have a baby, Nell," she said, not trying to hide her disapproval of her daughter's attitude. "I'll make a cup of tea."

"Your cure for all ills, Mother. Okay, if it will make you feel better, go ahead."

~ * ~

At work, Tom hadn't been able to concentrate. His colleague and mentor, Peter, had almost suffered with him. "How were you when you had your first, Pete? I feel sick all the time, and talk about being tired! I'm exhausted after I've been out of bed half an hour," he said peering over the top of his drawing board at Peter, who faced him, grinning broadly.

"It's only just beginning, mate," Peter assured him amicably. "Just wait till it's waking up every three hours to be fed and think about when it's older asking for money to go on a date, or to borrow the car for the day!"

"Job's comforter!" Tom groaned, grimacing at his friend. "There's something in this sympathy lark though. I've suffered all the niggling symptoms of Nell's pregnancy, morning sickness, physical exhaustion, the lot."

Peter shrugged. "I don't know about that, mate, but just look forward to night feeds and dirty nappies. They're real, Tom, not imaginary and you can't avoid them."

Tom frequently lay awake at night listening to Nell's steady breathing and feeling the tiny feet of the baby as he happily kicked inside Nell's ever-enlarging belly. "He," he said out loud. "I'm going to have a son."

"*We* are going to have a son," Nell reminded him. "I'm going to do all the hard labour in this. Your part was the easy bit."

He'd stared at the telephone on his desk, willing it to ring. "Ring, blast you!" he urged the inanimate object. Any other day, it would have rung half a dozen times before lunch, but today it was silent—damn it! The whole office was quiet. The others had all gone on site, and he had been left at his drawing board to prepare the plans for the proposed extension to their premises. It was a strategic move, since he needed to be available at a moment's notice, but today every moment seemed like a minute, every minute an hour. At two o'clock that afternoon, the phone went off like a bomb and Tom snatched it up. "Yes?" he asked eagerly.

"Tom, it's me, Margaret. We have just called for an ambulance. Her waters broke. She'll be at The Grange within fifteen minutes. Are you going up there?"

"Yes, yes, of course I am. I'll be right there. Thanks, Margaret," and he hastily put down the phone, made sure the secretary in the adjoining suite knew he was leaving the office and he was in his car within seconds.

When he arrived at the maternity home, Nell was already prepared and in the labour ward. "I'm a bit nervous," she admitted quietly and searched Tom's face for some reassurance.

"You'll be okay, sweetheart. You're a Scouser, don't forget. They have babies like shelling peas in Liverpool," he told her in an effort to make her smile, but all she could raise was a grimace. "You're a natural, love," he said, trying heroically not to show his anxiety as her face creased with another excruciating contraction.

"Thanks!" she said breathlessly. "I'm from the Wirral actually and we don't consider ourselves to be Scousers, if you don't mind," she told him haughtily, her self-assuredness still intact, Tom noticed. Nell prepared to combat another piercing pain, the intensity of which she could never have imagined. They were coming hard and fast now. Tom held her hand tightly to let her know he would share the pain if it were possible; after all, he'd shared everything else! When the nurse appeared, he felt quite desperate and looked at Nell as yet another pain wracked her body.

"Time to go, Mr. Winston," the nurse said as she ushered him out.

He kissed Nell and said encouragingly, "Keep your chin up, sweetheart."

She managed a wry smile. "Chin up, or down," she offered, "I'll do it as best I can."

Nell tensed as she was wheeled into the delivery room and felt a wave of panic sweep through her, but Joel Thomas Winston was born at six-thirty in the evening, a healthy seven and a half pounds and with a lusty cry as soon as his head appeared in the outside world.

"He was sure determined to have his say even before he was out," the midwife joked.

"Just so long as he does as he's told when he's older,' Nell quipped.

"He's amazing," Tom observed at visiting time. He was overcome with pride for his son and total admiration for his wife. He sat quietly by the crib and watched in awe as the tiny form slept, his little chest moving rhythmically up and down as he breathed in the clean air all on his own, a beautiful baby made by Nell and him.

"Wonderful!" he enthused. Tom would be on cloud nine for the rest of his life.

~ * ~

The next few weeks were both uplifting and tiring for the new parents. Nell was tired, yet was able to sleep when Joel slept. Tom was thankfully impressed that Nell took things in her stride, but *he* needed to go to work and was gradually becoming more and more weary. When Joel began to sleep longer through the night, he thought he would begin to feel better. Strangely, he felt worse. The pregnancy and the birth appeared to have taken more of a toll on Tom than it had on Nell.

Perhaps the myth of deferred symptoms is a reality after all, he thought. *But a man can't be seen to baulk at fatherhood.* His mind was filled with typically misplaced masculine pride, so he kept on pushing himself in the hope that eventually the tiredness would go and the anxiety disappear.

"Tom, you look terrible," Nell observed. "Shall I ask Mum to come over again so we can take a break, perhaps go away for a weekend to the seaside? Let's go to North Wales. It will be quiet at this time of year, and we love Snowdonia in spring."

"Sounds tempting," Tom had replied, but in truth, he didn't know whether or not he had the energy to make the journey. Under normal circumstances, he would have jumped at the idea, but he silently questioned the wisdom of going away for a weekend when he felt so tired.

"Come on, it will do us both good," Nell persuaded and so they had packed a weekend case and made for Betws-y-Coed. The air was fresh and invigorating. They sat by Swallow Falls and watched the rushing water as it thundered down the rocks towards the river below. They wandered through the village and had afternoon tea at the little tea-shop in the high street before wending their way back to the hotel for dinner followed by a quiet drink in their room. The Welsh air had indeed been rejuvenating, for Nell at least. Tom had found the whole episode a strain, but had put on a brave face for Nell's sake.

The weeks went by and she became more than a little concerned that his romantic intentions towards her hadn't resurfaced after Joel's birth. Nothing was said, however, and each went along with the charade for the other's benefit. *I know I should say something*, she thought, *but what if Tom has gone off me since I had Joel? I can't bear the thought of that. I'm scared.*

When Joel was six months old, the sleepless nights disappeared and Nell felt much more relaxed. "We ought to regain some semblance of normal routine now," she told Tom one evening over dinner. Tom nodded and smiled, not at Nell, but at some imaginary focal point beyond her. "Tom? What's wrong? You're miles away and you haven't heard a word I've said. You have been in a world of your own for weeks. Is it the baby? Is it me? Talk to me, please," she pleaded.

"What?" Tom sounded vague.

Nell was at her wits end. They had generally been open and honest with each other, but there was something very strange happening and it frightened her. "Tom!" She was shouting now.

"What is it?" he asked, completely unaware of his wife's concern.

"You haven't heard a word I've said," she repeated. "Is it the baby? Is it me?" She had heard that some new fathers felt jealous and rejected, but she was sure she hadn't neglected Tom.

"I love the baby and I love you...very much," he said with unmistakeable tenderness.

"Then what is the matter?" Nell continued, now that she had his attention. "You aren't yourself. Why don't you go to see the doctor? Maybe he'll give you a tonic."

"I'm just tired," Tom explained and he did, indeed, sound weary.

"That's it then. I'll make an appointment for you tomorrow. I want my husband back and Joel wants his daddy. We need you." Nell smiled at the man she trusted with her life. "I hate to see you like this."

~ * ~

Tom sat in front of the doctor's desk and told him how he felt. "I think I'm probably being soft," he said, trying to make light of it, "But I can't deny that I have felt pretty dreadful since Joel was born," and if he were being truthful, long before then. He related all the times when he was totally devoid of energy, when he was too tired to put one foot in front of the other. He went to bed exhausted and woke up exhausted after a night of restlessness. Sometimes it seemed that even when he was desperately tired, sleep eluded him. Other times, he felt that he was just going through the motions of living without actually taking notice of anything around him. "I have never felt so tired in my life, Doctor," he said, "I used to play rugby for goodness sake, before we came to Bolton. I'd like to think I might kick a ball about with Joel in a few months time."

Doctor Varsani examined him thoroughly. "You seem to be anaemic, Tom, but I can't be sure until we've taken a blood test, and you need to go to the Infirmary for that. In the meantime, I'll prescribe some iron tablets. They should give you extra energy until we know exactly what you need."

~ * ~

If World War Three had begun, it could not have shattered Nell's life more. She stood by Tom's grave holding Joel to her closely. Her family and friends surrounded her in silence as she threw two red roses onto the coffin, her mind completely devoid of rational thoughts. Tom would surely appear soon to show them it had all been a terrible mistake. She expected him to be waiting for them at home when they returned. Hot tears stung her eyes, and her pale face was expressionless as she turned to walk slowly into a desolate future. She had fluctuated from despair and desolation to anger and determination. As each new day dawned, she slowly came to terms with the fact that she had to accept her situation for the sake of Joel. Leukaemia had taken Tom, but one thing she knew more than anything else: she would spend the rest of her life devoted to their son. Joel was truly Tom's gift of love to her, and she would make damn certain their child would be his father's son in the ways she wanted him to be.

Nell shivered at the intensity of her thoughts and stood up quickly to free herself of the sadness of the past. "Goodness, four o'clock already. I'd better make Joel's tea." As she wiped away the tears of the past, she stood up and walked purposely forward in the present to what she felt was an uncertain future.

Three

Margaret had reluctantly accepted what Nell was saying about getting on with her life. "All right," Margaret agreed, trying not to show hurt that her daughter had more or less thrown her out. "We are only a phone call away, anytime, day or night, always remember that." And she had packed up her belongings and gone home to the Wirral to the husband she was only too aware she had neglected while she had considered the needs of her only child, Nell. In her heart, she knew she had to do as her daughter asked of her. Her own marriage had taken a battering recently and she had to show Bob her loyalties were still with him, despite the fact that their daughter's need had seemed far greater than theirs during the past few months.

"Nell's changed, Bob," she told her husband on her return. "Her eyes were cold and somehow unseeing. She seemed to be focussing somewhere way beyond reality, if that doesn't sound stupid. I'm worried about her. She hasn't a kind word to say to anybody. She even said our lives are boring. Why would she say such a thing?"

"Just give her time, Margaret, she'll come round. You know how stubborn she can be," Bob told his concerned wife. "She's old enough to decide what's right for herself and no matter what you or I say to her, she'll do what she wants anyway, so it's no use worrying about her. You know how strong-willed she is, too."

Still uncertain, however, Margaret left Nell to face whatever life had in store. Their parting had not been pleasant. *Cool* only just came close to describing the feelings between the two women as she had left Nell's Bolton home.

Nell was indeed a very different woman with a steely resolve to lead the life that only she could plan for Joel and for herself. She set her sights high; best schools to begin with, top universities, corporate management, Queen's Council, Prime Minister. *My son will be whatever I choose*, she thought as she watched the peacefully sleeping baby, a child too young to be aware of what the future had in store for him. "And," she announced to the room that was her world for now, "nobody will stand in my way."

~ * ~

When Joel was four years old, even though it was contrary to her plans, she had reluctantly placed him in a day nursery on the advice of her schoolteacher father. "He needs children around him, Nell," Bob had told her. "He'll grow up thinking he has to be with adults all the time, not to mention the fact that other children will shun him if they think he behaves like a little old man."

"What do you mean, Dad? You only have to look at him. He *is* still a child!" Nell answered defensively, unreasonably irritated by her father's observations.

"Of course, he is still a child and I want you to treat him as such," Bob said, his tone showing how desperate he was not to sound interfering, yet demonstrating all the time that he was.

"I *do* treat him like a child. How could I possibly do otherwise?" she complained. "What reasons have you to make a comment like that? I love you, Dad, and usually I would respect your judgment, but

I don't like what you are saying and I'm beginning to resent your opinion."

Bob smiled. "He told me this morning he was bloody fed up because that damned fool of a milkman had left you without milk for the second time this week! Hardly the comments of a four-year-old!"

"Oh, my word! What did you say?" Nell asked and realised she had indeed cursed under her breath and had also castigated the milkman when she had phoned the dairy to complain.

Bob was still smiling when he replied, "Joel isn't the first child to pick up on adult language and he won't be the last, but you really must think about ensuring that he has company of his own age so he can play children's games. A nursery school would be ideal."

Nell reluctantly accepted that he was right, but she also knew her conscience would play havoc with her own clearly defined sense of motherhood. "Palming him off on other people would suggest I'm neglecting my duty as a mother, and I'm not sure if I want to have to deal with that."

"Nell, I'm dealing with other people's children every day, children not much older than Joel. I see children who weep when their mothers leave, only to be laughing and playing as soon as Mum is out of sight. Children are good little actors. Their tears are for show, because they instinctively know Mum is uptight about leaving them. Cute little imps, they are! We don't always give them credit for their inborn judgment of their fellow human beings." Bob knew he was being a bit heavy and philosophical. "I know, Nell, you're trying to find a reason not to leave Joel in a nursery, but let me tell you again, I think it's the right thing to do. I know how stubborn you can be, but as your father, I have to tell you I'm right. I hope you'll use your common sense in this."

And so, Nell heeded her father's advice and enrolled Joel in The Lawns. On the first day, he went in and never looked back. Even though she found it difficult, Nell decided she would have to trust the professionals, but she couldn't help but notice that Joel was happy to leave her behind for a few hours. *Life is cruel sometimes,* she thought as she walked home after leaving her precious son with strangers, *and don't I know it?*

Nell's social life had diminished drastically after Tom's death. Eventually the invitations stopped coming, because she always had her excuse not to accept. For four years she had chosen to be on her own. She didn't see the need for other people to enter the equation. "My decision, my choice," she told herself frequently as she listened to the radio on lonely Saturday nights, or read a book when Joel was in bed.

"The mere thought of going out socialising is an unnecessary indulgence," she told her mother during their weekly telephone call, "and anyway, I wouldn't enjoy myself, so what would be the point?"

"But surely the odd night out would do you..." Margaret stopped abruptly, recalling the last time she had told Nell that something would do her good. "Perhaps you could get a job."

"Don't start, Mother. I don't need a job, and I get all the pleasure I need from my little boy. I'm still not sure about taking him to nursery school," she conceded. "It was only because Dad said Joel needed to play with other children that I agreed to him going to The Lawns. I still think I should be looking after him myself."

"That's understandable, but wouldn't you like a little job while Joel is at nursery?" Margaret continued. "This is nineteen fifty-one, Nell, and women go out to work these days, have done since the war was over," she urged.

"For goodness sake, Mother..."

"Just a thought, dear, just a thought," her mother said wisely. "I'll talk to you next week. Goodbye, dear." She made a necessary hasty retreat in order to avoid yet another confrontation.

"Damn you, Mother," Nell said to herself as she replaced the phone on the cradle. "You always have the irritating knack of getting under my skin. Job indeed!"

As she dusted the furniture for the third time that morning, she tried to convince herself that her mother was wrong. "I don't need a job. Joel is my job. He's my number one priority. I'm his mother and I know what's best for him. I won't have anybody else telling me how to bring him up." But her mother's words had struck a chord and they played on her mind.

~ * ~

If the paperboy hadn't pushed the *Evening News* through her door by mistake, she would never have seen the situations vacant and the part-time job that was advertised. Joel had long ago started school, and he was soon to have his ninth birthday. Her part-time job over at the doctor's surgery had indeed given Nell something other than Joel to occupy her thoughts and, indeed, her life.

"You've soon got the hang of it," Jackie, her new colleague, told her after her first week. "It took me ages to suss that filing system when I first started here." Nell wasn't sure whether or not Jackie had said it to make her feel good, but she had to admit she was beginning to feel human again and she realised very quickly that she had forgotten what being with other adults for most of the day was like. There were two doctors, a practice nurse and two receptionists, Jackie and Nell. Each day, she gained more confidence and she learned to laugh again without feeling guilty. After Tom's demise, she hadn't felt comfortable smiling, let alone laughing out loud. Jackie was the kind of person who was at ease with anyone and everyone. Her tiny frame seemed almost too small to house such a huge personality, but in spite of her small stature, she oozed confidence and joviality. Nell felt that Fate had perhaps led her to her new place of employment and provided her with a new friend.

"What are you doing tomorrow?" Jackie asked as they finished work one Friday afternoon. "Can you get a babysitter? The girls and I are going into Manchester for a bit of window shopping. Do you fancy coming with us?"

"Saturdays are for Joel, and we usually go to watch the Wanderers," she informed Jackie. "I can't possibly forego that for a bit of unnecessary girlie window shopping."

"But the change will do you good," Jackie told her. "At least think about it, Nell. I've asked you so many times over the past few years and your answer is always the same. I'd like you to meet my other friends. They're a good lot. You'll like them."

"Thanks, but no thanks. How many times will it take to make you realise that Saturdays are always for Joel?" she repeated. "No discussion."

Nevertheless, the job had given the only change she deemed necessary. She enjoyed the work and she never ceased to be amused by the way Jackie handled the most difficult of patients with skilful diplomacy. That in itself was an entertaining bonus and a welcome distraction from wondering what Joel was up to in her absence. She had a way with her that made Nell genuinely laugh again.

"You know, Jackie," she divulged quietly, "I had forgotten what it was like to enjoy a good belly laugh." Frequently she found herself having to hide behind the filing cabinet as Jackie dealt with Mrs. Awkward, or Mr. Obstreperous.

"Oh, Mrs. So-and-so," she would say, "Please take a seat. The doctor will see you when it's your turn."

"But I've been waiting half an hour already," the patient would complain.

"Oh dear, have you really?" Jackie would feign surprise. "Doesn't time fly when you're having fun? I'll tell you what ...help yourself to a cup of coffee and then it will be your turn by the time you've drunk it. Trust me."

The patient would generally retreat, placated. If that didn't work, Jackie would use Plan B—smile understandingly and inform the patient that the doctor was very busy and could only see one person at a time. If that failed, still smiling, she would shrug sympathetically with a fervent hope that the telephone would ring to rescue her from the difficult situation.

"The cup of coffee usually works," she told Nell one day at the end of surgery, "but I've had a couple throw up as a result of it when they've come in with an upset stomach. Wouldn't you think they'd know not drink it knowing that they felt sick?"

Nell pulled a face. "I hate being sick. I run a mile if I think anyone is going to throw up! Thank goodness Joel isn't a sickly child. I don't know what I'd do if he were."

"You'd just get on with clearing it up!"

"Yuk! Let's change the subject, shall we?" Nell said and just as the 'Yuk' came out of her mouth, Sean Flynn appeared at the reception desk. "Whoops! Sorry, Doctor Flynn," she apologised and strangely found herself blushing.

"I hope that expression of disgust wasn't meant for me, Mrs. Winston," he said with a friendly smile. "Are my calls ready?"

Strangely, Nell fumbled like an embarrassed teenager to find the list of house calls she had prepared. "Not at all, Doctor, it certainly wasn't directed at you." Changing the subject rapidly, she added, "You're going to be busy, I'm afraid. I think you'd better have a cup of coffee before you go." The significance of the remark hit them both at once, and she and Jackie burst out laughing again.

"I see," the good-natured medic said, "The joke's on me! Well, you two had better be here when I get back, or there'll be trouble, so there will."

Nell looked at him, aghast. "I finish at three in time to collect Joel from school," she said, making it clear that Doctor Flynn might make her late.

"In that case then, I'll have to call round to see you at home," he said tersely and with that he theatrically took his leave, the two receptionists standing open-mouthed at his parting gesture.

Jackie looked at Nell, who had shrugged at the thought of whatever they had done to upset Doctor Flynn was enough for him to reprimand her before the next day. She struggled to think what crime they might have committed apart from having a laugh when they ought to have been sorting out patient records in readiness for the next surgery. Surely Doctor Flynn wasn't so tyrannical as to object to a bit of light-hearted banter after work. Jackie's expression suddenly changed from being puzzled to blatant realisation.

"He's not going to tell you off," she announced. "He was looking for an excuse to call on you, the wily old devil. You mark my words, girl, he's on a mission! And ..." She winked. "Who could resist those green Irish eyes?"

"Don't be daft, Jackie!" Nell was aghast at the idea. "What would he want to do that for?" But she had to pick Joel up from school. Maybe he was just joking, and surely Jackie was allowing her imagination to run riot. Once out of the surgery, her priority as always was Joel, and Doctor Sean Flynn was pushed out of her mind.

Four

Sean Flynn had lived in the north of England ever since he had qualified at Manchester School of Medicine. His parents, Irish potato farmers, had encouraged him to go to university in England in order to find his true vocation away from the rural restraints of his native Ireland.

"'Tis experience you need, son," his daddy had told him. He was a man of few words, but when he spoke, it was usually to give sound advice and with good judgment. "Sure, you'll not gain much experience here on the farm other than which are the best murphies to send to market, and your mammy and I want more for you than that." Sean himself had realised as he was growing up that the world held much more in store for him than growing potatoes. His two older brothers knew farming inside out, had married into farming families and had accepted their roles in continuing the family business. He needed to spread his wings and he knew his parents would be behind him every step of the way.

He was going to be thirty years old next birthday and still hadn't asked Kathy to marry him. She had been a trainee nurse in Dublin when he left to go to Manchester. All through his training, he had corresponded with her and her letters had been a source of pleasure for him when he felt alone and isolated during his first year in university. Later, when he had established himself in his new surroundings, she still kept him in touch with home and he even spent all his time with her during the summer holidays on the farm.

Kathleen O'Connor was a dark-haired, green-eyed Irish beauty. Her olive skin made her look very European and yet no one could mistake the Irish colleen in her sparkling eyes. Sean had realised he was in love with her during that first summer back from university. She had run in the fields with him, sailed on the loch and fished in the pond, all the time smiling and chattering nineteen to the dozen about her life at the hospital and asking him all sorts of questions about his life as a medical student.

"How soon before you go on the wards? We are there all the time, well, except when we're in class with Matron, or the nurse tutor," Kathy told him. "Everything is so interesting, but the part I like most is seeing little children smile when the pain has gone."

"That's great, Kathy. We'll make a good team when we're both qualified," Sean replied, smiling as he noticed the sparkle in her emerald eyes.

"Sure we will, Flynny, but that's a long time away just yet," she said matter-of-factly. "There's a lot of hard work to be done before we can plan for the future. We're too young to be thinking that far ahead."

"I know, I know," Sean agreed, but he was always at ease in her company and that was very gratifying for an eighteen-year-old young man. He held her hand, shyly at first and then with growing confidence as she responded to his affection. He had kissed her on his last day at home at the end of that summer and the love he had felt then enhanced his dreams throughout the next few years. He had told her more than once that he loved her.

"Love ya back, Flynny!" she answered and he delighted in the fact that her feelings were as deep as his.

Kathy was always there for him when he went back to Ireland, but she had never wanted to leave the land of her birth. He had tried to convince her that the world was there for the taking and she would easily be able to find work in the hospitals in England, but she wouldn't listen.

"I love you," he told her, "and I want you to be with me." Even so, she had stayed in Dublin and refused to cross the Irish Sea to begin a new life with Doctor Sean Flynn.

"I'm not ready to leave home yet," she told him frequently. "You will just have to be patient."

"Is that meant to be a joke?" he asked in an effort to remove the tension between them.

"Ha, ha, Flynny! Very funny, but let's just leave it for now, eh? We go over the same ground time and time again and I just want to be able to relax when you're home. No pressure, please!"

"Okay, you win this time, but I won't give up." And yet in spite of her indifferent attitude, he had still felt a great affection for her. He had thought she loved him; she had indeed said that she did, but he wasn't so convinced anymore. He told himself that was the reason why he hadn't asked her to marry him. She had become a habit with him and he with her. The burning question for him now was, should he, or shouldn't he, ask her to be his wife?

Almost as if by telepathy, Kathy had telephoned one Sunday evening as Sean sat alone in his Bromley Cross home contemplating his future. "Hi, Flynny," she said, "I have some news."

"To be sure you've decided to come to England," he sang, emphasising his Irish brogue in an effort to make her laugh.

"Not exactly," she replied, her tone somewhat confusing. He decided later that he had detected an odd mix of elation and guilt, of happiness and sadness, with not one of those emotions coming through as the dominant factor.

"Well then, what?" Sean had asked, totally unaware of the bombshell she was about to drop to shatter his world completely.

"I'm pregnant," she announced.

"You're what?" Sean grabbed hold of the table, totally astounded.

"Do I need to repeat it? I'm pregnant and I want you to be the first to know."

"Kathy," he was almost at a loss for words, "we haven't slept together since last summer. Are you telling me it's someone else's child?"

"Flynny, you're a doctor. You know how babies are made." She was playing around with his emotions. "I've been seeing one of the senior obstetricians..."

"Like hell, you have! He does his job well then! And you didn't think to tell me before? I must be very naïve not to have read something in your lack of communication. I just thought you were busy working. Well, yes, I guess you were!" Sean was seething. He had put his faith in this girl and had thought that eventually she would want to be with him as much as he had wanted to be with her. How wrong could he have been?

"Don't be like that, Flynny. I never said I would follow you across the water. I was always honest about that. I didn't have to take a vow of chastity whilst you took on your duties as a GP in an alien country. If you really wanted me, you would have come home after you qualified, and you didn't do that. I hope that we are friends enough to accept that life goes on and we must go our separate ways. I'm going to marry Seamus and that's going to happen soon. I didn't want you to find out from your mother when she read it in the *Gazette*."

"Thanks for that at least," Sean had said. "Now if you don't mind, I've got work to do," and he rang off without so much as a goodbye. His pride was dented, but not smashed to smithereens. Kathleen O'Connor could go marry her senior obstetrician and have as many babies as she wanted. What did he care? It was her choice after all.

That was five years ago and Sean Flynn had stayed single. He gained much satisfaction from his work, played golf twice a week, accepted invitations to dinner from well-meaning wives of his golfing friends and enjoyed going to the Manchester theatres when time allowed. He had lots of friends, but never became involved in a relationship with any of his female companions, and secretly at the golf club he was known as Bolton's most eligible bachelor. He was tall and handsome with a profession that gained him respect in all walks of life. His soft Irish accent merely added to his attraction.

"At work, he's just Doctor Flynn," Jackie told Nell, "amiable, efficient, likeable and competent. His bedside manner is very reassuring," she said as she grinned mischievously at Nell. "For the patients, I mean," she continued, "but I have no idea what he's like at home. He's a very private person, as far as I can gather."

The day that he had asked Jackie and Nell to see him after he'd finished his house calls, he had received two tickets for *The Dresser* at the Palace Theatre in Manchester. He didn't wish to make it obvious that he would like to ask Nell to go with him, so he had addressed them both as he left. Jackie had a husband to go home to, but Nell was a young widow. He thought she might like a night at the theatre, although she did seem to devote all her time to her little boy. He wondered if babysitters were available, or would she, indeed, like a night out with him. On second thought, he decided he would leave it until another time. *Maybe I'll give the tickets to Mac and Irene at the golf club. They'd appreciate them. Yes, that's what I'll do.*

~ * ~

That same day, Joel was in tears when Nell collected him from school. She was devastated when she saw his tear-stained face, and she bent down to hug him and find out what was the cause of this very uncustomary occurrence. "What is it?" she had asked the unusually sad eight-year-old.

Joel took a deep breath and fought back his sobs. "G... G...Geoffrey F... F... Foster," he stuttered, "said only boys who are bad have no dads and he said my daddy had gone away because he didn't love us."

Nell was totally taken aback; she had not been prepared for such an occurrence and had never even thought about a situation where children's cruelty against each other could manifest itself in such a way. "Oh, sweetheart, that's not true at all. Geoffrey Foster can't possibly know that your daddy loved you very much and that he was so poorly that God had to invite him to stay with Him. That's what happens when someone you love dearly is very sick. Please don't cry. Mummy's here and I love you very much."

Joel wasn't easily convinced. "Geoffrey Foster said that his dad had gone to live somewhere else, and his mum had told him that it was because he and his brothers had been naughty. Had I been naughty to make my daddy go away?"

Nell was aghast. How on earth could a mother tell her children they were to blame for a break-up in a marriage? That was a terrible thing to do and certainly bore no comparison with the circumstances of Tom's death.

"Listen, darling," she explained again to her distraught son, "your daddy was really very, very sick and the doctors couldn't make him better. When that happens to people, God takes them into His care, but they live on in our hearts, because we love them. Don't you remember the story of Jesus I told you at Christmas and Easter?" She was clutching at straws and hoped with all her heart that a worried eight-year-old might grasp some grains of comfort from the story that even adults have to take on trust. "If Geoffrey Foster says anything else to you about your daddy, you may tell him that I'll be only too pleased to explain to him why your daddy is no longer with us, should he care to ask me."

"I don't think he'll say anything else, Mum," Joel said, brighter now that he had shared his problem. "Mrs. Blakeley heard him calling me a cry baby and she made him stand in the corner all through Art, and Art is his favourite lesson!"

"Oh," Nell said quietly and hoped that Mrs. Blakeley had realised why her son had been so upset. She was tempted to make an appointment to see the teacher, but decided that for the time being, she would allow Joel the space in which to grow up to understand that life is full of little knocks. One just had to deal with them as best as one could. She would deal with it later in her own way.

That evening, when Joel had gone to bed, she reflected on what had happened during the day and resolved to try to protect her little boy from the vagaries of life as far as possible. She would not stand by and see her child oppressed by the tyranny of childish taunts. She couldn't be with him twenty-four hours a day, but she could make damn sure he was equipped to cope with the nastiness of his insensitive, unfeeling and ignorant peers.

And by eleven o'clock, she realised that Doctor Flynn hadn't called after all.

Five

Joel couldn't remember being unhappy as he was growing up, but he always knew there was something missing from his young life. He had often watched other boys in the park with their dads and wished that his daddy could be there to kick a ball around, to fly his kite and to play rough and tumble games whilst they laughed and rolled about on the grass and wrestled for the ball. By the time he was ten years old, he had learned to live with the fact that he would never have that special feeling he presumed other boys shared with their dads.

He had been brooding for days. There was a lot for a boy to work out, but he knew he had a problem and he didn't know how to deal with it.

"Ben? What's your mum like?" he asked his closest friend casually one playtime at school.

Ben Mason regarded Joel through questioning eyes. "Why do you want to know?" Ben never discussed his mother with anyone, not even Joel.

"I just wondered if all mums were like mine, bossy. She never lets me do anything *I* want and I never get a say in anything," he confided with Ben, gaining in confidence as he shared his grievances with his friend. "It doesn't half get on my wick. And I hate Sunday mornings. I daren't say anything to her, otherwise she gets all high and mighty, and I hate that, too."

"Listen, Joel, I'm telling you straight, you wouldn't want to swap places with me. Just think yourself lucky to have a mum like you've got. You wouldn't want mine. But why Sundays?" Ben asked as they continued to kick the ball back and forth almost as if they were punctuating each statement. He was warming to the fact that Joel had decided to air his views with him, and Joel felt a kind of liberation from Ben's openness. "My Sundays are the best days of the week, because my mum doesn't get up till about teatime and then she goes out again as soon she's had a cup of tea and a cigarette. I'm glad to see the back of her."

"But you go to church, don't you, because I've seen you sitting at the back with your brother," Joel told him.

"I want to go to St. Luke's High School. I know I can get a place if I go to church and I can do that on my own. Anyway, my mum would never go to church. She thinks it's only for snooty, posh people."

"I'd give anything not to go to church every Sunday. It's boring, and you could always just do the entrance exam for St. Luke's, couldn't you? How do you know all that stuff, Ben? You sound so grown up when you talk like that.'

"I have to fend for myself. I've been told that going to church gives you extra points," Ben continued. "I know it's boring, but I really want to go to St. Luke's and it's something I can do by myself. If I go to St. Luke's, then my brother will be able to go, too. Going to church isn't that bad and I'd go every day if it got me a place at that school."

Joel stared in awe at Ben. He was full of admiration of his confidence, but he had to ask, "Why does your mum stay in bed all day? Who makes your dinner and tea then? Your dad's not there either, is he? Did he die like mine?"

Ben steadied the ball under his foot and appeared momentarily sad. "I can look after myself," he said adamantly. "My dad left when I was six and Michael was only three. We don't see him at all now. I don't even know where he is, but I don't care anymore. I just get on with what I have to do. When I'm old enough, I'm getting a flat and living on my own."

"Bloody hell, Ben!" He had never used strong language in public before. "I'm sorry," he said, though he wasn't sure if were apologising for swearing, or for the fact that Ben had to look after himself and his brother. He didn't know how else to react, but he admired Ben's attitude. He liked Ben and didn't understand why Nell wouldn't allow him to invite Ben for tea. She had made no bones about telling Joel he should find another friend.

"I don't like you playing with that boy," she told him. "Surely there are other boys in your class who would be pleased to be your friend."

"Ben's all right, Mum. Why don't you like him?"

"Because..." Nell told him. "Just because. Don't question my decisions, Joel. I'm your mother and I know what's good for you. End of discussion."

When Sunday came around again, he wondered how it would be if *his* mum stayed in bed all day. It would give him some freedom at least, but he braced himself for the usual tedious performance.

"Do I have to go to church, Mum?" he asked over breakfast. "One day you might just let me stay at home." His discussion with Ben had made him realise standing up for himself was an option he had previously been too timid to consider.

"Joel!" Nell replied, exasperated. "You ask that every week without fail. How many times do I have to tell you that we do have to go to church."

Joel continued to goad her. "But we never used to go to church. Why have you suddenly decided to go now?" Joel asked, not attempting to hide his annoyance.

"Joel Winston, are you questioning me again, young man?" Nell was becoming more than irritated by his attitude and, before he could voice his objections more strongly, she continued, "Don't make it seem like I'm forcing you to do something you don't want to do. I know you don't really mean to be so unenthusiastic and anyway," she conceded, finally revealing the real reason why church attendance was necessary, "it will get you a place at St. Luke's."

Joel felt smug. "I can pass the entrance exam for St. Luke's if it's that important to you. There are ways around it without sitting through purgatory every Sunday morning. Church is boring," he announced belligerently. His mother hadn't previously admitted that St. Luke's was the reason why they travelled across town to the parish church every Sunday, and her admission fuelled Joel with undisguised self-satisfaction.

"Look here, young man, St. Luke's is a church school, the best school round here, and we need to go to church if I want a place there for you. No argument, Joel. Just finish your breakfast, or we'll be late," Nell told him. "We don't want to set the wrong example, do we?"

"I don't have to go to St. Luke's. I can always go to the secondary modern," he suggested to his mother as they drove the couple of miles across town.

"Over my dead body, Joel. No child of mine is going to a secondary modern school, so just keep quiet, do as you're told, please, and no more arguments."

The boy's simmering resentment eventually boiled over just before his eleventh birthday and he defiantly stood up to his mother again, this time determined not to allow her to browbeat him into submission.

"But Joel, you always have a party at home for your friends. Why don't you want one this year? This is an important birthday and probably the last time you'll see of some of your friends from High Lawns. You are eleven, Joel. All eleven-year-olds have parties. You have to hang on to your childhood before it is gone forever. I won't allow you to grow up too quickly," she told him categorically.

"I don't want a party at all, Mum," he declared. "I'd rather spend it at the Scout Hut with my friends there." But Nell had formed this grandiose idea that he was best friends with everybody in his class, that he was the most popular boy in the school.

"What about all your friends in your class at High Lawns?" she asked.

"There's only Ben Mason—"

"How many times have I told you not to play with that boy? His mother..." She paused abruptly. "Well, I just don't like that family, that's all."

"Ben's my best friend and I'll play with him as much as I like. You don't know him, or his family, so don't talk about him like that," Joel continued obstreperously.

Nell was taken aback. "Watch your attitude, young man. Just show a little more respect. I'm your mother, or have you forgotten who feeds and clothes you? I can't believe you have suddenly become so rude."

Joel looked down at his feet to avoid eye contact with his mother. Ben was the only friend he needed. He went to Scouts with him, so he would have his friend there on his birthday. "I don't want pass the parcel, musical chairs, candles on a birthday cake and goody bags at the end of the party," he told her belligerently. "I'm not a baby. I'm eleven years old, damn it!"

"Excuse me, Joel Winston. Don't you dare use that sort of language to me! I bet that's how that dreadful boy talks. What is getting into you?" Nell asked, and realising that the ridiculous argument might blow up out of all proportion, she tried a different ploy. "Won't you have one last party just to please me?" she asked, fluttering her eyelids and pouting like a little girl.

Joel briefly considered the proposal and Nell waited expectantly. She knew he'd see sense eventually.

"No, I won't," he told her. "I really don't want a birthday party this year." But his thoughts really weren't with Ben at all. His mind was filled with Julie. She was his first girlfriend and was in the Girl Guides. She was going to St. Luke's, too, and he had kissed her on the lips behind the Scout hut. She always allowed him to catch her when they played "Kiss Chase" at school playtime. He knew his mum would be absolutely appalled if she thought he had a girlfriend, let alone that he had kissed her—and more than once! He certainly wasn't going to tell his mother about that. But oh, how he liked Julie! She made his skin tingle when she held his hand under the table as they sat together at supper on Wednesday nights after the Scout and Guide meetings. Keeping Julie a secret from his mother gave him a wonderful sense of power.

"Okay, sweetie pie, how about—"

"Mum!" Joel shouted petulantly. "Don't treat me like a baby! I don't want a party. How many times do I have to tell you? I don't want a flippin' birthday cake with candles on it. I just want to do my own thing!"

"And what might that be?" Nell asked forcefully, but feeling confused and bewildered at the thought of her son objecting to her well-meaning efforts to make his birthday an enjoyable occasion.

"Nothing!" Joel snapped, "Just leave it, will you?" and he stormed off to his room to avoid more confrontation. In his room, he smiled to himself. He felt a kind of exhilaration that he had dared to challenge his mother's wisdom. She usually had a way of intimidating him with a mere look, but he was determined not to allow her to interfere with his own plans to spend his birthday with the people he liked most.

"How hurtful can he be?" Nell said to herself angrily and she refused to accept that her little boy was indeed growing up and soon might not need his mother at all.

~ * ~

When September came, Joel settled quickly at his new school and quietly accepted that going to church had indeed helped him to gain a place at St. Luke's. He was a very bright boy and soon found his self-confidence. The progressive school allowed him the space in which to become his own person without his mother's input. He very soon realised that he was, indeed, in the best school and he accepted that his mother's insistence on going to church had reaped the benefits, though he did admit to himself, *I would never give her the pleasure of knowing she'd been right all along.*

The years up to being sixteen and the onset of his Ordinary level exams sailed by seemingly without a problem. His first love, Julie, was replaced by Angela, Angela was replaced by Kate, Kate by Amy and by the time he was ready to go into Sixth Form, he had established himself as a sociable and amiable young man without his mother breathing down his neck during school hours. The expected gawky teenage features never materialised; his hormones had been kind to him. He developed a love for music and found he could sing even when his voice was pitching a couple of octaves lower. His performances in school productions had made him very popular and he loved it. His dreams were full of becoming a pop star with girls all clamouring to get a piece of him.

"Look at you," Ben observed enviously. "The girls are falling over themselves to go out with you. Leave some for the rest of us, won't you?"

"Sorry, Ben. I can't help having the magnetic personality that the chicks love!" Joel joked.

"Don't get too cocky, mate," Ben advised light-heartedly. "Girls don't like arrogance—even I know that."

"Point taken, Benny boy, but for the time being, don't spoil my fun."

Ben shook his head slowly. "You know what, Joel? I think you might just fall flat on your face one day and I hope I'm there to see it," he said, wise words that he couldn't possibly have known would turn out to be profoundly prophetic.

Joel grinned. "You're a good mate, Ben, but I hope you're wrong."

Ben shrugged. "We'll see, Joel, we'll see."

~ * ~

The relationship between mother and son soon became a battle of wills. While Nell was vociferous in her control, Joel was more covert in his approach. She planned her every move on the road to Joel's future; he went with the flow in order to make sure his mother thought she was winning. She smiled at the thought that she had already orchestrated his prospects and, as long as she was in control, she would see that he achieved the best in everything.

When she spoke with her mother, whom she considered her ally in all matters Joel, her tone was more than usually agitated. "I'm his mother and I'm bound to watch out for him. I don't think he appreciates all I do for him." Their conversations rarely ventured on to any other topic.

"So long as that's all you do, Nell," Margaret replied. "There's a big difference between watching out and watching over. Don't confuse the two."

"What do you mean?" Nell asked, convinced that her mother was unnecessarily splitting hairs.

"Watching out is being aware of what might happen and watching over is interfering with what might happen. You need to understand that, Nell."

"My, my, Mother, that's very philosophical. Do you really believe that?"

"Yes, I do, and it might be worth remembering. I'm just giving a bit of motherly advice, that's all," Margaret told her.

Nell said her goodbyes and put down the phone. Her mother had touched a nerve—again. She didn't know why, but her greatest challenge was not allowing her head to rule her heart where Joel was concerned, and she uncharacteristically wondered if she would ever have the inner strength to let go. *He's my son*, she told herself over and over again. *I will never relinquish my hold on him.*

~ * ~

Nell never wavered from her mission in what she interpreted as being there for Joel. She always made sure he had what she wanted. She watched him develop into a strong and, dare she say it, a handsome young man. "Oh, yes, he is certainly handsome!" she observed, but when girls began to show more than a little interest in her son, she was determined she wouldn't be sidelined. She frequently took it upon herself to make sure the girls knew where they stood.

"Joel is too young for a serious relationship," she told Angela as soon as she manipulated the situation for private conversation. "He needs to devote his time to his studies, not gadding about with girls."

Angela smiled sweetly. "We're just close friends, Mrs. Winston. I have ambitions too, you know, and I know what I have to do if I want to achieve them."

"Let me assure you, dear, that I won't allow Joel to be distracted by any girl and it will be in your interest and that of your ambition if you tell him you won't see him again." Nell smiled knowingly and tapped Angela meaningfully on the arm as she said pointedly, "And if you repeat one word of this conversation to Joel, I shall make sure your ambitions will never be achieved." She walked away, her head held high and a triumphant smile on her face.

Angela never did find out the serious intent of Mrs. Winston's threat, but later unceremoniously dumped Joel, who was hurt and confused that his teenage heart had been broken. Instantly, Nell took up the reins again and gave him a hug, telling him, "There are plenty more fish in the sea," and sure enough, another streamlined aquatic beauty would be swimming close by before the surrounding waters had time to go cold. Nell was never far away, surreptitiously lying in wait like a predatory sea serpent to make sure he wouldn't get caught in the net again. Eventually, Kate and Amy were also given Nell's devoted mother treatment and Joel suffered the consequences.

"All girls are the same," she informed him. "They'll love you and leave you, you know, but despite their fickle ways, they all want to be treated respectfully. You do know what I mean, don't you, Joel? All mothers want to think their sons are perfect gentlemen."

"Oh come on, Mum! Girls are different these days," Joel argued amicably, feeling awkward about discussing such things with his mother, of all people.

"More forward, perhaps, but I think they still like to be treated respectfully. All girls want to think their boyfriends would move heaven and earth for them, whatever their age, and they don't want to feel that they have to be easy just because boys would like them to be. I haven't brought you up to be that kind of boy."

Joel shrugged, shook his head and grinned knowingly at his mother as he prepared to go off to college. "Well, I hope you would never let me down," she called as he left, but she sensed something different in his manner—something she couldn't fathom.

It was when Joel arrived home from college that the bombshell was dropped. "I'm not going to college anymore," he announced casually. "I've seen the principal today and he agrees I'm wasting my time and theirs if I continue with my A levels." Since the beginning of term, he had lost all his desire to continue with his studies. "Media Studies is okay, but I'm not really into English Literature. Shakespeare talks in riddles as far as I'm concerned and I have no interest whatsoever in Politics."

"You *are* joking, Joel." Nell's heart was pounding in her chest. She had definitely not been prepared for such a blow. In one devastating minute, Joel had shattered all her plans for him. He wasn't being serious. He couldn't be!

"No, I'm not joking, Mum. I've been thinking about it for weeks. I don't know why I did those subjects in the first place," he said in an effort to explain to his incredulous mother that he was doing the right thing in abandoning his studies.

Nell gasped. "You are doing them because I chose them," she told him. "I directed you to follow a course of study which would give you several career options."

"Oh, that figures then," Joel stated. He took a deep breath and blew it out forcefully. "Your choices, not mine!" he said in an unnecessarily scathing tone. "I wish I'd realised how I'd been manipulated at the time, but I went along with your wishes as usual." The harsh reality was that he knew his overzealous mother had underhandedly controlled him yet again and he had to admit that he had allowed her to do so. Joel sighed loudly, more out of frustration than resignation.

"I thought I was being helpful, Joel. I know I did the right thing. I've already lined up possible job prospects for when you have completed your Advanced levels and university course. I can't believe you are being so ungrateful."

"Ungrateful? Ungrateful?" he shouted, his resentment forcing him to release all the tension that had been building up for... for how long? For years, and now he was venting his true feelings. "Am I supposed to thank you for treating me like an idiot who can't think for himself? I'll start looking for a job tomorrow and I'll do it by myself."

"Everybody knows tomorrow never comes, Joel." Nell felt her anger rising. She couldn't remember when she had last been so angry. Maybe it was after Tom's death when her bereavement took her through the whole spectrum of emotions. "You cannot possibly have thought this through before you made the rash decision to quit college. I can't bear the thought of you becoming another government statistic—not *my* son. Tomorrow never comes, Joel," she repeated quietly, her anger giving rise now to anxiety. "You can't just walk into a good job these days. I thought you knew that, but apparently not. You need qualifications. I've already spoken to your form tutor about you doing the Oxbridge paper. How stupid can you be, how inconsiderate, how insensitive? It's total madness!"

"You have done what?" Joel exclaimed. "I don't believe this. Mr. Harris must think I'm an imbecile who needs to have his mother speak for him. God almighty!"

"Joel Winston! Don't you dare blaspheme in this house!"

They had never had a row like this. She had guilefully avoided many adolescent arguments, usually because she had reasoned quietly, compromised often, humoured even, so that she always had the upper hand without their relationship being strained. But this was different. Now, Joel was pushing her to the limits and she wasn't going to allow him to jeopardise his future on the mere whim that he was wasting his time.

She looked at him standing in front of her, tall and erect, strong and defiant, young and vulnerable. Her heart went out to him in a desperate desire to sympathise with him, to plead with him, to urge him to rethink his plans, if indeed he had any, and make him see the error of his ways. On the other hand, she had to be assertive. *I am his mother after all. I know best. Joel is no longer the little boy on whom I have lavished all my love and attention for the past eighteen years. He is a young man, a man ready to face what life throws at him, a man eager and determined to prove himself in a man's world, a young man destined to make good. I am absolutely certain of that. But he can't do it without my help and he's too stubborn to realise it,* she reasoned silently. Nell's anger subsided, her motherly intuition overpowering that moment of wrath. She inhaled deeply, her lips pressed together as if she were about to embark upon a programme of rigorous exercise. "We'll talk about it later," she told her rebellious son, and Joel visibly relaxed, knowing he had cleared the first hurdle in the race to his future.

~ * ~

The following day, Nell rose early. She left Joel sleeping as she slipped out of the house, taking into account the fact that she need not be at work until eleven o'clock. She drove into town with some purpose and, having completed her task by ten-thirty, she arrived at work, unexpectedly feeling relieved. The mission she had set herself during her long, sleepless night had been fairly successful. The clerk in the employment agency had been very helpful and when Nell had been directed to Grinsberg, Grinsberg and Green, the eminent firm of solicitors, she was very confident that she was making the right overtures for her son's future.

"When he has finalised everything at college today, ask him to come and see us," Oliver Grinsberg Jnr. had said to Nell.

She had taken great pains to impress upon the gentleman that she had only called in at the employment agency to see what options were open to Joel—"To save him the time," she fibbed—but the solicitor was very amenable and at least didn't dismiss her as an overbearing mother. Common sense had later made her wrestle with her conscience as regards interfering too much, but it was easy for her to reassure herself that she was only doing what any caring mother would do.

When she arrived home from work that evening, Joel had been into college to tie up the loose ends and he had a cup of tea ready for her as soon as she walked in.

"I'm sorry if I upset you, Mum, but I really did hate the course." He was trying to make his mother understand how he felt, and his basic upbringing in being mannerly had not completely deserted him. "My heart wasn't in it and I couldn't see where it was leading. I want more out of life than going along with the flow just because the current is forcing me in that direction."

Nell smiled. "Very eloquently put, Joel." But she stopped him before they got into a heavy discussion about the rights and wrongs of his actions. She needed to choose her words carefully so Joel wouldn't accuse her of interfering again. She needed to be the very epitome of diplomacy. "The problem has been solved, Joel. You won't be swimming against the tide any longer," she told him. Joel listened as she explained the situation. She looked directly at him, trying to read the changing expressions on his face as she related her morning's exploits. At one point, she almost gave up, seeing what she thought was a look of extreme bitterness in his eyes.

She still continued to try to justify her actions until Joel suddenly stood up in disbelief, his arms flapping up and down as if he were about to take flight.

"Why have you done all that? You've made it look as though I'm a cretin who can't speak up for himself. That's twice now and for all I know, it may be more! For crying out loud, stop interfering in my life, Mother," and with that he stormed out and up to his bedroom. She heard his heavy footsteps on the stairs and she felt that the whole house was coming down upon her.

He grabbed a rucksack from the back of his wardrobe and put in as many of his clothes as he could manage. He had to get away. If he were to prove his worth in this world, he would do it on his own without his mother looking over his shoulder. He would stay at Ben's tonight and start his quest tomorrow. Then he smiled to himself ironically. He recalled what his mother had said about tomorrows, but told himself, "My tomorrow will come. Just you wait and see."

Nell was beside herself. When Joel came downstairs with his rucksack and his guitar strung over his shoulder, a look of complete defiance in his eyes, she pleaded with him to reconsider. She grabbed hold of her little boy and begged him not to go.

"Where will you go? What will you do?" she implored until the tears prevented her from presenting a logical argument for him to stay.

"I'll go to Ben's tonight," he told her. He owed her that at least. "And then I'll decide what I am going to do in my own time."

"But—"

"No buts, Mother." He knew she hated that formal title, but he felt so estranged from her at that moment that any words of endearment would diminish the depth of his true feelings. She had to know he was determined to stand alone on this and if it meant hurting her feelings in the process, then so be it. He was not falling for the guilt trip thing again. "You have to accept that I am no longer a child," he told her. "I have to demand that you respect my decision this time. I can't stand all this interference and the sooner you realise that, the better." They were strong words aimed at having an impact that should not be taken lightly and Nell felt the full force of his onslaught.

"You're being too sensitive, Joel. You are just like your father—"

"Don't you dare use my dad to make me feel guilty! That's typical of you, Mother. Never your fault. You're always right and woe betide anybody who disagrees with your decision."

When the door slammed in his wake, she dropped to her knees and sobbed. She ought to go after him, but he needed time to calm down, to see the error of his ways. Maybe tomorrow, he'd come back with his tail between his legs, realising she had been right all along. But what had she said about tomorrows?

"Oh God, what have I done?"

Six

As he had predicted when he was ten, Ben Mason moved into his one bed flat as soon as soon as he left school. It was by far preferable to watching his mother entertain first one deadbeat after another each night. Against the odds, he had gained a string of A grades in his exams and had managed to get a job in the bank. The money wasn't good, but it was enough to put food on the table and with a subsidy from the local council, he had rented a one-bed apartment in an area that was desperately in need of renovation. Ben decided it would do for the time being. He worried about his younger brother. Michael had to stay with a mother who was more concerned with buying a new mini-skirt than with making sure her youngest child was ready for school each day. Michael, at fifteen, was already regularly arriving late for school when his mother failed to surface in the mornings.

"Michael," Ben had advised, "just try to sort yourself out, kiddo. As soon as I can move into a bigger place, you can come to stay with me. I promise."

"You have no idea what she's like, Ben."

"Yes, I have. That's why I'm here."

"But I'm sick of waking up to ...." He stopped, embarrassed. How could he tell Ben what he heard coming from his mother's bedroom every night? The very thought of hearing the grunts and groans of the obnoxious fat bastards his mother took up with made him feel sick to the stomach.

"I know, Mickey, I know and I will help as soon as I can, but please try to block out all that stuff and get to school on time. You don't want old Hepworth calling you into his office anymore, do you?" Ben could only encourage his young brother to be strong in the face of adversity until he was able to rescue him from a life of hell. "You can come and do your homework here if you like, then at least you'll be well on the way to getting good grades." Michael had been momentarily placated with that.

When Joel knocked on the door, Ben had just arrived home from work. "Hello, mate," he said, surprised that Joel even knew where he lived.

"Hi," Joel said, not trying to hide the desperation in his voice. "I need a favour."

Although Ben had been Joel's friend for as long as he could remember, they had never actually visited each other's homes. He had always thought Joel lived at the other side of the track from him, the side that had everything and wanted for nothing. He had stopped calling at his house when he realised Joel's mother never invited him in. It didn't take a super brain to work out that he wasn't welcome. His friendship with Joel had always been strong, solid enough to withstand the teenage differences and petty jealousies that arose. Joel was never short of girlfriends and Ben had been quite envious of him. His only romance had been with one of Joel's cast-offs and it had lasted just a couple of weeks, because he couldn't afford to pay for her at the cinema. However, Joel was okay. He had liked his sense of fun and his popularity with his peers. That he should turn up here was a complete surprise to Ben.

"What can I do for you?"

"I need a bed for the night," Joel stated bluntly. "The settee will do if you don't mind me crashing out with you."

"You'd best come in. I'm not that sure that it's up to your standard. I try to keep it clean, but it's hardly the Hilton," he said to cover his embarrassment. "Beggars can't be choosers, can they?"

Joel cast a quick eye around the room, "It looks pretty good to me. It's just for one night, though and I'll move on tomorrow. I've had a run in with my mum and I just need some space, that's all."

"I'm not going to have her hammering on my door in the middle of the night, am I?" The thought of somebody else's parent bringing strife into the little place where he had created his own refuge wasn't in the least bit inspiring. Even his own irresponsible mother had not been allowed to do that. He had no intentions of allowing Joel's mother to shatter his peace.

"I don't think so..." Although Joel wasn't sure anymore what she might do. He briefly, very briefly, put Ben in the picture and emphasised again that he would be on his way the next day. He would have to spend the night working out his next move. All this was unplanned and the task of sorting out his future while he lay uncomfortably on Ben's threadbare sofa for one night was totally daunting to him.

It was well past midnight when the two friends stopped talking. With a few beers inside them and their tongues loosened, they had put the world to rights without touching on the finer details that directly affected each of them. "Remember when you told me I was too cocky, Ben?" Joel asked in a moment of self-assessment.

Ben looked embarrassed. "Yes, I do, but I was only jealous that you were going out with Amy at the time and I fancied her rotten!" he said.

Joel smiled knowingly. "My mother frightened Amy off ... and Angela...and Kate, but I was a bit of a pain in the backside, wasn't I? I know that now and hopefully I can change. I hate cocky bastards!"

The two young men laughed as they opened another bottle of Worthington E. Strangely, in spite of their alcohol-fuelled brains, they had both managed to keep their innermost thoughts to themselves. Ben had not talked about his brother, or his mother, and Joel had deliberately kept his mother's underhandedness out of the conversation. When eventually Ben went to his bedroom, leaving Joel to familiarise himself with the broken spring in the settee, their heads were full of teenage memories that had kept their spirits high during their adolescent years. Once alone, they both lay awake for hours, each making a bold effort to find some semblance of reason in his seemingly impossible situation. For Ben, it was easy. He had already begun to map out his own way in life. As for Joel, he had nowhere to go, no job and no idea where to start.

When daylight broke, Joel had reached no conclusion. He had looked at the possibility of going to Merseyside to seek the advice of his grandparents, but he thought that Grandpa Bob would be the proverbial soothsayer and would predict doom and gloom should he try to go it completely alone. Granny would nod in agreement without saying much at all and then she would give that look of disapproval to try to make him feel guilty. He loved them both dearly, but it always seemed that each had his own agenda for him and he felt trapped whichever way he looked at it. Merseyside was out of the question... or was it? He questioned his own wisdom in writing off Liverpool when he realised what opportunities were on offer. Liverpool was a thriving city. Joel's mind raced. "It's a place where young people are establishing themselves in the music industry. There are opportunities for everybody who shows some inclination to make the big time. Everybody knows about the Maria Morenzi Theatre School in Liverpool. I've seen some of her pupils on All Your Own," he told Ben. He grew excited as he recalled the talent show on television and the times he'd heard some of her pupils with fabulous voices on the Carroll Levis Discovery Show on the radio.

"I could be mixing with the likes of that new girl singer in Liverpool, Cilla Black. Somebody told me she had been at the theatre school, too, but I don't know how true it is. I did all right as Billy Bigelow in Carousel," he enthused, "and as Curly in Oklahoma, but they were hardly Broadway productions and not really what I could claim as theatrical experience."

"Ah well, think positive, Joel. That's the only thing you can do."

He looked directly at Ben as his excitement grew and said, more to reassure himself than to inform his friend, "The jam sessions with my music teacher always gained praise. My skills on the guitar are on a par with some of the groups that are coming out of Liverpool at the moment," he said confidently. Joel's heart leapt and he thought he could see his way forward.

Ben was incredulous at Joel's hastily made plans. "It's madness, Joel. What will your mum say?"

"Mum won't know, Ben. I've got to swear you to secrecy. If she turns up here, and I don't believe she will, but if she does, you don't know where I've gone. I'll call her to tell her not to worry and that I'll be in touch when I'm settled. She won't like it, but it's what I have to do. Promise me... please, Ben." Joel thanked his mate and headed for the station.

~ * ~

He took a train to Beat City and found his way amid the clamour of young voices all seeking the spotlight, all vying for that elusive place in the hearts of the teeny boppers and the dream of stardom. *Well, it's a start anyway.* Sitting on the crowded diesel train in Wigan Wall Street station, he couldn't help sensing the excitement in this outrageous adventure upon which he was embarking, the overwhelming feeling of independence, the reckless act of freeing himself of the shackles his over-protective mother had applied for as long as he could remember. He ought to feel guilty that he had left her bereft, not allowing her to know where he was going. In fact, he felt wonderfully liberated. *I'll call her eventually, but not until I've established myself in my own domain... my choice, my decision, my future.*

He closed his eyes and allowed himself to be carried away with the rhythmical beat of the train's wheels on the track, but was roused from his reverie as somebody pushed into the small space between him and the elderly gentleman who had not looked up from reading his newspaper during the whole journey. Wriggling around to squeeze her small frame into the gap of no more than six inches, the newcomer tutted and sighed as she put her oversized holdall on the floor of the compartment close to her feet. She was clearly disgruntled, at odds with the world.

"What's happened to good old-fashioned chivalry?" she muttered under her breath. "What's a girl got to do before some knight in shining armour comes to her rescue? I've been standing in the corridor since I got on the train in Wigan. The carriages are all crowded and nobody has the decency to help with my heavy luggage, and to top that, nobody has moved an inch to let me sit down." She sighed deeply and loudly. "If you sat up straight," she said to the young man looking as if he were lost in thought and sprawled diagonally across two seats, "another person would be able to sit down!"

Joel sat up immediately and moved as close to the window as he could so the girl could fit in between him and the avid newspaper reader. "Sorry," he mumbled without looking up.

"And so you should be. Whoever said the age of chivalry wasn't dead was way off the mark. You wouldn't have got far in King Arthur's court, that's for sure." She was trying to make conversation, trying to relieve the stress she had been feeling not just because she couldn't find a seat on the train, but also because of the row she'd had with her mother that morning.

As the train pulled into Lime Street station, there was an uneasy silence between the two young people. Joel picked up his guitar and his rucksack, jumped down from the train and, following the exit signs, set off confidently into the unknown. He had no idea what was in store for him, but he was not deterred. First he would find a place to stay and then he would set out his stall.

The girl watched as he left her in his wake. She looked around for Penny, who was supposed to meet her at the station. Typical! Penny was nowhere to be seen, late as usual.

Joel made a hasty decision to turn left as he walked to the exit. There was no rocket science involved, just a simple imaginary flip of a coin. *I'll go right if I see a policeman, left if I see a cab.* The cab won and Joel made his way down Lime Street towards the city centre.

I guess I'd better find a phone box, he thought, *but then I can do that later when I've found somewhere to stay.*

Seven

"What shall I do, Mum?" Nell appealed sorrowfully to her mother. "He just packed his bag and left. I can't believe it." She wanted to say 'after all I've done for him,' but stopped short of sounding like a martyr to the cause.

"Leave him for a couple of days and see what happens. At least you know he isn't sleeping rough. He'll come to his senses and realise which side his bread is buttered. Kids these days just seem so ungrateful. I don't know what gets into them. Who is this Ben, anyway?"

"But Joel isn't just any kid, Mum...he's my son and Ben is one of his friends from school. Not my choice of friend, I can tell you. His mother is ... well, let's say, she isn't too fussy about the men she takes up with and I never liked Joel mixing with him. I vaguely remember Joel saying he had moved into a bedsit somewhere round Deane Road. Can't blame the boy for leaving home really, having a mother like that. I don't know where he lives, but it wouldn't be too difficult to find out."

Her mother was aghast. "Don't do that!" she advised, "You'll make matters worse if you go looking for him. Where's your common sense gone, Nell? Joel is a man, albeit a very young man, but he can be a train driver if he likes, or go down the mines, and he can marry if he so wishes and we can't do anything to stop him. Give him time and space..."

"How will I cope without him?" Nell wailed.

"You'll cope—you'll have to. If we still had conscription, he'd have been called up by now so just be strong and it will all turn out right in the end."

Her mother had been unusually calm and controlled. At the very least, Nell had expected her to raise her voice in despair as she herself had done, but Margaret had been uncharacteristically down to earth and all without her husband's logical input.

"Leave the lad alone," Bob said after Margaret had given him her version of Nell's plight. "If I'm being totally honest, it doesn't surprise me that he's rebelled. He's been mollycoddled and pampered all his life. Some of those who've been indulged as children become feckless wimps. Others become rebellious and make a stand to prove their strength of character. Thank God Joel's showing some independence, that's all I can say."

"Bob!" Margaret cried, "Can't you see what it's doing to Nell? We have to be there for her. She's distraught. Our little girl is devastated."

"There you go, Margaret," Bob said defiantly, "like mother, like daughter. She isn't our little girl anymore, she's a grown woman and if she's making mistakes, she has to have the courage to put them right. I know she's our daughter and I love her dearly, but I don't always like what she does. She knows we're here for her if she needs us, but she has to work things out for herself as far as Joel is concerned. We can only hope she has the sense and good grace to admit her faults."

Margaret wasn't so sure. "I think I'll go to Bolton tomorrow. At least I'll be moral support for her."

"All right, all right, but I think you're making a mistake. You are getting involved with something you can't do anything about, but if that's what you want to do, go ahead. I only hope I don't have to say 'I told you so' later." Bob was sceptical about his wife's involvement. Nell would manipulate her mother into thinking that Joel was in the wrong. He knew his women and there was nothing so sure.

"I won't take sides," Margaret assured him, but he knew very well she would.

~ * ~

Nell was on the telephone as Margaret walked through the door. She signalled to her mother to go through to the lounge and indicated that the call was important.

"But where are you?" she asked the person at the other end of the line.

"I'm in Liverpool, not a million miles away, and it's a place I'm familiar with so you've no need to worry. Please don't make this any more difficult for me, Mum." Joel was still not in the mood for his mother's antics, but felt he should at least try to be civil.

"But where will you stay? Couldn't you live at Granny and Grandpa's? It's only a ferry ride to the city centre. I think that would be ideal and—"

"You still don't get it, do you, Mum? *You* think it would be ideal, *your* decision, *your* choice. All this has to be my choice and my decision. If I make mistakes, they'll be *my* mistakes and I'll deal with them," Joel insisted. "I'm going to apply for a place at the City Theatre School, so I'll let you know how it goes. Bye for now, Mum." He replaced the receiver before Nell played the emotional card again. He wasn't ready for all that sob story stuff just yet.

Margaret stood at the door and watched her daughter as she stared at the telephone in her hand, dumbfounded. "He hung up on me before I could plead my case," she cried. "He's in Liverpool!"

"Is he? Well, he could stay with his grandpa and me, couldn't he?" Margaret relaxed a little, thinking she had solved the problem before she'd even taken off her coat.

"That's what I told him, but he rejected the offer without any consideration whatsoever. I tell you, Mum, he's totally out of hand. I feel so angry with him. I don't understand him anymore." Nell was in despair again, but her anger was spurring her on.

"Nell, calm down. At least he's called to let you know he's all right. We have to be thankful for that," Margaret reasoned.

"I can't believe you are so matter-of-fact about it, Mum," Nell complained. "Can't you see what it's doing to me? I would have thought that you above all people would be on my side."

"I don't intend to take sides, Nell, but as your mother, I'm here to support you. I don't like what Joel is doing, but I'm trying to keep a level head. Your dad thinks you and I are going to join forces and become hell bent on bringing Joel to heel, but I haven't got a magic wand and I have no idea how to deal with this at the moment," Margaret told her distraught daughter.

Nell sighed. "I feel useless," she stated, "useless, helpless and redundant. I am having great difficulty in getting my head around this. It's Joel we're talking about. Not some unloved, dragged up, aimless individual whose life means nothing. These things happen to other people, not to us."

"Did he say he would let you know what he intends to do?" Margaret asked.

"He said something about applying to the Theatre School, but surely he can't just walk in and ask for a place." Nell was gradually trying to make some sense out of her wayward son's reckless decision. "I have to try to go along with him, if only for some peace of mind."

"That sounds a reasonable plan for both of you," Margaret told her. "Now, let's have a cup of tea and decide what we can do to make this sorry affair more bearable."

Eight

Liverpool in June was alive with the hustle and bustle of day-to-day routines, with traffic that was noisy, but not intrusive, with ships' sirens echoing across the city from Pier Head. Lively, vibrant sounds were bellowing from every store and from every transistor radio carried by the young people who were unwittingly creating musical history. Joel, his guitar slung over his shoulder and his rucksack on his back, looked overloaded, but not out of place. He stood at the bottom of the steps of the Adelphi Hotel listening to the guitarist whose pitch outside the main entrance of Lewis's seemed to be drawing lots of attention. The cap strategically placed at the musician's feet was full of coins: pennies, three-penny bits, sixpences, shillings and on closer inspection there were even half crowns in there. The young man was about Joel's age, long haired and really not, Joel noticed, very adept at picking out the chords on his guitar, but his voice was pleasant enough and some young girls were jiving on the pavement, lending a party atmosphere to the gathering gloom of the summer evening.

Joel looked at his watch. *Half past four already*, he thought. He trundled to the bus stop where he could see several young people waiting in the queue. The one at the end had his hands pushed deep in his pockets and was shifting his weight from side to side as if he were desperate to use the toilet. Amused at this thought, Joel tapped him on the shoulder. "Excuse me," he said to the young man who was hopping around at the back.

The boy turned round and glared. "What?" he snapped.

"Blimey. Forget it," Joel told him, thinking he'd ask somebody else who didn't give the impression that he'd attack a bloke just for looking at him. Joel knew his limits and decided to turn away from a possibly hostile situation.

"Who d'yer think you are?" the angry young man asked the somewhat bemused Joel. "Talk to me like I'm dirt on yer shoe and I'll rip yer 'ead off yer shoulders." He grabbed at Joel's jacket lapels and butted him straight between the eyes. Reeling, Joel took a step back, completely disoriented. The next thing he knew, he was on the ground looking up into a sea of concerned eyes, angry voices rallying in his defence.

"Hey, you thug! Leave the kid alone. He didn't do anything to you."

"Mind yer own fuckin' business," the bully spat at them and instantly turned and ran into the crowd, pushing his spoils into his pocket.

"Where are the bizzies when you need 'em?" one of Joel's Samaritans asked. "Are you awright, wack? Do yer need the ozzy? There's a bit o' blood on yer 'ooter."

Joel felt his nose and shook his head. "I'll be okay," he said, "but maybe you can help me." This lad looked reasonable and he had shown some concern for Joel.

"No wonder he decked yer," the boy said grinning mischievously. "Talking like that, he musta thought yer were a shirtlifter! Yer not, are yer, la?"

"A what?" Joel asked uncomprehending for a moment and then realisation made him laugh raucously. "Definitely not, mate. You've no need to worry on that score."

"Didn't think you were, but yer accent isn't Scouse. Where've yer come from?"

"Only Bolton, so it's not that far away," Joel told him and silently cursed his mother for making him speak properly. He stood out like a sore thumb in this company. "I'm Joel," he told the lad.

"Posh name too!" he teased. "Hiya, I'm Gerry, not Marsden, but it's good for leadin' the judies on, yer know, when I'm at The Cabin. Gerry Marsden's goin' to be famous one o' these days. Now, what is it yer want, wack? I'll help if I can."

Joel eased himself on to the bench in the bus shelter. The queue had dispersed and he and Gerry were the only two left.

"Have I made you miss your bus?" he asked apologetically.

"Nah. Me mam won't have me jam butty ready yet," he joked.

"I'm looking for somewhere to stay," Joel told him. "I can pay—"

"Wayo, wack," Gerry interrupted quietly. "Don't say that too loud. They'll rob yer blind round 'ere if they 'ear yer saying yer flushed."

"Well, do you know of anywhere?"

Gerry thought for a moment and as the bus drew up next to them, he said, "Come on, get on 'ere with me. I'll find yer somewhere to get yer 'ead down for a few nights."

They were on the bus for about fifteen minutes and the two young men didn't say much to each other apart from Joel finding out that Gerry was a few months younger than he was and was looking forward to turning eighteen so he could have a legal bevvy without the bizzies givin' him the evils and asking for his birth certificate. "I usually go for a leak when I see a tall hat coming in the door!" He grinned at Joel. "I can always duck down the jigger through the back if I think they're on to me. Any road, they've seen me chuckin' arrers and not bothered so long as I haven't got a pint in me 'and."

"What's a jigger?" Joel asked. He had visions of Gerry with his head down the toilet.

Gerry looked at him wide eyed. "Did you come down in the last shower, La? It's the alley at the back of the pub. Come on, this is our stop."

Joel picked up his guitar and his rucksack from the seat in front. He looked around for any pointers to tell him where he was so he wouldn't have to show his ignorance again to his benefactor. He looked up at the street sign riveted to the wall on the side of the corner shop. They'd just passed Princes Park so he vaguely knew the location. Elsie Street to the left, Doris Street to the right. They stopped at the shop and Gerry pointed to a notice on the door. 'Room to Let. Apply Within.' "Come on, let's apply within."

"Ullo dur, Gerry. 'ow yer doin', our kid?" the young woman behind the counter greeted them. "Who've we got 'ere? Looks like he's bin ten rounds wi' Cassius Clay!"

"Muhammad Ali now, our Chrissie. Get yer facts straight."

Joel looked from one to the other, totally unaware of what Gerry had in mind. He directed his words to Chrissie. "I'm Joel..."

"Ooo er! That's a posh name, even though you do look a bit rough," Chrissie told him. "'ave you bin 'avin a barney wi' somebody?"

"Not really," Joel informed her. "I walked into a lamp-post."

"Oh yeah and the queen's our ol' granny!"

"Shut yer gob, Chrissie. Some lowlife welcomed 'im to the Pool with a Kirkby kiss and then legged it before we could call the bizzies. He's lookin' for somewhere to stay, so we're applyin' within." Gerry cocked his thumb towards the notice on the door.

"Oh, right then," Chrissie became more businesslike. "The room's in the attic above the shop. It's small, but clean and there's a separate bathroom and lavvy up there. You can eat with us if yer like, but that'll cost a couple o' quid more a week. With food, the rent is five pound, without food, it's three.'

"Sounds great," Joel told her, silently thanking his lucky stars Gerry had been at the bus stop on Renshaw Street.

"Our Gerry'll show yer up. 'is room is just below yours so yer can stamp around as much as yer want." Just then the shop door flew open and a crowd of noisy school kids came in.

"Hey, youse lot! Behave, or gerrout!"

"Come on, Poshman." Gerry winked good-naturedly. "Let's get yer settled in and then we'll have our jam butties with a cuppa tea."

They climbed up the stairs at the back of the shop to the first floor. At the top of the stairs was a long corridor with several doors on each side. The first door on the left was open and through it wafted a delicious smell of roast beef. A lady whom Joel guessed was in her early forties called out from the kitchen as they passed. "You got somethin' to tell me, our Gerry, or are yer just goin' to walk past without introducing me to yer mate?"

"Awrigh', Mam," Gerry greeted her, "This is Joel..."

"That's a posh name... 'ow are yer, love? Yer look as though yer've done ten rounds—"

"With Muhammad Ali... yes, I know. That's what Chrissie said," Joel agreed. "I haven't been fighting though, Mrs. ... Blimey, Gerry, I don't even know your last name."

"I'm Mrs. Connolly, love, but call me Maggie, everybody does," Gerry's mother invited. "We don't stand on ceremony 'ere."

"Thanks, Maggie." Joel liked her already. "I really appreciate your offering me a room. I won't be any trouble and I'm trying to get a place at the Theatre School."

"A student, eh? Well, we like students, don't we, Gerry? We hope they'll teach you some common sense, don't we, Gerry?" Maggie eyed her son lovingly. "He's a good boy really. While he's doing his apprenticeship down the docks, he'll be able to study at night school for a diploma. Then he can look after his ol' girl in 'er old age."

"Gerroff, Mam," Gerry told her. "Stop showin' me up in front of my new mate. Take no notice of 'er, Joel, she's off 'er 'ead most of the time!"

"No wonder either, wi' you and our Chrissie," she joked, "but I loves yer both to death and don't yous both know it!"

Maggie Connolly was indeed a very young mother. At thirty-seven, she had a daughter of twenty and a son, *God bless 'im,* who was almost eighteen. She looked a little careworn, but still had a reasonable figure and, with the services of a good hairdresser, might still pass as being very attractive. Her dress sense left a little to be desired since the trendy mini-skirt didn't hang well over her shapely hips and the tight sweater only emphasised her matronly bosom, but everybody who knew her said she had a heart of gold and would move the earth to please her husband and her children.

At the far end of the corridor, Gerry led Joel up another flight of narrow steps to the attic. The room was indeed small, but had a single bed, a chest of drawers and a chair. There was a built-in wardrobe for his clothes and through a narrow door where the roof slanted sharply, a dormer room had been erected to house a surprisingly spacious bathroom with a bath, washbasin and toilet. The fittings were obviously new and Joel was delighted with what he saw.

"Will it do, Poshman?" Gerry asked. He'd adopted the nickname for Joel, who took it all in good part. He realised Gerry was just being friendly and he willingly accepted the camaraderie that was on offer.

"It's great," Joel replied and offered his hand to this Liverpudlian saviour who had asked no questions and welcomed him into his family. "Thanks, Wacker," he said and from then on, Poshman and Wacker were best mates, cronies, allies, the most unlikely partnership that fostered respect and unconditional loyalty from the start.

When the shop closed at six o'clock, they sat round the kitchen table and ate roast beef and three veg. Maggie had made a huge chocolate cake for afters and as Joel savoured every mouthful, he listened to the family banter from the Connolly clan.

Maggie had married her man when she was nearly seventeen and she'd had Chrissie straight away. "I had a big, wide frock that covered the bump," she joked. "A few snooty neighbours looked down their noses at me, but I didn't care. Me and Paddy were madly in love. He had to go to sea soon after the wedding. He was in the Merchant Navy, if you can call the Isle o' Man boats the navy." She grinned. "He's still crossing the Irish Sea four times a week, but he goes to Dublin these days. He says it's like going home. I only get to see him one night a week, but I reckon that's why we're still together." Joel listened politely. Chrissie watched him as he nodded in agreement, or shook his head in dismay as Maggie related her exploits during the war.

"Paddy set me up in the shop when he'd made enough money from the boats. He used to get all sorts of stuff from the docks that I could sell off. I only sold it to my mates, though, the ones whose fellas were away fighting. It wasn't legal, but I got away with it. I think the bizzies weren't bothered so long as it helped them in need."

"How old are you, Joel?" Chrissy asked him. "What do your mam and dad do?"

Alarm bells rang in Joel's head. How much should he say? He didn't want these kind-hearted people to think he was a delinquent who had run away from home. They might want to ship him straight back to where he'd come from. "I'm eighteen," he told them truthfully. "My dad died when I was a baby and my mum is a doctor's receptionist. My parents came from the Wirral originally."

"Oooo, no wonder you're posh! Over the water, no less!"

"They moved to Bolton when they got married, but my grandparents still live in Heswall," Joel told them. "They suggested I live with them while I was in Liverpool, but I want to be independent. I don't think I could stand them fussing all the time." He hoped he sounded credible.

"Well, you'll be okay 'ere, la," Maggie reassured him, "and there's a phone box on the corner if you want to call home."

"Shall I pay you now, Maggie? I can give you a month's rent in advance and then I'll look for a part-time job to fit in with my studies ...when I start college. Maybe I'll call my mum now." He pushed up his sleeve to look at his watch. "That's funny. My watch has gone..."

"It'll be that lowlife what decked yer this affie," Gerry interjected. "That's why he took off so quick. Do you want to report it?"

"It was my dad's watch, not worth a lot, but it was valuable to me," Joel told him. "If he's looking to make money on it, he won't get much." He was sad that his father's watch was gone, but common sense told him the memories planted in his heart by his mother would always be there, watch or no watch. "No, I won't report it. I don't think it would be much use. The police won't be interested in a bit of pick pocketing and that's all it is, really. At least he didn't get my wallet. I'm thankful for that."

Joel offered to help with the washing up before he went to find the phone box. After being made to feel like part of the Connolly family, his conscience bit him and he knew he should call Nell to tell her he had found somewhere to stay. Much as he needed to be away from her just now, he felt he owed her that at least.

Nine

The telephone call was strained. Joel tried to keep the conversation light by being cheery about the Connollys.

"How did you find their place in Princes Park?" Nell asked. "Are you sure it's a decent area? Wait till you see it in daylight before you make a decision to stay. You can still go to Granny's, you know."

Joel took a deep breath. "It's fine, Mum," he said with forced composure.

"Well, how did you find it?" she repeated, determined to ascertain that Joel wasn't lowering his standards just to prove his independence.

"I met Gerry Connolly at the bus stop near the Adelphi and asked if he knew of anywhere I might stay." He felt it sensible not to mention the incident.

"Well, I'll have to take your word for it," Nell conceded, "but I shall certainly come and visit you soon to make sure. Have you got a cold? You're talking down your nose."

"Mum!" Joel said, unable to hide his irritation. "I'll call you again later when I have secured a place at college. And I might have a bit of a cold coming on. My nose is a bit blocked. Cheerio and don't worry."

Nell stared incredulously at the telephone in her hand. "Don't worry?" she asked the inanimate object she was firmly holding onto. "How could he do this? How could he?"

When Joel returned to his room, Gerry was getting ready to go out. "I'm going to The Bull with my mates. Do yer want to come, Poshman?"

"I think I'll just settle in if that's okay, Wacker. It's been a big day one way and another. I'll come out with you next time. I think I just need a good night's sleep," Joel explained and then wondered if he'd offended his benefactor. "If you really want me to..."

"Nah, it's okay, mate, but I'll tell 'em about you, though. They're a good lot. A bit rough round the edges, but good mates," Gerry told him.

"Thanks, Wacker, I appreciate what you've done. I shall be eternally grateful."

Gerry looked embarrassed. "Look, mate, don't get all soppy on me. I know a good sort when I see one and you are one of 'em. It'll be like havin' a brother in the 'ouse. I'll see yer later."

Joel went down to the living room where Maggie and Chrissie were watching television and knocked gently on the door before he went in. "Eee, lad, you don't have to knock," Maggie said. "Just make yerself at home. Come and watch a bit of *Coronation Street*. That Ena Sharples is a right old battleaxe. She'd do a good job down Scottie Road, she would. She'd have all the scallies sorted out, that's for sure!"

"I just came down to pay my rent, if that's all right, and then I'll have an early night. It's been a big day today and that bump on the nose hasn't helped."

"Do you want a couple of aspirins?" Chrissie offered. "I can get a tape of Aspros from out the shop. It's no trouble."

"No thanks. I'll be okay when I've had a sleep. Here's twenty pounds, Maggie. That should cover me for four weeks," Joel said and offered four crisp fivers to his new landlady.

"Thanks, love. I'll make out a receipt and give it to you termorrer. We'll have to do it proper so you know we're not on the fiddle."

"I know you're not on the fiddle," Joel told her. "I'll be off then. Goodnight, Maggie, 'night Chrissie. See you tomorrow."

The women smiled and said, "Good night then, la. Sleep tight and mind the bugs don't bite."

Joel sat on his bed and looked around. This room bore no resemblance to his bedroom at home, but it felt comfortable. He took up his guitar and removed the instrument from its case, stroking it fondly and enjoying the familiarity of its form. He placed his fingers on the neck and strummed a few chords quietly. He softly hummed the tune ... *'Are you lonesome tonight, Do you miss me tonight, Are you sorry we drifted apart...'* thinking of his childhood and all the reasons that had brought him to this place. Setting down the guitar by his side on the bed, he slowly removed his clothes, deliberately throwing them on the floor to leave them there until morning, and then he drifted off to sleep.

Outside his bedroom door, Chrissie Connolly listened to the soulful voice of their new lodger. *He's good*, she thought, *He's bloody good.*

~ * ~

The City Theatre School had been in existence for several years. A local dance teacher had seen the potential in those youngsters without inhibitions and recognised the advantages for children who needed a confidence boost. Maria Morenzi, a child of Italian immigrants, born in The Dingle, Liverpool, had herself been a Windmill girl and had appeared at *Les Folies Bergere* in Paris just after the war. Later, as a principal dancer at the London Palladium, she had learned every aspect of the entertainment industry, including choreography and theatrical direction. Her school introduced live theatre to her beloved Liverpudlians. The school began in a church hall off Scotland Road and then took over premises on the Docks Road. The old warehouse was built of bricks blackened by the smoke and grime from surrounding factories and the river, but its big double doors opened up to offer wonderful opportunities for talented children in the world of entertainment. Maria Morenzi was well into her seventies, but she still had an influential role to play in her establishment. Her pupils performed in the Christmas pantomimes at the Empire Theatre and several of them had gone on to take leading roles in the West End and on Broadway. The theatrical world loved and respected her work.

Armed with his guitar, Joel stood and stared at the enormous red doors that oozed ostentation. They were painted to depict stage curtains partially opened to reveal the most elaborate sign in gold lights: CITY THEATRE SCHOOL WHERE DREAMS COME TRUE. The double doors were no longer functional and a smaller sign indicated that the entrance was to the left of the building down a side street. The side stage door was the entry into the school. Joel was impressed with the authenticity. He pressed the bell on the intercom. "Yes?" a husky voice responded.

"Hello. My name is Joel Winston..."

"Ooo, that's a posh name...!"

Joel grinned. He'd never considered that his name was posh, but since it was the fourth time he'd heard that comment in the last two days, he acknowledged that perhaps it was a bit out of the ordinary. He coughed and started again. "My name is Joel Winston ...call it posh if you like... but may I speak to the principal, please?"

"Well, that depends," the faceless voice replied.

"I can make an appointment if necessary, but I just came on speck. I know I'm being presumptuous and—"

"Hold on, Joel Winston. Slow down a bit. Push the handle on your right and I'll release the catch. Let's have a look at who's talking."

Joel did as instructed and pushed open the door. Inside was a reception hall with a long polished oak desk behind which sat an elderly lady surrounded by theatrical posters of yesteryear and pictures of entertainers unknown to Joel. In the distance, he could hear piano music and a female voice instructing, "Watch your head, Josephine, and point those toes, Marilyn. Stop, stop! Start again and perfect this time, please, ladies. I despair!"

The lady noted Joel's interest. "That's Miss Elvira. Do you dance?"

"Only when I think nobody's watching," Joel admitted, "but I have been known to strut my stuff around the stage a bit in school productions and my drama teacher thought I had good co-ordination and rhythm. I can't imagine myself as a ballet dancer, though."

"If you come here, you'll have to do a bit of everything before you graduate. Good performers are multi-talented, you know. See that picture there," the lady said, pointing an arthritic finger towards a dapper gentleman in striped blazer and straw boater. She leaned forward as though imparting a great secret and beckoned Joel to come closer. "Maurice Chevalier," she told him proudly. "I worked with him in Paris." She winked and touched the side of her nose knowingly.

Joel smiled. "That's wonderful," he said. "Who's the little guy in the glasses?"

"Oh, that's Arthur Askey, one of the best loved comedians Liverpool ever produced. I loved that little man." She winked again. "Only he was married and I didn't stand a chance! He's still going, you know."

"You seem to have had a very eventful life, Miss… sorry, I don't know your name."

"You don't need my name. I thought you wanted to see the principal," she reminded him. "Well, just take a seat and I'll see if he's available. You can fill out an application form whilst you're waiting. Here you are. There's a pen there on the desk." With that, she glided through a door behind where she had been sitting, her diaphanous robes floating behind her and leaving in her wake a smell of expensive perfume on the air.

Joel filled out the form carefully. It was fairly straightforward and although there was space for academic qualifications, the emphasis seemed to be on experience in entertainment and that worried him. His only experience had been in school productions. His Ordinary level in Drama might help. All he wanted was a chance to perform and gain a place on the course.

He had been sitting there for about ten minutes before the door behind the desk opened again. A very tall, theatrical-looking gentleman appeared, wearing a crisp white shirt and sporting a very colourful cravat round his neck. His very upright stance gave him an air of superiority and Joel assumed he was the principal. "Good morning, young man," he said offering a well-manicured hand. "Theodore Pendennis."

Joel stood up and shook the gentleman's hand firmly, silently thanking his grandfather for that vital piece of information regarding etiquette. "Never offer a limp hand, my boy. Gives the impression that you are weak and ineffectual." Smiling confidently, he replied, "Good morning, sir. I'm pleased to meet you."

"Let me see your application, please. You must be keen if you've come here to apply in person. I like a bit of initiative." Pendennis studied the sheet in silence apart from the intermittent grunts that didn't inspire Joel with confidence at all. "Hmm, O level results pretty impressive. That's useful because you have to do theory in some of our subjects, particularly music." He paused briefly and took out a large desk diary from under the counter. Flicking through the pages, he said, "Let's see... are you able to come back on Friday for an audition?"

"Yes, sir," Joel replied enthusiastically.

"Bring references and make sure you have audition pieces prepared. Four-thirty Friday and your name?"

"Joel Winston, sir."

"Hmm, that's a posh name. A good stage name. See you on Friday and please be punctual." With a flourish of his right hand, Pendennis left the room.

~ * ~

"Our Chrissie heard you singing last night," Gerry told him when he arrived home from work. "She says you're pretty good as well."

Joel blushed. He hadn't realised anybody could hear. "She wasn't supposed to be listening," he said, but unable to keep his good news from Gerry, he blurted out, "I've got an audition at Maria Morenzi's Theatre School on Friday."

"Well done, Poshman. I'm made up for yer. Yer can sing for us after tea. It'll be good practice."

"Okay, I'll see, but I'll have to go out tomorrow and find a part-time job. The term doesn't start until October and my savings won't last forever. I'll apply for a study grant once I get a place at the college—if I get a place, that is."

"From what our Chrissie says, you'll be the next Cliff Richard, but he's a singer for girls so will yer try to be a bit more like Elvis?" Gerry looked at him, curling his top lip to emulate the King of Rock and Roll. With his hips gyrating and his rubbery legs bending and twisting in all directions, he did a reasonable imitation of Elvis's 'Blue Suede Shoes' and it made Joel laugh.

"Maybe you should come to the audition with me," he said, grinning at his mate.

"Not me, Poshman," Gerry replied. "I'd need a few bevvies inside me to sing in public!"

Maggie came into the living room. "Here y'are, love, yer receipt! How did yer get on today?"

Joel thanked her and told her about the college, the old lady behind the desk and Theodore Pendennis. "He must be the principal, I think, so at least I've had a look at him before my interview. I have to have audition pieces ready for Friday."

"You'll be fine, love," Maggie reassured him. "Our Chrissie ..."

"Yes, so I believe," he interrupted.

Maggie smiled, a warm welcoming smile that made Joel feel comfortable and at home. His mother had often smiled at him, in fact she smiled at him all the time, but Maggie's smile was different, not patronising, nor condescending, just homely.

After they had eaten, Chrissie dared to ask, "Will you sing for us, Joey?"

"Joey?" Maggie questioned.

"Well, Joel's too posh for the likes of me. Joey's more Liverpool, so I'm going to call him Joey from now on, if you don't mind." She looked at Joel with raised eyebrows and waited for an answer.

"You can call me anything you like," he told her, "within reason. I don't think I'd answer to Ratbag or Wet Nelly, and please don't call me Winnie. I hate Winnie!"

"Only when I want to annoy you, Joey. So that's settled then. Now will yer sing for us or not?"

Joel went to get his guitar from his room, feeling more than a bit embarrassed, but he reasoned silently that he would have to overcome any show of nerves if he intended to make it in the world of show business.

The family sat in the cosy living room for a couple of hours listening to the young lad who had appeared from nowhere and was allowing them to be privy to his talent before his audition. Joel's confidence soared with their appreciation and he decided that his audition pieces would be "Can't Help Falling in Love," the Elvis version, Cliff Richard's "Nine Times Out of Ten," which would give more scope to show his pop side and then he would finish with his own composition, "Flight of Fancy." The words would be perfect:

> *'There's a place in my heart where fantasy dwells,*
> *There is hope that I'll always be free,*

To follow my vision that gives me the chance,
To follow that dear flight of fancy.

Chorus: Don't say it's a pipedream,
Don't tell me I'm wrong,
Don't shatter illusions
When I sing you my song.

There's a wish that I'm wishing deep in my soul,
There's a consuming yearning within,
Belief ever urging and making me dance
To the tune of my dear flight of fancy.

Chorus: Don't say it's a pipedream, etc.

This was Joel's song, and nobody had heard it before. He sang it soulfully with eyes closed most of the time and as he finished, he looked up to see Maggie wiping away a tear.

"That's beautiful, lad," she said. "Sing like that and you'll be number one in a flash."

"I don't know about that. My main aim is to do what I want to do and convince my mother I don't need her to show me the way." It seemed harsh, but Joel felt the need to be brutally honest.

"That's a bit hard on yer mam, Joey," Chrissie told him. "She did bring you into the world, after all."

"It's complicated, Chrissie." He didn't want to get involved in the whys and wherefores of his hasty departure from the home where he'd grown up. This was *his* life and he had a lot to prove.

The telephone box on the corner of Doris Street was out of order. Somebody had jammed pennies into the slot and button B wouldn't press in at all. "I need a telephone, Maggie. Where is the nearest one after Doris Street?"

"Oh, lad, it's down at Childwall Valley, or back into town. I could ask Mrs. Lafferty next door. She's had a phone put in and she'll let yer use it, I'm sure, if it's important," Maggie told him. "Now that you're staying here, I might be able to afford one myself. It'll be more convenient for us all."

"I don't want to be a nuisance, Maggie, but if I don't get these references for Friday, I'll be right up the creek without a paddle," Joel said.

Maggie grinned, her eyes twinkling like a mischievous schoolgirl. "That's a more polite way than our Gerry would have put it. He'd describe the creek by using the stuff that's flushed down the lav! But come on, I'll ask Mrs. Lafferty and tell her it's an emergency."

While Maggie Connolly and Nora Lafferty caught up on the latest gossip, Joel called his drama teacher and asked for a reference. He arranged to return to Bolton the following day to collect it. He also called the head teacher of the college and the vicar of his local church, although he couldn't be certain that his mother wouldn't have gone to him for spiritual guidance in dealing with the present situation concerning her wayward son. It was a risk he'd have to take, as references from parish priests were important for confirming that he was a person of moral substance and reliability. He knew he might get a lecture, but if so, he'd tough it out.

On the journey back to Bolton, Joel planned his itinerary for the day. He would go to college first and then the vicarage. After that he would call to see his mother and put her in the picture. He didn't want her turning up in Liverpool just yet. If he went to the surgery, she wouldn't be able to make a scene. He wanted to be back at the Connolly house before dark.

The visit to college was extremely encouraging. Roberta Davenport, his drama teacher, was thrilled that he was applying to the theatre school and gave him a few tips for the audition. "Be confident, not cocky," she advised pointedly. "Project and perform, smile when appropriate and use your talent for wit to your advantage. You can do it, Joel. Have you got your audition pieces ready?"

"I have three musical pieces and I thought you might advise me on a dramatic piece," Joel replied. He knew he would need to practise a reading before he arrived at Maria Morenzi's on Friday.

"Try Billy's speech at the end of act one of Keith Waterhouse's *Billy Liar*. It will give you the scope to show a change of attitude and mood. The one that ends with 'Some of us, Mr. Duxbury, belong in the stars.' That's quite appropriate, don't you think?"

"Thanks, Miss Davenport. I appreciate your input," Joel said to the teacher who had always encouraged him. "Now I'd better go and see the principal and hope he has found something complimentary to say about me." He grinned. "My O level results were okay, so hopefully he'll say I worked hard to achieve them. Thank you for your reference, Miss. Thanks very much."

The reference from the principal did indeed compliment Joel on his academic ability, but not without adding that he (the principal) was disappointed that Joel had not completed the advanced level course he had begun earlier in the school year. He did, however, wish him success in whatever he chose as a career. Now it was time to face the vicar.

Reverend Copeland was pleasantly amenable and provided the character reference that Joel required. "And how is your mother, Joel?" he asked as they said their goodbyes.

Joel was taken aback. "She's fine, sir," was all he could say, thankful that she had obviously not seen the vicar recently to discuss her situation.

"Good, my boy. No doubt we'll see her at communion on Sunday."

"Probably, sir. Thank you for your help. I very much appreciate it." Joel made a hasty retreat to avoid an awkward conversation developing. Anyway, he would have to go to the surgery and face whatever his mother had in store for him.

He stood across the road from the medical centre for what seemed ages when in actual fact it was only a few minutes. He checked his watch, the one Gerry had lent him until he could replace the one he'd had stolen. Quarter to two. Afternoon surgery started at two o'clock so he would just have time to speak to his mother before she had to open up for the first patient. Taking a deep breath, he crossed the road and headed for the entrance. Nell was on reception, head down, checking patient files were in order for the afternoon appointments. "Just a moment," she said without looking up. "Mr. Braithwaite, is it?"

"Winston," Joel told her.

"Joel!" she gasped. "What are you doing here? You should have let me know. I could have asked for an hour off. We need to talk. I need to make sure you're all right. Have you got enough money? Are you staying the night? I haven't aired your bed. Oh goodness, I haven't got enough chicken out for tea..."

"Mother, slow down before you give yourself a heart attack."

Nell was beside herself. "Jackie, can you cover for me for a few minutes? I need to speak to my son."

Jackie nodded and looked pointedly at Joel. No words passed between them, but her disapproval was written all over her face.

"I won't keep her long," he said nonchalantly, not caring what Jackie thought about him. She only knew one side of the story and anyway, it was none of her business.

Nell ushered him outside and round the side of the building for privacy. "I knew you'd come to your senses," she said, giving him a hug and then, holding him at arm's length, she delivered the rehearsed speech she had kept in her head for the last couple of days. Joel looked all around, unable to hold his mother's gaze. "Joel, I only want what is best for you. Anything I do—did—was to steer you in the right direction. That's my right as a mother and you should not ignore my advice—"

"STOP!" Joel shouted.

"No! You listen to me, Joel Winston," Nell's voice rose in a crescendo.

Joel freed himself from Nell's grasp. He spoke quietly to try to diffuse the inflammatory situation that was developing again. "I came back to pick up references from school and from the vicar—"

"Oh, nice impression I bet the vicar's been given. I'll never be able to show my face at church again," Nell commented.

"This isn't about you, Mother, and since you mention it, the vicar doesn't know anything about this unless you've told him, in which case he was very diplomatic and didn't say a word."

"I haven't been to church since you left. How could I? It's only been a couple of days, but apart from that, I have been too upset to face people. Coming to work has been very difficult for me, but you wouldn't care about that, would you? All you think about is yourself" She hesitated. "...after all I've done for you."

"You mean like choosing my A level subjects for me and going to beg for a job at the solicitor's office?" Joel spat the words in her direction. "Like making me have childish birthday parties and insulting my friends ..." It sounded very futile, but how could he relate all that had happened during the years of being dominated by a possessive, interfering mother who really didn't know her son at all?

"I never insulted your friends, Joel. How can you say that?"

"I can say it because it's true. You told me Ben couldn't come into our home, because you'd heard his mother had several boyfriends who stayed in her house at night and you never welcomed Angela, or Amy, or Kate when they came to tea except to tell them I wasn't old enough to have a serious girlfriend. You made it pretty clear you disapproved of them. No wonder they dumped me soon afterwards," Joel told her.

"Well, they weren't good enough for you," Nell insisted.

"Who says?" Joel asked. "And anyway, this is not about my friends, or whether you accepted them, it's about me doing what I want to do and in my own way. I'm not coming home. I've found some good digs in Liverpool and I've got an audition on Friday at the Maria Morenzi Theatre School. Now that you know what's happening, I have a train to catch." He looked directly into his mother's eyes, eyes that weren't at all sad, eyes that still showed anger, eyes that said, 'how dare you?'

"Let's not part on bad terms," Nell said catching Joel off guard. "I can see you're determined to do your own thing, so I'll go along with it for now, but I hope I won't be saying 'I told you so' in a few weeks time." She took hold of his hands and kissed him on the cheek. "You're my son and I love you, but I don't like you at the moment. Good luck. Call me at the weekend."

"Okay, but just try to accept that I have a brain in my head and I don't need you to run my life. Thanks for giving me some space at least," Joel said, relieved that his mum had at last accepted an uneasy truce. "I'll call."

Nell didn't wait to watch as Joel turned and walked away. When she returned to the reception desk, she thanked Jackie and merely shrugged. She threw herself into her work with an air of haughty maternal superiority to hide the simmering anger and anxiety she felt inside.

Joel went to his house to pick up some clothes and odds and ends he'd left behind in the rush to leave. He travelled by bus to Wigan this time and the train journey from there to Liverpool seemed much shorter. His heart was lighter and, although he hadn't exactly been given his mother's blessing, they had at least parted on reasonable terms. He read through his audition pieces and tried to memorise the speech from *Billy Liar*—"Some of us, Mr. Duxbury, belong in the stars!"

Ten

"Eee, you look nice, lad," Maggie told him as he prepared to leave for his audition.

"Thanks, Maggie. You don't think I'm over-dressed? Do you think I should leave the jacket off?" Joel asked. He'd decided to wear a suit, but now he was uncertain. "Maybe I should go more casual. What do you think?"

"I can't say really," Maggie told him, "but yer do look very smart. I always think if yer look well dressed, you create a good impression without even opening yer mouth. Yer could always take yer jacket off while yer playin' yer guitar. It might look more casual like."

"Good idea. I might just do that and then I'll feel more relaxed. Good one, Maggie. Thanks." The previous night, Joel had performed his audition pieces for the Connolly family, who were very appreciative and did his confidence a power of good.

"Well, good luck, lad, or should I say break a leg? Funny thing that, isn't it? Breaking yer leg is the last thing yer'd want." She winked at him good-naturedly. "Just do yer best, lad. I'm sure yer'll knock 'em dead!"

Arriving at the theatre school at four o'clock gave him time to hand in his references at the desk and then compose himself before his audition and interview. The friendly lady who had been behind the desk on Monday had been replaced by a younger woman who was rather brusque, but efficient. "Thank you," she said curtly as Joel presented her with the documents.

"Name?"

"Joel Winston."

She raised her pencilled eyebrows and looked at him carefully without smiling. "Good start, anyway. Name's appropriate, at least. Take a seat and you'll be called when they're ready for you. Toilet's down the corridor, third door on the right."

Joel turned and smiled to himself. "Seems my mother did one thing right at least," he mused and repeated, "Name's appropriate ... posh too, from all accounts."

At four-thirty on the dot, the receptionist called out his name. "Joel Winston, come this way, please." She beckoned him with a hand that displayed blood-red nails like long claws, and Joel couldn't help but momentarily think he was being led into the lion's den.

To his surprise, Joel walked into an empty room with a low dais at the far end. Above the dais was a notice in big red letters. 'THIS IS WHERE IT ALL BEGINS!' and there was an arrow pointing to a white spot painted on the floor of the platform. Joel looked around. His instinct was to call out, "Is anybody here?" but he walked slowly forward and intuition told him to go and stand on the spot. The moment he stepped on the stage, house lights were dimmed and the spotlight was on him.

He hadn't noticed the three chairs placed strategically in the centre of the hall and as if by magic, the occupants had placed themselves comfortably to watch his performance. Joel peered into the darkened room and heard the gently encouraging words,

"You may begin." The voice was that of Theodore Pendennis. Joel recognised the confidence of the military-like gentleman and he instantly took heart from it. "Please give us your name and introduce yourself."

Joel took a deep breath and began ... "My name is Joel Winston ..."

"Some of us, Mr. Duxbury, belong in the stars." What had seemed like hours was in reality only minutes. His introduction was brief. He recalled Miss Davenport's advice: "Be confident, not cocky," and he even remembered her other advice to use his sense of wit, so he said, "and if I don't get a chance to tread the boards, I'll just have to walk the plank!" which brought a smile to the faces of his adjudicators. He breezed through his songs and felt happy that his voice had been mellow and clear. He had memorised the *Billy Liar* speech and, though he had never actually read the play, he had seen the film and taken pointers from Tom Courtney's portrayal of the ambitious but ultimately lazy young man. Joel didn't take a bow. That would have been too presumptuous, but he smiled into the darkness, taking a step out of the spotlight to indicate he had finished.

"Thank you, young man," Pendennis boomed. "If you would like to wait in Reception, we'll discuss your performance and let you know our findings forthwith." As the lights went up, Joel saw who his judges were. Along with Pendennis were the elderly lady whom he met on Monday and a younger man with glasses who gave no clue as to his reason for being there.

During the wait, all the pent-up anxiety revealed itself in hot sweats and an urgent need to visit the lavatory several times as the clock on the wall ticked by minute after apprehensive minute, all adding to Joel's nervous anticipation. *This is it*, he thought. *If I don't get a place, I'll just have to rethink. There's always teacher training college, or the bank, or down the docks with Gerry and if all else fails, I could do a bit of busking.* He decided there would be something for him to do. He had to be prepared for the big letdown, especially since it was taking them ages to decide his fate.

If I'd done okay, they would have decided straight away, he thought. *Please, hurry up!*

After three quarters of an hour, the door opened again and Pendennis himself asked him to return to the room. His expression gave no inkling of what had been decided and Joel feared the worst.

"Thank you for your performance. We enjoyed it very much, but I'll leave it to Miss Morenzi to inform you of our decision," the principal told him.

Joel's mouth was dry and he felt the sweat dripping down his back. He tried to smile, but knew he would most likely be displaying a grimace instead of the optimistic expression he wished to present to his judges. Facial muscles don't behave when nerves are taut and he made a bold effort to look confident, despite his insides being attacked by millions of marauding butterflies.

The old lady began quietly. "I'm Maria Morenzi," she said and it brought a smile, a genuine smile to Joel's face.

No wonder she wouldn't give me her name, he thought.

"We have deliberated long and hard..." she continued. Joel's heart missed a beat and he felt the disappointment at the bad news he knew she was about to impart.

I knew it, he thought, his spirits sinking into the depths of despair. *I was too cocky, I was too arrogant. What did I tell Ben about cocky bastards? You stupid fool, Joel, you stupid, stupid fool.* It was a rude awakening to self-assessment and he didn't like it.

"...and Mr. Music here..." she cocked a thumb towards the bespectacled young man who still gave no intimation of his feelings. "... Mr. Powell, has argued strongly against..." Joel's heart sank further. "...our desire to offer you an acting scholarship as he desperately wants you to major in music."

"Does that mean...?" Joel asked incredulously, his mood quickly changing from utter despair to complete joy.

Miss Morenzi nodded and smiled. "Yes, it does. You will major in music and take acting as a subsidiary subject along with basic dance. Are you happy with that?"

"Yes, Miss Morenzi, I am very happy. Thank you so much."

"We begin the new term on October fifth. Speak to Deirdre on Reception and she'll give you all the details. Good luck, Joel Winston." She stood and floated off to the right of the stage, turning round to call enthusiastically, "Good name!" as she left.

Eleven

Joel set out his stall on the corner of Tarleton Street, opposite Marks and Spencer's. He'd borrowed a flat cap from Gerry and he placed a few coppers in it to encourage the punters. It was ten thirty, Monday morning and there was a steady stream of shoppers going in and out of the store. Self-consciously at first, he went through his repertoire of popular songs, his young voice echoing around the streets enclosed by high, stone buildings that cast long shadows across the old grey cobbles when the summer sun shone brightly in a clear, blue sky. Nobody seemed to take any notice of him, and he wondered if he should change his pitch and go to Lime Street station. He decided that the people there would be more intent upon getting to their destinations instead of stopping for a while to listen to his performance, so Marks and Spencer's it would have to be.

By lunchtime, he had collected almost a pound, so he picked up his takings and went to the nearest coffee bar for an espresso. The place was nouveau chic, but empty apart from two girls sitting chatting as he walked in. "Well, look who it is," the girl said as he found a table near the window.

"Excuse me," Joel said noting that there was a guitar resting against the chair next to the louder of the two girls, "but do I know you?"

"Not really, but I know you," she told him. "You weren't very polite when you were on the train last week. I had to squeeze between you and an old man reading a newspaper and I had to ask you to move your feet. A girl shouldn't have to ask for a seat. A gentleman would have offered her one."

Joel vaguely recalled the situation and excused his behaviour as he had been preoccupied at that time with thoughts of his immediate future. "I'm sorry I gave you that impression," he said. "I'm not usually bad mannered. My mother would be disgusted if she thought I'd mistreated a lady," he joked, realising that his mother would indeed be aghast at his attitude, "but since she's not here, I'll make amends before she finds out. Can I buy you another coffee?"

The girl grinned and nudged her companion. "What do you think, Penny? Shall we let a stranger buy us a drink?"

Penny smiled shyly and nodded. "Okay," she said quietly, almost cowering behind her large coffee mug. "Cappuccino, please."

"Is that two cappuccinos then?" Joel asked.

"Thanks," the girl replied, seeming more humble now and much more attractive. "I don't mind if I do."

Joel went to the counter, ordered three cappuccinos and returned to the table in the window. "Do you mind if I join you? I'm Joel—"

"Oooh, that's a po—"

"—posh name?" Joel asked.

"How did you know what I was going to say? Are you psychic or something?" the girl asked.

"Sort of," Joel replied. "You must be the sixth or seventh person to say that in the past week."

"Well, it does sound a bit posh. I'm Belinda and she's Penny."

"And you're saying *my* name's posh! Belinda and Penelope…"

"Oh, don't call me that," Penny cried, suddenly becoming animated. "I hate it. Penny's bad enough and I've even been called ha'penny by my dad when I was little, but Penelope! God knows where my mum found that name."

Joel grinned. "Okay, let's call a truce. Discussion of names forbidden in any future conversations. Agreed?

"So we're going to have future conversations, are we?" Belinda asked.

"I don't see why not," he told the two girls. "Do you live in Liverpool?"

The two girls seemed eager to talk. He discovered that Penny was in Notre Dame Sixth Form and lived with her parents in Maghull. Belinda was staying with her until she decided what she was going to do with her life. "I'd love to work in the theatre in some capacity," she told Joel. "I sing a bit, but I wouldn't mind being a set designer or make-up artist. My mum has fallen out with me because she says working in a theatre isn't a proper job. She sort of threw me out of my home in Aspull and told me not to go back until I come to my senses."

"I know the feeling," Joel agreed without explaining further and Belinda didn't press him as she was too preoccupied with her own problems to notice that she had found a soul mate.

"Is that your guitar?" he asked.

"It is," she told him. "I was going to do a bit of busking, but I lost my nerve."

"I can't believe that," Joel teased. "You aren't backward about coming forward with your opinions, from what I can gather."

"Don't you be so cheeky, posh Joel!"

"Well, come on then. Let's put a few chords together and see what we come up with," he suggested. They strummed quietly as the café proprietor nodded his approval and gradually, the coffee bar filled up with customers who were drawn in by the music. Belinda and Joel grinned at each other and Belinda's eyes shone as they sang a few popular songs, mainly ballads—then '"Travelling Light," "Theme for a Dream," "It's All in the Game" and the Elvis great, "Jailhouse Rock."

"I'm Vic Santorini. I own this place. Will you come back tomorrow about the same time?" the café owner asked. "My takings have trebled in just half an hour. I'll pay you ten percent of my lunchtime takings between you, Monday to Saturday. Deal?"

The young performers couldn't believe their luck. "I will," Joel answered at once. "I need a job for the next couple of months before I start college. How about you, Belinda?"

She looked at Penny for reassurance.

"Go for it, Bel. My mum will be okay with it. She promised your mum she'd make sure you earned your keep and she loves your singing so..."

"Okay, I'll give it a try," she said, "but we'll have to practise."

Joel arranged to meet them outside Lewis's at six o'clock. "I'll have to check with my landlady to see if it's all right for you to come to my digs to practise. She's a good sort, so I don't think there'll be a problem."

Penny looked concerned. "I'll have to come with Bel, if that's okay with you. My mum wouldn't want her travelling home on the bus on her own at night."

"That's fine by me," Joel told her. "You can give us your opinion on what we sound like and we might need a referee when we fight over what songs to sing."

"I won't sing any old rubbish," Belinda said adamantly. "See you at six then."

~ * ~

"You don't mind if I bring two girls here tonight, do you?" Joel asked Maggie.

"My, my, you're a quick worker, Joel Winston," Maggie replied with a wink. "So long as they don't stay over. I don't think yer mam would approve of me parenting skills if I let you have two girls in yer bedroom."

Joel blushed. He wasn't used to anybody talking openly about girls and bedrooms in the same breath. "They'll only be here for an hour or so. We've got a regular gig in the Casa Bellissimo and we need to rehearse. We'll practise in the living room, if you like."

"What, and interfere with *Coronation Street*? No you won't. Your room is all right, but you know my rules. I don't want you getting caught like I did. I know what it's like to struggle with babies before you're old enough to realise what it's all about."

"I won't let you down, Maggie. I only met them today, but this gig is too good to miss. It'll pay enough for my rent and leave some for my savings." He paused, remembering his grandfather's wisdom again: "Always make sure there's enough in your bank account for a rainy day. You never know when you'll need a few bob to see you through."

"I won't let you down, Maggie," he repeated.

He met Belinda and Penny at six as arranged and ushered them onto the bus to take them to the shop. They entered through the side door as the shop was closed and he led them along the dark corridor to the stairs at the back. "It's only me," he called out as they climbed the stairs.

Maggie popped her head round the kitchen door. "Okay, lad. How yer doin', girls?"

The two girls smiled. "We're fine, thanks," Belinda spoke first and Penny smiled shyly.

"You're a bonny little thing," Maggie told Penny. "I like yer mini. Wish I had legs like that!" and she winked at Joel as he beckoned the girls to follow him up to his room.

Half an hour into the rehearsal, Gerry peeped round the door. "Can I come and listen, Poshman?" he asked, his eyes fixed on Penny.

"If you like, Wacker, but are you talking to me, or taking in the scenery?" Joel grinned at his mate.

"Well, put like that, the view is pretty gorgeous from where I'm standing. Hello, darlin'. I'm Gerry. Do yer mind if I sit next to yer?"

Penny looked shyly from under her dark eyelashes. "Hiya," she said coyly and patted the edge of the bed as she moved over to make room for him.

By half past seven, Belinda and Joel had decided on their programme and were delighted with the harmonies they produced.

"I can't believe we can sing so well together," Belinda told Joel as they packed away their guitars.

"Well, our music teachers would be delighted with us, wouldn't they?" Joel said. "I know mine would be. I used to have jam sessions with him, so they obviously paid off. I can't wait to start college in October. The music tutor there requested I major in music and I'm chuffed about that."

"You didn't tell me you were going to college to do music," Belinda told him. "I'm dead jealous. You lucky thing!"

"You didn't ask, and anyway, I did tell Vic at the café, so you mustn't have been listening."

Belinda pulled a face and stuck out her tongue. "Well, I'm still dead jealous. I might even try for a place at college myself."

After much deliberation and with input from the enthusiastic Gerry, they came up with the name Beljolinda. "What a cracker!" Gerry said. "Can I be yer manager? I'll get a few tips from my mate Brian Epstein!"

"Will you do it for free?" Joel asked him.

"Will I 'eckers! Ten percent to start with and then when you get famous, I'll up it to forty."

"On yer bike!" Joel told him. "I'll manage myself at that rate! Come on, girls, I'll take you back to the station to catch your bus home."

"I'll come with yer," Gerry said eagerly and he handed Penny her jacket as she stood up from the edge of the bed. On the bus into the city, Joel sat with Belinda to finalise the arrangements for the next day. Gerry was delighted and sat close to Penny on the seat behind the others.

"Will yer go out with me?" he whispered. Penny nodded. When she slipped her hand into his, he thrilled with pleasure and squeezed it gently to confirm his interest.

"But Belinda will have to come too, because my mum might not like me going out on my own," she said quietly. "I've never been out with a boy before."

"No problem, darling. Poshman will probably get off with Belinda anyway."

"Why do you call him Poshman?" Penny asked.

"Because he's posh and I'm not. Are we on for a date then? How about Saturday night? We can go to The Cabin," Gerry almost pleaded. His heart was beating fast. This pretty little thing had his senses reeling.

They arrived at Central Bus Station ten minutes before the Maghull bus was due out. Gerry, now firmly holding on to Penny's hand, made no secret of the fact that he fancied her.

"We're going out on Saturday," he told the wide-eyed Joel and Belinda. "I hope you two are up for going to The Cabin, 'cos that's where we'll meet at half past seven."

They looked at each other and shrugged. "I suppose we have no choice, have we?" Belinda reasoned, knowing she would have to accompany Penny anyway.

As the bus pulled into the station, Gerry turned to Penny. "Can I kiss yer goodnight?" he asked, but before she could answer, his lips were on hers and he held her tightly as she responded.

Joel looked at Belinda, shrugged again and kissed her on the cheek. "Goodnight," he said. "I'll see you tomorrow at ten-thirty outside Lewis's."

~ * ~

The following weeks were hectic and happy. Beljolinda brought in the customers to Casa Bellissimo and thus brought in the money for the two young singers. Gerry and Penny were rarely apart and Joel and Belinda went along for the ride.

"I've told my mum and dad about you," Penny said unexpectedly as she snuggled up to Gerry while Beljolinda tried out new songs.

"Blimey," Gerry replied, "I bet that gave 'em a shock, didn't it?"

"They want to meet you. Are you up for it?"

"Er ... well, yeah, I suppose so. They're not expecting a millionaire, are they? I mean, all that's important is that I love yer and want to look after yer, isn't it? What will I wear and when do they want to see me? Do they know I work down the docks 'til I can get into college to do my ONC? Will I 'ave to talk posh? I can, yer know ... listen to this." He coughed affectedly, stuck out his chin and said, "My favourite meal is chicking and chips. HI'm never 'appier than when HI'm 'aving hit with hall the trimmin's."

The others fell about laughing. Gerry grinned. "Gotcha!" he said. "I'm not that ignorant, but I promise I won't let yer down, Penny, love."

"I know you won't," Penny told him, "And anyway, they'd see right through you if you tried to be something you're not. Now come on. I'm back at school tomorrow so I'd better have an early night."

~ * ~

The first week in September when all the students were back in school didn't decrease the number of customers at the Casa Bellissimo. Vic knew that come October, Joel would be at college, but asked Beljolinda if they would come in on Saturdays.

"Of course we will," Joel answered for both of them and when the final week arrived, Belinda spent each afternoon with Joel in his room before leaving to meet Penny as she came out of school. It was Friday afternoon when it happened. Excitement about their success and the pure emotion of the situation overwhelmed their sensibilities. They kissed passionately for the first time and as their kisses became more urgent, more forceful, events took their natural course.

"That wasn't supposed to happen," Joel said as they scrambled to find their clothes to hide their nakedness.

Belinda looked stunned. "You didn't enjoy it?" she asked, confused at Joel's reaction.

"I didn't say that," Joel snapped, "but we're not an item."

"We could be," Belinda told him wistfully. "It's not as though we're complete strangers."

Joel looked at his musical partner. She was nice, kind, attractive and endearingly honest to the point of being forthright on occasions, but that was it. He felt no hint of sexual chemistry really. What had just happened was a heat of the moment thing. "No, we're not strangers, certainly not now..." He paused in order to make sure the words came out right. "I like you Bel..."

"What makes me think there's a 'but' coming?" she said.

Joel looked at the girl whose attractive blue eyes showed a hint of desperation. "I don't want to get involved, Bel. I don't want to say that the last half hour was a mistake either, but it was a one off."

Belinda snatched up her bag and headed for the door. "You posh boys are all the same. Think you are god's gift and every girl is yours for the taking. Well, stuff you, posh Joel." She opened the door and ran down the stairs, hot tears misting her view.

Maggie had gone to the suppliers and Chrissie was in the shop unaware of what was happening upstairs. She had just directed a young man to Joel's room and Belinda collided with him at the foot of the stairs.

"Hey, slow down," he said gently. "Can I help?"

"Sorry, but no," she told him. "Just let me out of here." She ran down the street towards the bus stop. She needed to meet Penny at four o'clock.

As Joel sat on the edge of his bed, his head in his hands, he heard a gentle knock on the door. "Come in," he called. "It's not locked."

"Hello, Joel," the visitor said. "How are you?"

Joel looked up. "Ben! What the hell are you doing here?"

Twelve

Nell decided to visit Joel at the Connolly place before he began his first term at the Maria Morenzi Theatre School. If she arrived unannounced, they wouldn't make any special preparations and she might see how Joel really was living.

"Will you come with me, Mum?" she asked Margaret. "I'll come to you for the weekend and we'll go over on Saturday afternoon. He says this Saturday job he has finishes at three o'clock so we'll be there in time for tea."

"Do you think we should intrude?" Margaret asked.

"Of course we should intrude. This woman is supposedly looking after my son, but I'll give her a call beforehand. At least they've had a phone installed now. What sort of a shop could it have been without a telephone?" She sighed in exasperation.

"Goodness, Nell, how you've changed. What happened to the quiet, caring girl we used to know?" her mother asked, doubting her daughter's motives in visiting Joel at the place in which he had chosen to live. "Couldn't we just arrange to meet him in town and have tea at the Adelphi?"

"Mother! I know what I'm doing. If this Connolly woman isn't providing suitable accommodation, I'll find him a place myself."

Margaret sighed. "All right, dear, but please don't get on your high horse. You know Joel won't take kindly to your interfering and anyway, most Liverpudlians are good sorts, homely and down-to-earth."

"That may be so, Mum, but I have to make sure my son is living in the way to which he is accustomed."

Margaret sighed again, this time more deeply and audibly.

"Stop it, Mother! Just come with me as my support. That's all I ask." Nell was certain in her mind that the two of them would stand united in the face of the enemy.

When they drew up at the corner of Doris Street, Margaret was pleasantly surprised. The terraced houses were clean and welcoming. Sparkling windows with brightly coloured curtains, donkey-stoned steps and polished doors with shiny brass fittings gave the street a friendly glow in the autumn afternoon sun. "This is nice," she commented to a steely-faced Nell.

"They're terraced houses, Mother!" she said with disdain.

"But they're nice terraced houses, dear," Margaret said, hoping she might keep the situation in check.

Nell chose not to reply and looked pointedly at her mother. "We're here," she announced. "This is the shop. Oh my goodness, it's—"

"It's very clean," Margaret rejoined, "and how beautifully the window display is set out. Did you call as you said you would?"

Nell cast a disparaging eye over the shop window. Grudgingly she admitted to herself that it was indeed pleasing to the eye, but had no intentions of openly acknowledging the fact. "No, I forgot to phone," she said. *Deliberately,* she thought. She pulled round the corner away from the front of the shop, locked the car and looked around to make sure no loutish individuals were sussing out the situation before they entered the shop. When the bell rang, Chrissie was taking her break and Maggie was behind the counter.

"Hullo there," she greeted her customers, whom she imagined could be nothing short of royalty. "What can I do for you?"

"Are you Mrs. Connolly?" Nell asked as pleasantly as she could muster.

"That's me, love, and who might you be if it's not a rude question?"

"I'm Mrs. Winston, Joel's mother, and this is his grandmother, Mrs. Benson. We've come to see Joel. Is he in?" She baulked at asking if he were *home,* because that way she would be publicly acknowledging he no longer lived with her.

"He's due home anytime soon," Maggie told them as Nell flinched at the word she herself had avoided. "Do you want to come up for a cuppa tea while you wait?"

"I suppose it can do no harm," Nell replied and waited until Maggie lifted the counter top to let them through to the stairs at the back.

"Chrissie!" Maggie shouted as Nell flinched again. "Can you take over, darlin'? This is Joel's mum and 'is gran come to see 'im. I'll just make 'em a cuppa tea."

Chrissie came out of the kitchen wiping her hands on her apron, her face flustered at the sight of the two elegant ladies climbing their back stairs. "Hullo there, Mrs. Winston." She hopped around not quite knowing whether to bow or curtsey, but decided against both and offered her hand instead.

Nell smiled condescendingly, but Margaret took the girl's hand and said, "Hello, dear, how are you?"

"Okay, thanks, Mrs...?"

"Benson, dear."

"I'm fine, thanks, Mrs. Benson." She made a hasty retreat into the shop. Her mother could deal with this on her own.

Joel returned with a placated Belinda just as Maggie was taking tea on a tray into the living room. "Is the Queen here for tea?" he asked with a grin. "China cups too! What are we celebrating?"

Maggie tried to warn him, but a voice from within the living room called, "Joel? Is that you?"

Joel's eyes opened wide, his jaw dropped and he stood rigid on the landing. "Mum?" he mouthed to his landlady.

Maggie nodded and winked reassuringly. "Come and look who's 'ere," she said and allowed him to pass in front of her to greet his mother before she took in the tea. Belinda stayed on the landing, mortified by the domineering voice coming from inside the living room.

"Hello, Mum. What are you doing here and Granny too?"

"Hello, darling," Nell cooed, making Joel cringe and Maggie smile. "We thought we'd give you a surprise."

"You've certainly done that," he told her. "I wasn't expecting visitors today. I would have made my bed and tidied my room if I'd known you were coming."

"You take no notice of 'im, Mrs. Winston. 'is room is always clean and tidy. More than I can say for our Gerry's.'

"Oh, you have a son then?" Nell asked. Her mind was working overtime. *I bet he's a scallywag and leading Joel astray,* she thought irrationally. *I'd better get him out of here at once.*

"I told you it was Gerry who brought me here, Mum. You have forgotten, obviously," Joel said, embarrassed that his mother should make out that he hadn't told her how kind the Connolly family had been to him.

"Did you, darling? Sorry. I must have had other things on my mind at the time," she said, directing a telling look at her son and taking a sip of the tea Maggie had poured. She looked over her teacup, a surprisingly delicate Royal Albert Moonlight Rose design, and surveyed her surroundings. The living room was bright and clean, neatly furnished and not at all like Nell had expected. "How do you manage to keep your lounge so tidy with a business to run, Mrs. Connolly?" It almost sounded like a compliment.

"I keep anythin' to do with the business downstairs. We used to live at the back of the shop, but when we 'ad the extension built, all the living accommodation was transferred up 'ere. It's separate, see and like goin' 'ome from work instead of livin' with the job. And call me Maggie. Everybody does." Maggie was surprisingly at ease with this hoity-toity woman who had descended upon her house. *'ow on earth can she 'ave produced a lovely lad like Joel?* she thought. *Maybe 'e takes after 'is dad. God rest 'is soul.*

"Do you think Joel could take us to see his room, Mrs. Connolly?" Nell asked as she stood up and moved towards the door. "His grandmother and I would like a few minutes alone with him since we haven't seen him for weeks." Joel moved quickly to open the door for them only to find Belinda still on the landing waiting for him.

"Oh, we have an intruder!" Nell cried, blatantly looking Belinda up and down.

"Mother!" Joel was aghast. "This is my friend, Belinda, and she is waiting for me."

"Hello, Mrs. Winston," Belinda said shyly. "Pleased to meet you," then silently adding, *I think.*

"Hello, young lady." Nell smiled before she added, "Joel has a few years of studying ahead of him, you know. He has no time for girlfriends."

Joel took a deep breath and marched off up the stairs. Margaret took hold of Nell's arm and pushed her forward to follow Joel before World War Three broke out. She directed a conciliatory smile towards Belinda and Maggie, who put an affectionate arm round the girl, led her into the living room and closed the door.

Nell stood framed in the doorway of Joel's room. Joel stood staring through the skylight onto the sea of rooftops before him. He was determined not to raise his voice in this house. He turned to face the woman with whom he was finding it difficult to relate and he spoke quietly, but forcefully. "I can well imagine why you have come here, Mother, but your mission has failed. I hope you can appreciate this lovely home in spite of your supercilious ways. Maggie has shown me what it is to be humble without depreciating your values."

"That woman has hoodwinked you into thinking you're a nobody," Nell told him scathingly.

"Don't you dare call her 'that woman' in her own home! She is warm and kind and human, and she has brought up her children to be well-mannered, well-adjusted, confident free spirits without dominating their every move. Now you have seen where I live, you may leave." Joel was in no mood for confrontations. "I'm sorry you had to see and hear all this, Granny, but now will you please take my mother home?"

Margaret took hold of Nell's arm again, but Nell wrenched it free and wagged a tyrannical finger at her wilful son. "You'll regret all this one day, my boy. Just you wait and see. And while I'm here..." She turned to look down the stairs towards the living room where the door was still firmly shut. "That girl is a gold-digger. It's written all over her pretty face. You were always a sucker for big, blue eyes." With that, she marched down the stairs and through the shop without as much as a glance at Chrissie standing behind the counter.

Once in the car, Nell and Margaret sat in silence for a few minutes before Nell started the engine. Securing the new seatbelts Nell had had fitted, Margaret turned to face her daughter. "Well, you handled that very well, dear," she said, her tone pointedly sarcastic.

Back in the living room, Maggie and Belinda sat in silence, each with their own thoughts. They had not discussed the woman from whom Joel had run away. "We'd best not discuss what we know nothing about," Maggie suggested and they sat in silence until Joel reappeared.

When he stood framed in the doorway, they both smiled at him, warm, welcoming, understanding smiles. "Sorry about that," he apologised. "You can choose your friends, but not your relatives."

"It's okay, love. Don't apologise for something you can't change," Maggie reassured him. "Let's call our Gerry and Penny down. They've missed all the fun while they've been canoodling to music in his room! I could hear Elvis putting in his two-penn'orth while our visitors were 'ere.'

"We'll go up to them, Maggie," Joel told her. "The girls have to go back to Maghull to get changed before we go out."

As they took the girls to catch their bus home, Joel informed the others he'd invited a friend along for the evening. "His name's Ben and he's my mate from school. He works for the Provincial Bank and he's been transferred to the Allerton branch for a year. They've found his digs for him and everything. He rents his own flat in Bolton, but his younger brother is looking after it for him while he's here, and Ben will go home every other weekend anyway."

"Is 'e posh like you, Poshman?" Gerry enquired, "'cos if he is, I'd better be taking elocution lessons!"

"Don't be daft, Ger," Penny said as she punched him playfully. "Anybody who can talk to my mum and dad like you did doesn't need elocution lessons. You should have heard him! All his aitches in the right places! My mum loved him and my dad said he wasn't bad for a Liverpool supporter. All my dad's family are Everton fans, so I reckon Gerry did all right."

Gerry grinned and gave Penny a hug. "Our dad's home tonight, so we'll make ourselves scarce," he told them.

Paddy Connolly hadn't been home all summer, doubling up on shifts so that he could make enough cash to take Maggie on the holiday of a lifetime. He wanted to surprise her for her birthday and whisk her away on a Caribbean cruise for two weeks in December. He'd planned it with Chrissie and Gerry months ago and tonight he was going to break the news.

"No problem," they agreed and arranged to meet outside The Cabin Club at half past seven.

"You can sleep over in my room if you like, Ben. Maggie has lent me a camp bed and I've got a sleeping bag and travel rug so you'll be quite cosy. How about it? I owe you anyway for coming to my rescue when I needed you," Joel told his friend while they were waiting for the girls.

"Thanks, that'll be great. It'll save me walking to Allerton Park from your place. The last bus goes at quarter to eleven. I can't wait 'til I can afford a car. I'm already taking driving lessons," Ben informed his companions. "And thanks, guys, for inviting me tonight. It's no fun being on your own in a strange place."

"And Liverpool is very strange," quipped Belinda as she and Penny joined the group, "like most of its inhabitants!" and she playfully stuck out her tongue at Gerry.

"Watch it, Belinda Robinson. You've no room to talk. You come from Wigan!" Gerry reminded her and a minor skirmish ensued.

Joel introduced Ben to the girls. "Wigan, eh? The place with the imaginary pier and a reasonable rugby league team," Ben joked, ready to join in the fun.

"Actually I come from Aspull on the way to Haigh Hall from Bolton. Do you know it?" she asked the newcomer.

"I've been near there to visit an old auntie who's in a home at Parbold," Ben told her amicably.

"What is this? A geography lesson? Come on, you lot, let's get to The Cabin before it gets full," Joel urged. "Cilla Black is supposed to be on tonight, so it'll be packed to the seams."

"I hope she is," Ben enthused. "I've heard she's good, different from all the other girl singers from the States."

"If she's from the Pool, she's good. No doubt about it," Gerry said proudly. "Come on then, let's get a move on."

~ * ~

Later as the two school mates lay in the darkness in Joel's room, they talked well into the wee small hours. "That Cilla Black is something else, isn't she?" Ben said dreamily. "I could go for her!"

"Not my type, mate, but yeah, she's got what it takes," Joel answered. He drifted into his own world, on a stage with thousands of screaming fans urging him to sing his number one hit.

Ben continued to talk into the darkness. "What's with you and Belinda, Joel?"

Joel snapped out of his reverie. "Nothing," he said, "absolutely nothing. We're singing partners, that's all."

"She likes you."

"And I like her, but not in that way. We make good music together. Come to the Casa Bellissimo next Saturday," Joel suggested.

"It's my weekend at home next week. I can't leave Michael alone in my flat for more than two weeks. I trust him and he needs to be there for his own sake..."

Joel nodded, understanding Michael's home situation, but felt no need to comment.

"...but I'm not sure about his mates," Ben continued. "I'll come the following week, though. I'm no judge, but you were pretty good at singing in school."

"I'm hopeful, Ben, but I don't want to be too confident. My audition went really well, but ...well..." Joel paused pensively.

"Blimey, you've changed a bit, but what's up?"

"I've grown up a lot. I've had to and it's not been easy, but as regards my singing... well, I don't want the Casa Bellissimo bubble to burst. This is just between you and me though. Going to college will delay what I want. The course takes three years to complete and what's happening in the music world at the moment could be over and done with by then," he explained.

"Oh, I see," Ben replied, "but what's the alternative?"

"That's the problem." Joel fell silent.

Taking the hint, Ben turned over, made himself comfortable and said, "Goodnight, mate."

"Goodnight, Ben." But Joel lay awake for ages thinking about his ambitions and strangely, after what had happened the day before, not of Belinda.

Thirteen

Nell took on her duties at work with renewed vigour. Much as she regretted what had happened, she conceded she would have to live with it for the time being at least. "Are you going shopping on Saturday?" she asked Jackie during their break.

"Not this week. It's Dave's birthday and I'm taking him away for the weekend," Jackie told her. "It's a surprise. We're going for a leisure weekend at St Anne's, dinner and dance all in."

"Sounds lovely," Nell said trying to cover her disappointment.

"Aw, sorry, Nell. You've obviously bitten the bullet in deciding to go out. Next week, I promise." Jackie realised Nell was doing something she had hitherto refused to consider at all and she noted that this change of events had occurred since her visit to Liverpool, but she didn't want to pry.

"That's okay, Jackie," she replied. "It'll keep."

When Friday came, she went home after work and decided to do absolutely nothing. She would normally have done the housework, cleaning, washing, the lot, but tonight she wasn't motivated at all. She kicked off her shoes, undid the top few buttons of her blouse and opened a bottle of Burgundy that had been in her drinks cabinet since her birthday in July. Taking a glass from the cupboard, she poured the wine and took it into the lounge where she flopped into her favourite chair just as the doorbell rang. "Who on earth can this be?" she said out loud, slightly irritated that her relaxation had been interrupted before it had begun. She opened the door. "Yes?"

"Hello, Nell. I hope I'm not intruding."

"Doctor Flynn! What brings you here?" Nell was taken aback. She fumbled with the buttons she had undone only minutes before.

"May I come in?" Sean Flynn asked. "Or are you going to keep me standing on the doorstep?"

"Oh, sorry. Come in... please." She led him into the lounge where her shoes were in the middle of the hearthrug exactly where she had kicked them. Hastily placing them neatly by her chair, she very formally invited the doctor to take a seat. "Will you sit down?"

"Thank you," Doctor Flynn said, equally as formal.

"What can I do for you, Doctor? I have to admit I'm a bit flummoxed that you are here. Is there something I need to do for work?"

"No, nothing to do with work at all. On the contrary. It's a social call," he conceded.

"Oh, I see," Nell told him, although she didn't understand at all. "In that case, will you join me in a glass of wine? I have some smoked salmon and green salad in the fridge. You are welcome to have dinner with me if you haven't already eaten."

"Sounds good to me. I love smoked salmon," the doctor said, "and thank you."

They sat at the kitchen table. Several glasses of wine later and having dispensed with all the small talk, "I guess that now we're more relaxed, we are ready to put the world to rights. Now tell me why you really came here," Nell coaxed. "I'm sure it wasn't because you guessed I was having smoked salmon for dinner."

Sean reached across the table and took hold of Nell's hands. She stiffened. No man had touched her like that for eighteen years. "I came to invite you to dinner," he said.

"Oh?" Nell was surprised, not shocked, but she delicately pulled her hands away from his.

The wine had done a good job, however, in making her unwind and she began to feel at ease with the attention she was getting from her employer.

He went over to where he had thrown his coat on the settee and brought a bottle of Mateus Rose out of the deep pocket. "Shall we?" he asked mischievously.

"Why not?" Nell hadn't felt like this for years and she was enjoying Sean Flynn's company.

"Will you go to dinner with me sometime, Nell? I have waited for a long time to ask you, you know."

"I haven't been out with a man since my husband died. I didn't want to and I never felt I should. Joel was my priority, but now he has made it very clear he doesn't need me," Nell disclosed.

"Do you want to talk about it?" Sean asked her gently.

Nell nodded and they moved into the lounge and sat on the settee in front of the fire, their wine glasses replenished and placed on the occasional tables by each arm of the sofa. She drew up her knees and settled back comfortably as she described her relationship with her son. "I have been a very silly woman, Doctor."

"How do you mean? And please call me Sean. We're not at work now and I think we know each other well enough to be on first name terms," he stated amicably.

"We don't really know each other at all, do we?" Nell said pointedly. "I think you wouldn't want to invite me to dinner if you knew what I've done."

"I don't think you could have done anything so bad," Sean told her, but she looked sad, very sad, and he wanted to comfort her.

"I have, you know, and I despise myself for it. I have made my son hate me. I set myself up as this tyrannical, obsessive, control freak of a mother and it has taken a Liverpudlian shopkeeper to make me realise why my son has left home," Nell admitted. She related her visit to the Connolly house. "Maggie Connolly didn't actually say much to me at all, but I judged her before I even met her. I assumed that she would be uncouth and unrefined when all the time she was respectable and very considerate. She is looking after my son, *my son*, as she looks after her own. It took Joel to show me that children can grow up to be 'well-mannered, well-adjusted, confident, free spirits' as he put it, without their mother dominating their every move."

"Can't you tell him how you feel, Nell? Surely he is intelligent enough to accept that you know where you've gone wrong."

Nell thought for a moment. "I don't think he's ready for that yet. It's been going on for too long. I went into the Connollys' home with an attitude that can only be described as supercilious at best, arrogantly pretentious at worst. To be honest, I don't think I could face Joel either just at the moment. He needs to find himself. I realise that now."

Sean took hold of her hands again. "The death of a partner can do weird things to us, you know. You felt the need to dominate to show that you were strong. Joel has been your only connection with Tom and your need to hang on to him," he explained gently.

"But I made a conscious decision to rule his life. It wasn't as though I didn't know what I was doing. I worked out what I wanted for him, not only choosing his career path, but telling him who his friends should be. No wonder he rebelled, and my father warned me over and over again not to smother him," she revealed. "I really must try to stay out of Joel's life for a while."

Sean inched closer to her. "You're not alone. I'm here for you and now it's my turn to reveal my secrets. We are all hit with the vagaries of life, you know. Even doctors aren't immune."

Nell smiled. "I'm listening," she told him, "Something I've not been good at for the past few years."

Sean Flynn was equally honest about himself. He didn't blame Kathy for breaking his heart. "I mishandled the situation. I expected too much of her and was too wrapped up in my own career. Even so," he explained, "I am happy with my lot. Sometimes I'm lonely, though I've never felt awkward about my single status. After all, there are enough well-intentioned women at the golf club who would willingly pair me up with their single friends if I'd allow it!" He grinned. "Somebody set me up on a blind date once. What a disaster! The woman nearly ate me alive!"

"You never struck me as a blind date contestant," Nell told him, "not that I've ever thought about it. Well, I always imagined that doctors live very confined, staid lives."

"I almost invited you to the theatre years ago, but something I couldn't fathom about your situation prevented me from doing so," he divulged.

"I would probably have refused," she admitted. "I wouldn't even go shopping with Jackie and her friends. How unsociable is that?"

"I never felt the time was right after that, for you, or for me," Sean told her. "Tonight it just felt right so I grabbed the wine and..."

"...and here you are."

Sean looked at the clock. "Goodness, it's quarter to eleven. I hope I haven't outstayed my welcome."

"Not at all. That invitation to dinner turned into a counselling session, but it's been good. Thanks," Nell said.

"Can we do this again?" Sean asked.

"What? The counselling?"

"No, silly! Dinner."

"I'd like that.

"How about we go out tomorrow night?" Sean suggested. "There's a new restaurant opened at Cranberry Fold and I've heard the food's excellent. I'm not on call this weekend so we'll be able to dine uninterrupted. A rare treat."

Arrangements made, he bid her goodnight with a kiss on the cheek. As she closed the door, she couldn't help but wonder how tonight had happened.

Joel didn't hear from his mother for weeks. She kept a discreet silence and Joel presumed she was sulking. "It's strange she has suddenly stopped talking," he confided with Ben, who had been a regular visitor at the Connollys' place recently.

"Are you worried?" Ben asked. "You could always phone if you're bothered."

"No, I'm not worried. My grandpa phoned me soon after her visit and said to keep a low profile for a while. He's usually pretty clued up and he'd have called again if anything was wrong. With starting college and everything, I haven't had time to worry about my mother. Anyway, why should I?"

"How's Belinda?" Ben enquired. "She hasn't been around here for a while."

"I only see her when we do the gig on Saturdays. Gerry sees more of her than I do as he's always at Penny's these days. Got it really bad. I reckon I'm going to be best man soon!"

"You're joking!" Ben exclaimed. "Surely not! What does Belinda think?"

Joel looked at Ben wide-eyed. "What's this with you and Belinda? Ask her yourself. Why don't you ask her out? I'm not interested in her in that way, so you won't be treading on my toes." He grinned knowingly at his friend.

"She likes you. I told you before," Ben said adamantly. "She wouldn't give me a second look."

"Belinda knows where she stands with me. I've never led her on. Not my style," Joel explained. "Since she got a place at the College of Art, she hasn't even bothered coming round to rehearse. Maybe you can ask her on Saturday afternoon if you make an effort to come and see us in action at the Casa," he suggested.

~ * ~

When Saturday came, Joel arrived at the Casa Bellissimo in good time before the lunchtime rush. Ben was already there. "Blimey, you're keen," Joel teased.

"Just thought I'd get here early to get a good seat!"

"Yeah, and I'm a Dutchman," Joel said. "Belinda won't be here for about half an hour. She's always on the last minute."

Ben grinned. "No problem," he said and ordered a cappuccino while he waited.

Beljolinda usually started their gig at eleven-thirty. Joel looked at the clock at eleven twenty-five and there was no sign of his partner. Vic strolled over to ask what was going on. "Bel's not here. I don't know what's happened," Joel explained. "Shall I start without her?"

"Well, the place is full already. I think you'd better make a start," Vic instructed. "I hope you can hold the punters on your own."

"I'll give it a go," Joel told him. "Wish me luck."

Performing without Bel was a liberating experience and Joel liked it. He sang a few Buddy Holly numbers and a couple of Adam Faith's, all top tens. The regulars at the Casa loved him. When he'd finished the session, Vic came over, followed by a man in blue jeans and sleek silver grey crew neck sweater. "Great, young 'un," he enthused. "This is Ray Greenwood. He wants a word with you."

Joel felt mildly threatened. He didn't know why. "Hello, sir. How are you?"

"What's with the *sir*?" Ray asked, gently nudging Joel's arm.

"Sorry. Strict upbringing, I suppose," Joel told him. "You're not the music police, are you? I took a liberty in singing Buddy and Adam, I know that."

"Nah, don't worry about that. I'm a talent scout for The Cabin management. I'm interested in you. Will you come and try out?" Ray offered.

"You're kidding! 'Course I'll try out. When?" Joel could hardly believe his luck. "If it's mid-week, I'll have to juggle my lectures at college, but I don't think it will be a problem."

"Are you at Morenzi's?" Ray enquired. "They'll be okay. We've dealt with them before." He patted Joel on the back. "You're good. We'll be in touch."

Ben had hovered in the background whilst Joel talked to Ray Greenwood. He wasn't so much interested in Joel's good fortune. "I wonder what's happened to Bel," he said as Joel packed away his gear. "She wouldn't miss a gig unless it was something major."

Joel stopped what he was doing and faced Ben. "I'm not impressed, so don't expect me to be worried about her. She could have phoned Vic at least. You don't just let people down like that. As it stands, she's missed out on a great opportunity. Her own fault, so she'll have to live with it."

Ben wasn't so sure. His concern was born out of his secret love for her. "Let me have her number, Joel. I'll give her a call."

Joel handed over the number. "You're doing this for yourself, not for me. If she asks, you can tell her I'm pissed off with her and don't tell her about The Cabin."

Fourteen

Nell and Sean went out together regularly. Love was growing, albeit slowly, but there was definitely a connection between them. "I never thought this could happen to two forty-something-year-olds," she told him. "I think I'm falling in love with you, Sean."

"I *know* I've fallen in love with you," Sean replied as he drew her close, finding her waiting lips with his. "This is so right for us, Nell."

She closed her eyes as he cupped her face gently and allowed the heat of the moment to overtake them. He stroked her neck with soothing fingers, her shoulders with tender hands. She held him in her arms, caressing his strong back and feeling the powerful urges that were inviting them to take this as far as it would go. "Sean?" she murmured.

"Darling Nell." His voice was throaty, sensuous, filled with longing for her.

"Are we ready for this?" she asked.

He didn't reply, but took her hand and led her to his bed.

"I love you," he told her afterwards as they lay there still gently caressing each other's torso, arms, breasts, thighs.

"I love you, too," she responded, "but can I tell you something?"

"Anything," he said, "anything at all."

"I had forgotten how wonderful making love can be. No words can describe that complete, all-consuming rush of emotion that penetrates the very soul. But..." She paused.

"There's a *but*?" Sean asked, his surprise not hidden.

"Only a little but... but I'm glad our first love-making was in your bed and not mine. I'm going to buy a new bed before I allow you to stay over at my house." She didn't need to explain further.

~ * ~

In Princes Park, Joel was composing a rock and roll song as part of an assignment when Maggie called him to the phone. "It's your mum," she said, her eyebrows raised in bemusement.

"Oh no," Joel whined. "I'm not ready for this. Does she sound mad?"

Maggie shrugged and left him to it.

"Joel? It's me!" Her voice sounded remarkably light and there was something very strange about her.

"Mum? You sound different. What's wrong?"

"Oh Joel, let's say I've had a make-over. Doctor Flynn has worked wonders on me," she divulged.

"Are you saying you've had therapy?" Joel asked, totally confused by what he was hearing.

"Not therapy in the medical sense, but I'm happy now. Let's not go over all the bad stuff. I know how wrong I was to try to make you do what I wanted. It was really that visit to see you that told me a few home truths," she explained. "I'm not asking you to forget, but I would like you to forgive."

Joel was stunned. "I don't know what to say. I'm not sure if I'm ready for all that yet, but I guess I can work on it. What did Dr Flynn do to transform you?"

"He fell in love with me."

Silence.

"Joel?" Nell knew she had shocked her son. "I'll go now. I wanted to tell you what is going on. See you later." And with that she rang off.

Joel slowly replaced the receiver. Maggie came into the living room. "Aw right, lad?" she asked the nonplussed Joel.

"I'm not sure," he told her. "That person wasn't my mother."

"Do yer want to talk?" Maggie questioned.

"Not just now, thanks, Maggie. There are a few things I need to sort out in my head," he conceded. *Doctor Flynn for starters*, he thought.

~ * ~

Joel informed his music tutor about his meeting with Ray Greenwood. Dafydd Powell was sceptical. "Don't let him turn your head, boy. It's easy these days to get swept along with the tide. There are so many singers coming out of, not just Liverpool, but Manchester, Birmingham and London itself. I'd hate to think of you being a one-hit wonder. You're better than that. Just be careful, Joel."

"I will, but I can't miss the chance to perform at The Cabin, can I?"

Dafydd Powell looked straight at Joel. "If that's what you want, I can't stop you, but I'll tell you again, be careful."

When he arrived at The Cabin, it was half past two, Wednesday afternoon. Inside, it was dark, dingy almost, but the coloured lights round the little stage transformed it, Joel thought, into a palace of dreams. Ray was talking animatedly with a guy in a camel overcoat and yellow scarf. He sounded as though his finger were right on the pulse. "If that's what you want, go ahead. We'll be getting the four Liverpool lads back from Hamburg soon. They're going to be big and we've one or two more hovering as well." He looked up and saw Joel. "Ah Joel, come in, come in. See yer, Jimmy. Take care."

Audition over, Ray told Joel straight away that he could have a fifteen-minute spot on Thursday night. "Sing a few Bings and one or two Vera Lynns. Our Thursday nighters will love it."

Joel tried to hide his disappointment. "Will I get to do some of the modern stuff, too?"

"Later, if you're any good on Thursday. Don't run before you can walk, lad. We all have to start at the bottom of the ladder."

"Okay, if you say so, I'll give it a go," Joel said, "but if it doesn't work out, I want to walk away."

"Cocky little bastard, aren't you? That's what I like to see, somebody with balls. See yer Thursday and don't be late."

~ * ~

Joel arrived early so he could get the feel of the place before his session.

"Jeez!" he whispered when he saw the clientele. There was nobody under forty, and his heart sank. He stood at the back feeling more and more confused as he watched the unlikely acts that went before him: a magician, a female impersonator and a stand-up comedian.

"Hey there, Joel," Greenwood greeted him, a look of smug complacency on his face. "Think you can cope with this lot?"

"Not my scene, Ray, but since you've obviously got me here, I'll do what you ask. You leave me with no choice," Joel said leaving Ray under no illusions. "I'll not welsh on an agreement, but unless I can sing to the young ones, I'm not up for your Thursday nighters as you call them. My grandparents look younger than some of these." He wanted to call him a sneaky bastard, but he wouldn't want to give Ray the pleasure of knowing he was upset.

"The oldies loved you," Ray said to him at the end of the session. "Come back stage and we'll give you a treat." He led Joel through a door at the side of the stage and then out through a door at the back into a narrow alley. It was dark, but they found a grubby green door that opened onto an equally grubby little shed. Sitting on up-turned crates, three young guys were smoking and filling the air with a noxious smell that made Joel's head spin.

"This is our new recruit, guys. Show 'im the ropes. Give 'im a good time," Ray instructed the three smokers and then left.

The nearest of the three handed Joel a cigarette. "I don't smoke, thanks," Joel said and yet at the same time he was being drawn into the atmosphere, the fumes seemingly encouraging him to light up and join them.

"You do now," another of the three told him. "Sit down and light up and stop yer fuckin' bleating."

"All right, all right," Joel agreed, "I'll give it a try."

The first couple of puffs made his head reel, but then he began to feel as though he were flying, rather like when he'd had too much to drink and the bed spun round and round in the darkness.

"This is bloody lovely," he announced to nobody in particular. The other three faces stared and grinned manically and all four of them began to laugh uncontrollably. He looked through misted eyes at the smallest of the three who was known as Ratty. "I know you from somewhere. Where do I know you from? I've met you before, I know I have. I have met you before, haven't I? Come on, tell me where I've seen you. At the Casa? At College? I know I've spoken to you, I know..."

"Shut the fuck up, yer posh bastard. Give me another joint, Ratty," and the loud boy guffawed again enveloped in the smoke that was their euphoria.

Some five hours later, Joel found himself in a bus shelter at Pier Head. He felt as though he'd been drinking heavily, but he knew he hadn't. The last thing he remembered was Ray taking him into a shed and leaving him there with some other lads. Slowly, he unravelled his confused brain. "Shit!" he exclaimed, "Shit! Shit! Shit!"

~ * ~

"Ben's here, Poshman," Gerry called up the stairs the following morning. "I'll send him up, okay? I'm off to work. See yer later."

Ben took one look at Joel as he clung tightly to the bedspread under his chin. "My god! What happened to you?"

Joel's mouth was dry and he found it difficult to open his eyes. "Nothing," he croaked.

"Well, whatever it was, I hope it was worth it. You look like shit," Ben told him. "I came to have a serious talk with you, but I'll come back after work when you'll be awake properly. God, Joel, you don't half make me feel like thumping you at times!"

"Sod off, Ben. Come back in a couple of hours. I'll be awake then."

"Shouldn't you be at college?" Ben asked.

"Oh shit. I've got a drama lecture in half an hour," Joel exclaimed. "Out of my way, Ben. I'm in deep shit if I miss it."

"Seems to me like you're in deep shit already. I'll see you later. I'm off, or I'll be late too," Ben said caustically.

Joel crawled out of bed carefully. He swilled his face with cold water. His eyes were red and his tongue was rough like sandpaper. He hadn't time to run a bath, but rushing around to get dressed seemed to make him feel normal again. His thoughts were still confused. *Did I really smoke pot?* he asked himself. He smiled. *I remember feeling high. I liked it, bloody hell! Drama, here I come!*

Janice, the drama tutor, set the task. "Today we are having a row," she told the group. "Find a partner and don't decide in advance what the row is about, let it evolve."

"You look like you've been on the tiles all night," Ken told him.

"What do you mean?" Joel asked bristling.

"Well, just look at the state of you. You need a shave, your hair is hanging in grease, your eyes are swollen and sorry to have to say this, but your breath stinks!" Ken remarked pointedly.

The onslaught touched a nerve with Joel. "Who do you think you are?" he shouted squaring up to the lad he had only just met a few weeks ago when they both started college. Their raised voices were drawing the attention of the others in the group.

"If you've got any sense, you'll see that I'm a friend," Ken replied.

"Friend? I don't think so. Friends wouldn't be so insulting—friends would be more discreet," Joel cried, his face red with anger.

"No, you're wrong, Joel. Dead wrong! Friends would be honest and that's what I'm being with you. You look like shit!"

Where had he heard that before? Joel's mind was in a whirl and his head hurt. He couldn't think straight. "I don't give a tinker's cuss what you think, Ken. Just piss off and find a partner to get on with this row we have to have..."

Loud applause echoed round the studio and Janice came forward to congratulate the pair on a very good performance. "Come on, the rest of you. Get on with it."

Joel excused himself moodily and went to the washroom to swill his face. Catching sight of himself in the mirror, he grimaced. "My god, Ken, you were right," and he returned to the class to apologise.

"No problem, mate, but clean yourself up. I've been there and it isn't worth it."

~ * ~

Ben returned after work with a very serious look on his face. "I've been with Belinda for the past few days..."

"Good one, Ben. I'm happy for you. I knew you'd get off with her."

"Shut up and listen, Joel," Ben continued. "I haven't slept with her, if that's what you're implying, but you did, didn't you?"

"Is that what she told you? Ben, it wasn't like you think..."

"Exactly what do I think, Joel? I'll tell you *not* what I think, but what I know. Belinda was in love with you, maybe still is. She didn't turn up for the gig because she was sick that morning and has been sick every morning since then. Get the picture, buddy?" Ben was seething.

Joel paled. "Shit! Oh shit!"

"Is that all you can say? How about, how is she now? How about, I must go to see her? How about, I'll stand by her?" Ben raged.

"But my career..." Joel cried. "What a mess!"

"You selfish bastard, Winston, and I thought you'd changed. From now on, you just keep away from Belinda. Do you hear me? Keep well away." With that, Ben stormed out.

Joel threw on a pair of jeans and a sweater. He raced into town to find Ray. "Ray! Ray!" he called breathlessly as he rushed into The Cabin.

"Hold on, lad. What's yer hurry?" Ray said grabbing hold of Joel's arm to keep him from running through the club like the proverbial bat out of hell.

"Take me to the green door," he instructed and waved a couple of pound notes in Ray's face. "Take me to the green door now."

~ * ~

When Gerry arrived home from work, Joel was spaced out on his bed. Gerry didn't wake him. "Poshman, you've let me down," he whispered to the sleeping mess in front of him. Throwing the note he'd written on the bed, he left the attic room, very sad and completely dejected.

Joel read the letter three or four times to make sure he hadn't misinterpreted:

Dear Poshman

What can I say? I'm happier today than I have ever been because you brought Penny and me together. I'm also sadder today than I have ever been, because you have betrayed our trust—mine, my mam's and our Chrissie's. You know what you've done so I won't spell it out to you. Not only that, you have brought the smell of pot into my home and that's despicable. We might not have much, but we're above all that rubbish.

When we met, I thought I had found a true and loyal friend, but it seems I was wrong. I have to ask you to leave.

I'll tell Mam when she gets back from her trip that your gran is sick and you need to spend time with her. Don't let me down. Pack your things and be out by tomorrow. If you stay, it will affect my relationship with Penny and I'm not prepared to risk that. Even now, when Bel looks at me, it's like she blames me for what you've done.

I don't wish you any harm, Poshman, but sort yourself out before it's too late.

Gerry

"Shit!" Joel said again. "That just about sums up my life just now. One big heap of unadulterated shit!" He folded the letter, stuffed it into his pocket, gathered his things together and went to find Ray's green door again.

Fifteen

Scan appeared on Nell's doorstep one Saturday morning, his face flushed as though he'd run a marathon. "What are you doing here at this time in the morning?" Nell asked him.

"I have some news," he announced, "news I've been waiting for, for months."

"Come in then and let me share it. By the look on your face, it must be good."

They went into the kitchen and Nell put on the kettle. "Coffee?" she asked.

"Afterwards." Sean sat at the breakfast bar facing Nell as she remained by the hob.

"Would you like to sit down," he invited. "This might take some digesting."

Nell shook her head and stood very still. "I'm not sure I'm going to like this," she said. "There is something ominous about the look in your eyes."

Sean smiled. "Ominous perhaps, but exciting. I've been offered a job in Sydney."

"Sydney, Australia?" Nell was puzzled.

"It's a consultancy. I need to do the training course when I get there, but I'll enjoy that. Two years on-the-job training in the largest orthopaedic hospital in Australia," Sean explained. "What an opportunity, Nell!"

Nell looked at him, his eyes shining with expectation.

"I want you to come with me, Nell, to be with me on this new adventure," he said.

"Is that a proposal?" she asked, knowing that it was, but not yet ready to hear it.

"Of course it is. I'll get down on one knee if necessary, but please will you marry me, Nell? I love you and this is the best thing that's happened to me in my life."

"This love, or the opportunity in Australia?" she asked quietly. "There can only be one best, can't there? Is it our love, or the job?"

Sean didn't answer right away. He was confused. "What do you want me to say, Nell?"

"If you have to ask, then I'm not going to tell you. I can't answer *your* question either just now. I can't believe you haven't told me about this before. I need time to think. It's such a massive decision. Perhaps we'd better skip coffee. I need to be alone." She kissed him on the cheek. "I'll call you later."

"Are you sure?" Sean asked, somewhat bemused by Nell's attitude.

She nodded, her strong, confident expression making it clear she was in no mood to argue.

"I'll call you," she repeated as she held open the door. "Later."

Nell leaned on the door she had just shut on the dejected Sean. She breathed in deeply, not really comprehending what her next move should be. She walked into the kitchen and poured herself a glass of wine. She didn't look at the clock. That it was only nine thirty in the morning didn't matter. She sat at the breakfast bar and twirled her glass between her fingers, intermittently taking a hearty gulp to help clarify her muddled thoughts.

The gall of him! she thought unreasonably. *Coming in here and expecting me to make a decision like that without thinking about it.*" She closed her eyes and slowly shook her head in an effort to find answers. *But I suppose he felt I loved him enough to respond quickly. Do I? Do I love him enough to drop everything, sell up and move myself body and soul to the other side of the world?*

And what about Joel? He and I are just beginning to understand each other again, even though I don't know what he's up to in Liverpool. He never thinks of calling me. Out of sight, out of mind with him. I could be lying dead on the floor of my bedroom and he wouldn't know, or care. Selfish little so-and-so. She took another swig of her wine. It felt good and warmed her throat as it went down. She took the bottle and her glass and went into the lounge where she sat on her favourite chair. It was comfortable and homely, familiar and reassuring.

She closed her eyes and tried to sort out her thoughts that were becoming more and more entangled. *If I sit here, I'll be asleep in two minutes.* So she paced the floor like one waiting for something to happen imminently. *What it comes down to,* she thought, momentarily more lucid, *is who needs me more, Joel or Sean? Joel? Well, he's my son, the child I raised, the boy who rebelled and the young man who appears to be standing on his own two feet. Sean? He's the man I have fallen in love with ...* She took another drink and sat down again. She held up the bottle, noting that it was half full. *Or half empty,* she thought and giggled as she filled her glass again.

When she woke, it was dark. She staggered to the bathroom and looked at her reflection in the mirror. "God, Nell, you look a mess," she told herself. "You need a drink."

Somewhere in the distance, she could hear the telephone ringing. "Will somebody answer that phone?" she called out and, as if by magic, the ringing stopped. When it started to ring again, she stumbled in the direction of the sound and lifted the receiver.

"Go away!" she shouted. "Just go away." Placing the receiver on the table, she went back to her bottle.

~ * ~

Sean looked at the telephone in his hand. "Oh Nell," he said out loud. "What are you doing?" He replaced the receiver and went to his study. This was his favourite thinking place. Somehow it offered him room for sensible contemplation. It was where he had sat when Kathy delivered her bombshell and where he resolved he would never allow a woman to play with his emotions again. "Oh, my God!" he said. "Not again, surely not again."

The thought of Nell sounding so drunk that she was unable to speak coherently prevented Sean from opening his bottle of Glenfiddich. He had to make his decision within the next forty-eight hours. He would have to talk to Nell when she had sobered up. "What on earth are you thinking about, Nell?" he said quietly, looking up at the heavens. "This is a chance of a lifetime for us. Why would it be so difficult?" He sat with his head in his hands until he fell asleep at his desk. He woke with a start when the clock struck midnight and he went to bed, resolving to call her the next day.

Sean went to early Mass that Sunday morning. He hoped he would find some divine inspiration in spite of his not attending Mass for many years, but as he knelt at the back of the church, he felt no rush of the Holy Spirit, only the burden of decision-making that filled his heart and mind.

He stood at Nell's door again, the place where she had shut him out the day before. With indescribable trepidation, he rang the bell.

"I can't come with you," Nell told him. "It's too much. I have to be here for Joel when he needs me."

"Nell, Joel hasn't been home for months. He wouldn't care whether you were here, or in Timbuktu!" Sean exclaimed. "You need this. I need this. We need this. Surely you can see that."

"Don't you dare tell me what I need and how to deal with my son," she cried. "He's *my* son and I know that he'll need me again eventually. I have to be here for him."

"No, you don't, Nell! I need you and we are good together."

"Between the sheets? Is that what you want me for?" she barked.

"For God's sake, Nell. You know that's not what I want you for."

"Oh, so you're saying I'm no good in bed now that you've had your fun," she continued irrationally.

"I can't talk to you when you're like this. I'll come back later when you've calmed down. I have to leave next week. I'm leaving the country, Nell, and I want you to come with me." Sean looked at her and shook his head in despair. "Call me when you're ready to talk, but don't leave it too long. There are flights to book." He left and didn't look back.

Nell opened another bottle of wine and poured herself a glass. It tasted good and, after two or three mouthfuls, she began to relax. *I have to choose. I never thought I would ever be in this situation*, she thought as she finished her wine and then poured another glass. "Joel or Sean? Sean or Joel?" she repeated out loud over and over again. When she had drained the last drops from the bottle, she picked up the phone.

Sean's telephone rang just before noon. "Don't mess me around, Nell. I won't let you play with my feelings. One woman did that a long time ago and I'm not prepared to let it happen again. Will you marry me?"

Nell's head was swimming. The wine that tasted so good was now invading her brain with long knives, but she knew what her answer would be. "I can't marry you and I can't go to Australia with you," she said surprisingly calmly.

Sean gasped. "Can't, or won't? Okay, that's it then. I love you, Nell, but I'm not giving up this opportunity to prove it. I have resigned from the practice, so I won't see you again. Be happy, Nell. Just be happy." He sighed deeply and replaced the receiver. Now he had urgent things to do.

~ * ~

"I'll show you, Sean Flynn. You aren't the only fish in the sea. I can get another man if I want to. Just you see if I don't."

Nell didn't go to work after that weekend. She called in sick and Jackie understood the situation without asking. "It's perhaps best that you recover for a few days," she told Nell when she phoned. "The new doctor will be settled in by then and you'll be able to adjust to any changes when you feel better."

Nell's hackles rose at the mere mention of a new doctor. *I'll make damn sure I don't get to know him*, she thought and took a gulp of the glass of wine she kept topped up during the day. Come the following Saturday night, she decided she had hidden away for long enough. She showered, did her hair and make-up and put on her prettiest dress before she called a taxi at nine o'clock. "Drop me on Bradshawgate," she instructed the driver.

For a moment or two she felt lost as she stood on the pavement outside the camera shop and stared around her. She'd already had a couple of glasses of wine and was beginning to feel the need of another urgently. She crossed the road and headed for the Wine Lodge. It looked warm and inviting and there was a lively atmosphere inside even though the lights were dim. She made her way to the bar. She'd never been alone in a pub, but she was determined that she would show the world she was strong.

No man will ever get the better of me, she told herself as she found a vacant bar stool at the end of the bar away from the main body of the room and inched herself onto it, her dress sliding up her shapely thighs as she made herself comfortable. "Red wine, please," she told the bartender, "a very large one," and she smiled at him seductively. The barman smiled back knowingly.

"Hello, beautiful," the man next to her said. "What's a lovely lady like you doing in a place like this?"

It was approaching eleven o'clock and she had drunk several large glasses of house red. "Are you talking to me?" she asked, squinting through glazed eyes.

"There's only one beautiful lady round here and she's only inches away from me, so it must be you, darlin.' What's your name, sweetheart?" He leered at her and she was flattered by his attention.

Nell giggled. "I'm Nell."

"That's a nice name. Can I call you Nellie?" the man asked, thinking Nellie was more appropriate in a town centre pub. "Nell sounds a bit posh for in here."

"No you can't!" Nell told him indignantly. "I might be a bit tiddly, but not so much that I'd become a common—"

"Feisty little madam, aren't you?" he interrupted and moved his stool closer in order to place his arm around her shoulders. "I like a bit of life in a woman."

Through her alcohol-fuelled gaze, he looked quite a handsome guy and she felt relaxed in his company. "And what's your name, big guy?" she slurred.

"Stan. Stan the man!" he joked. "Can I buy you a nightcap?"

Nell thought for a moment and then said, "Why not? I'll have another glass of red, please," her mouth curling upwards into a strange sort of smile. It was more a grimace, but still encouraging her admirer.

She remembered walking out into the cold night air and then nothing until she woke up in her bed with a bald-headed, overweight man snoring repulsively beside her. There were thousands of drummers in her head, all banging on their big bass drums at the same time. She crawled from under the duvet, revealing her naked body. Stepping over her clothes strewn across the floor, she found her way to the bathroom and took a couple of aspirins to ease her pain. She grabbed her robe from behind the door and returned to her room where the sleeping whale had not moved. Repulsed by his voluminous underwear hanging precariously on the door handle and the disgusting condom on the floor by the bed, she shook him vigorously.

"What the...?"

"Wake up, you great oaf. I don't want you here in my bed. I don't want you in my house. Get up and get out!" she screamed, her head pounding with every word she uttered. She hastily picked up his grubby clothes and throwing them at him, she shouted again, "Come on, Mr. whoever you are. Get out of my house—*now!*"

Stan was slowly coming round. "You weren't saying that last night, you little tart. You couldn't wait to let me into your posh knickers."

"Don't be so obnoxious! I don't know how you got here, but you'd better leave before I call the police." Nell was beside herself.

"All right, all right, I'm going, lady. Don't get yer knickers in a knot." He rumbled around the bedroom repulsively breaking wind as he bent to pick up his clothes. "Can I have a cup o' tea before I leave?" he asked the distraught Nell.

"*Out!*" she yelled and hung onto her head in order to stop the incessant throbbing in her temples as she followed him down the stairs.

Stan glared at her and wobbled to the foot of the stairs, puffing and panting as though he'd just run a marathon. As he opened the door, he turned and said, "A word of advice, lady. Don't offer yourself on a plate if you don't want a man to have his fill. You were gagging for it last night. But thanks, missus. You were a good lay!" He grinned sickeningly and closed the door behind him with a flourish.

Nell fell to her knees and clasped her arms around her to stop herself from throwing up. She took a deep breath and crawled to her favourite chair. Curling up in its warm, soft cushions felt familiar and comforting. She closed her eyes. The aspirins seemed to be working and she could move her head without feeling horses stampeding through her brain. She dozed for a while and when the phone rang, she was startled, but her pain had gone, the pain in her head that is. She didn't know if the pain in her heart would ever disappear.

"Nell? Is that you?" It was her mother and she was completely overcome with distress, her words tumbling out in torrents and making them indecipherable.

"Mother, what is it? Slow down. My brain can't take in all this gabbling," she told Margaret.

"Oh Nell, it's your dad. He's had a heart attack. I'm at the hospital. They don't know if he's going to make it and I don't know what to do. Can you come to Heswall General? I need you, Nell."

"I'll be there as soon as possible. Hold on, but it's going to take an hour at least for me to drive and I'll have to have a shower. Don't worry, I'll be there," Nell told her agitated mother. *Oh God,* she thought, *I could do without this today of all days.*

She stood in the shower and covered herself with the sweetest smelling shower cream she could find. *I have to wash away the stench of that repulsive individual who found his way to my bed last night,* she thought. She shivered as she covered herself in the perfumed foam and allowed the warm water to flow over her body, making her feel clean and respectable again. "I haven't even time to blow dry my hair. I'll just have to leave it." Her naturally curly hair never looked unruly, but if she didn't spend time on her appearance, she felt slovenly and unkempt, and it wasn't in Nell's nature to be slatternly. "Still, Mother needs me and..." She paused as the realisation hit her. "Oh, my poor dad!" she gasped. "Don't die, Dad. Please don't die."

~ * ~

Her mother coped very well. It was almost as if as you grow older, you learn to accept that you'll be left alone. "You go back to Bolton, Nell. I'll be fine," Margaret told her daughter. "I have my friends and I promise you I'm not going to crawl under a stone. I'll see you in a couple of weeks and we'll speak on the phone before then."

Nell drove home in a daze. *What next?* she thought. *First Sean leaves me and then Dad. Joel hardly spoke at the funeral and couldn't wait to run back to Liverpool. He looked a mess, too. Hair too long, pale, nervous, yes, nervous. What was that all about? And he didn't even ask about Sean. Well, I'm not going to tell him. He's obviously not interested.*

Going back to work was bittersweet. Jackie was pleased to see her, but the new doctor had changed everything and the filing system she had mastered so quickly in the beginning was difficult to initiate. Everything had to be cross-referenced, sometimes in duplicate, the drugs records in triplicate.

"Are you all right, Nell?" Jackie asked, concerned that Nell looked tired and drawn. "You seem to be "away with the fairies!"

"I'm fine, Jackie. Nothing I can't deal with," Nell told her colleague and simply carried on with her work quietly.

Once home in the evening, she opened a bottle of her favourite Burgundy and drank away her depression. She began to look forward to seven o'clock when she could kick off her shoes and forget who she was for a while. Sometimes she would fall asleep in her favourite chair and wake up cold and hungry in the small hours of the morning. A few water crackers and French onion dip kept her going and another glass of wine warmed her so she could crawl up to bed and sleep until the alarm went off at seven in the morning. Then her day-to-day routine would start all over again.

Friday nights were always lonely and she would find solace in drinking herself into oblivion. It was Joel's birthday. Nell hadn't heard from him. She never heard from him. His twentieth birthday and he hadn't bothered to call. She'd sent a card to the Connollys' place and she supposed they were all celebrating together.

"I can't call there," she said out loud, "not after the performance I put up last time. Ah well, Nell, have another drink." She topped up her glass and raised it to Joel's picture on the wall. "H-h-happy b-b-birthday, Joel," she sobbed. "Here's to you, you selfish, little swine! Here's to you, my darling boy." Tears coursed down her cheeks as she finished her second bottle of red before she collapsed in a heap on her bed.

Sixteen

When Joel heard of Belinda's pregnancy, he had been a mess. He'd raced down to the shed to find Ray so he might smoke himself into another world for a while. "Ray! Ray!"

Ray had caught hold of his arm. "Slow down, lad! What's your hurry?"

"Take me to the green door. Take me to the green door now."

Snatching the two-pound notes out of Joel's fingers, Ray grabbed him by the shoulders and pushed him towards the back room of the club. "Be quiet, you dumb bastard. We don't want the world to know what we're about," he said in hushed tones. Pushing roughly past Joel, he slowly opened the door that was half hidden by a filing cabinet and cautiously peeped out. "We can't be too cocky in broad daylight," he told Joel.

"Can't you hurry up?" Joel pleaded. "I need a joyride and fast!"

Ray was not expecting what happened next. Two plainclothes policemen were frog-marching Ratty down the alley. Joel could see the lad being man-handled and his coat sleeves were roughly pushed up to his elbows revealing his watch—Joel's dad's watch. In a flash, Joel recognised Ratty for the first time. He was the roughneck who'd head-butted him the day he'd arrived in Liverpool. The green door was wide open and hanging off its hinges. "Run!" Ray shouted to Joel. "Run, or you're in deep shit!"

Joel turned and ran through the club to the front door. He had no idea what was happening, but Ray sounded panic-stricken and he knew he had to get away. Suddenly he felt an almighty shove in his back and he went sprawling on the floor. Ray jumped over him so that he might get to the door first and if the cops were coming after them, they'd find Joel on the floor after Ray had fled.

Dazed, Joel looked up to see Ray throw open the door and run straight into the arms of two burly policemen. Joel rolled behind the bar and was hidden. He eased himself into a sitting position, leaning his back against the crates of beer stacked beneath the bar, breathing heavily. Nobody had come in through the back door so he remained hidden until he thought it would be safe to move.

"Not so fast, lad," the club manager said as Joel made to leave.

"Who are you and where did you come from?" Joel asked nervously, thinking that he hadn't escaped arrest after all.

"I'm in charge here and who might you be? Do I have to call the cops again?" the manager replied.

"I'm Joel Winston, sir," Joel told him, his up-bringing automatically coming to the fore. "I haven't done anything wrong. Why was Ray running from the police?"

"You know Ray Greenwood then, do you?" the manager asked, signalling to Joel to take a seat at one of the small tables next to the bar. "Are you all right, lad? That was a mighty tumble you took."

"I'm okay thanks, but I have no idea what's going on."

"Are you sure? You were with Ray. I heard you shout for him when you came in. I was in my office," the manager told him.

Joel was confused. He had been in a panic when he arrived at the club. Ray had seemed pleased to see him and eagerly took his money.

"How do you know Ray Greenwood?" the man asked again.

"He gave me an audition to perform at The Cabin. I did a spot a couple of Thursdays ago," Joel informed him. "Unfortunately, the oldies scene is not for me."

"What oldies scene?" the man asked incredulously.

"Thursday nights' over thirties! He said I went down a bomb and that they loved me, but it wasn't for me. I want to perform for the young ones," Joel explained.

The manager sighed. "The sneaky bastard!" he said. "That night there was a private party for somebody retiring from the office next door. Ray's our doorman, that is, he *was* our doorman, but not anymore. What did he tell you?"

Joel explained about the Casa Bellissimo and how Ray had approached him as a talent scout for The Cabin Club. He chose not to mention the green door, but the manager already knew.

"That excuse for a man has set himself up as second-class drugs lord in an old shed in the back alley. Kids are not safe with him around. I only found out a couple of weeks ago just after the private function. I was off for a few days that week and left Ray in charge of the opening and closing of the club. He'd got it all worked out, hadn't he? He took you for a ride, lad, I'm afraid."

"Yes, he did. I should have known that opportunities like that don't come so easily. My tutor at college did warn me," Joel conceded. "I'm sorry I got mixed up with him."

"Look, lad, you just go back to college and finish what you started. We don't do auditions here without being approached by an agent. I have to disappoint you," the manager said apologetically.

"That's okay, sir. I know where I stand."

"Do you? Well, I hope so. My advice to you is to keep a level head. Some things seem good at the time, but mess you up later. Get my meaning, lad?"

Joel looked embarrassed, but nodded. "Thanks, sir. Point taken. Thanks again." He shook the guy's hand as he left.

The manager pushed his hands deep into his trouser pockets and rocked back and forth. *Nice lad*, he thought. *I hope he steers clear of the likes of Ray Greenwood from now on.*

~ * ~

Joel found himself contemplating his future again. His run-in with Ray Greenwood and subsequently the manager of The Cabin Club had left him completely bewildered, but he had learned a very important lesson from it. He needed to talk to somebody he could trust.

Dafydd Powell, Joel's music tutor, was aghast when he related the events of the weekend. "I told you to be careful," he said, "but I had no idea that was going on. Thank goodness you came to your senses." He paused and stood up from behind the piano. Walking over to where Joel was standing, he placed a reassuring hand on the boy's shoulder. "Let's go for a walk," he suggested.

The cold December air down by the river made Joel feel refreshed. The kindly Welshman listened before he spoke. "I know how much you want to perform, Joel, but my advice would be to finish the course and then see where the music scene is going. The whole world is alive with rock and roll just now. Music is a funny business. Some of the top twenty hits we're hearing at present will be forgotten next month. Some of them are bloody good." He paused as if he were about to make an announcement. "A friend of mine in Hamburg sent me a demo tape of a group from Liverpool and I reckon they're going to be big. I'm not supposed to have it, so I'm swearing you to secrecy. This group is different from the rest."

"Why are you telling me all this?" Joel asked. "Is it because I haven't got what it takes?" He respected his tutor's opinion.

"It's not that at all. I think you're good, but you need to have that extra *je ne sais quoi*. I'm not sure you're quite there yet. Now, first things first. We have to find you somewhere to stay if we are going to carry on with your education. Do you think the Connollys will forgive and forget?"

"I doubt it. I'm not Gerry's favourite person at the moment and I'm not sure he'll ever forgive me. I've been very stupid and I've lost his trust," Joel confessed.

"What about your grandmother. Would she allow you to live with her? She might enjoy you being around, especially now."

"Sorry DP. That's not an option," Joel told him, but he chose not to divulge the strained relationship he had with his mother. The less he had to think about that, the better.

Mr. Powell thought for a moment. "Look," he said quietly, "I wouldn't normally do this, but I think you're a good kid and I know my wife would love to mollycoddle you for a while. How about I talk to her and see if she'll take in a lodger. We have the room and..." He regarded Joel with a knowing look in his eyes. "...you'll never to be able to skip lectures and I'll make sure you do your assignments on time! Deal?"

Joel scrutinised his tutor carefully. "Are you joking, sir?" he asked. "Because if you are, please don't offer me a sweet with one hand and take it away with the other."

"No joke, Joel Winston ...good name, by the way." Dafydd grinned like a mischievous schoolboy. "You can have the back bedroom. It's out of the way, but near enough when you need company. I hope West Derby is ready for the next Cliff Richard!"

"Sounds great to me," Joel told him and they shook hands firmly.

Later that night as he lay in his new bed, he thanked his lucky stars that what had happened to him in the past few weeks had not done any lasting damage. He'd lost a couple of friends in the fallout and he still had to come to terms with his continuing uneasy relationship with his mother, but he determined that he would get over the next three years and set his sights on his future.

~ * ~

Those three years flew by. Dafydd Powell was like the father Joel never had. They went to Anfield to watch the Reds every week, went to see all the movies that Mrs. Powell didn't fancy, played music together with a passion and, much to Joel's amazement, DP taught him to drive. Joel secretly basked in the special feeling he had discovered with DP, the feeling that had been missing when he was a boy. The tutor allowed the young man space when he needed to be with his friends and having eventually sussed that Joel's relationship with his mother needed to be rekindled, he encouraged Joel to visit her once a month.

"You need to see her, Joel, even if it's only to let her know you are all right. Maybe eventually, you'll patch up your differences," the kindly gentleman told him.

"Okay, I'll go to see her, but there's still a lot of baggage to clear out before I can begin to think about going home," Joel conceded. "She doesn't exactly make me feel wanted anymore. She never wants to talk on the phone. She didn't even send me a birthday card last year. There's no doubt about it, DP, we have grown apart."

Each month he made the journey on the train to Bolton. Sometimes he arranged to meet his mother in town and they had lunch together at the Swan, or the Pack Horse. "What happened to the doctor?" he dared to ask.

"Oh, he left the practice and that was that," she said and neither of them pursued the subject further.

Occasionally, they met at Granny's house on the Wirral and often conversation was strained, but they had a tacit understanding that they would always try to part as friends.

"I'll see you next month, Mum," Joel said as he left. "Take care." And with a fleeting kiss on the cheek, they went back to the lives into which both felt they had settled comfortably without each other.

Joel continued with his gigs at the Casa Bellissimo every Saturday lunchtime throughout his time at college. When he qualified with honours and began to look in *The Stage* magazine for jobs, he had to tell Vic he wouldn't be able to continue.

"I'll miss you and so will the punters," Vic told him, "but I knew you'd have to move on eventually."

"I'll see if there's anybody at college who can take over, if you like," Joel suggested.

"That'll be great," Vic agreed. "I might be able to keep up my takings, especially if they're as good as you've been!"

"I'll do my best," Joel reassured him. "And thanks for everything, Vic."

Seventeen

Nell managed to keep going to work at the surgery. Jackie had given up inviting her to the shopping jaunts with her friends and although there were no harsh words, the atmosphere between them was cool. Nell did what she supposed to do, but she didn't say much other than discussing matters of work.

Jackie was surprised, shocked even, when Nell announced one Friday, "I'm hitting the town tomorrow night. Do you fancy coming with me, Jackie?"

"Sorry, Nell, I don't do women on their own in pubs. Not my scene," Jackie informed her. "And to be honest, I'm surprised it's your thing. Are you sure about it?"

"Of course I'm sure. What would you know about it, Jackie?" Her retort was harsh and uncalled for, but she didn't care. "It's your loss. I'll go on my own. I usually find somebody to talk to." She winked at her dumbfounded colleague. "Know what I mean?"

Jackie was speechless and wondered what was happening to the woman who had set herself above the rest when it came to socialising—here she was, going out to town centre pubs on her own and …she hated to think it, but… picking up men!

"Saturday night is for enjoyment," Nell told herself as she stood in front of the mirror putting the finishing touches to her make-up. Her glass of wine was perched precariously on the edge of the dressing table. As she reached out to get her hairbrush, she nudged the glass. With remarkable dexterity, she managed to catch it before it spilled its contents onto the beige carpet. "Jeez!" she exclaimed and began to laugh hysterically. "You silly idiot, Nell. This stuff is too precious to throw around the room." She drank down what was left and called a taxi.

She sat at the bar in The Black Horse and ordered a drink. "Give me the bottle," she told the barman. "It'll save me keep waiting to be served." Finding a table in the corner, she set down the bottle and made herself comfortable.

"Are you Joel Winston's mother?" the woman asked.

"What is it to you?" Nell enquired.

"I'm surprised to see you in here," the woman continued. "I'd heard you were too posh and stuck up to be seen in a pub, especially in the town centre."

"Look, lady, I don't know who you are, but sit down and have a drink. I feel like a bit of woman talk. Makes a change from the sleazebag men who usually talk to me. Pull up a chair," Nell invited her would-be companion.

"Don't mind if I do, seeing as you're paying," the woman said. "I'm Connie, Connie Mason."

Nell looked at Connie through squinting eyes. The wine was taking effect and she found it difficult to focus. "Hello then, Connie. I know somebody called Mason, but I can't think of his first name."

"Ben?" Connie asked her.

"That's it! How did you know that?" Nell nudged her new friend and laughed. "You must be psychic. Clever thing, aren't you?"

"Not clever, dear. He's my son, not that he has anything to do with me these days. He moved out as soon as he left school. I never got so much as a penny from his wages, the little toe-rag. And now he's leading our Michael away, too."

"Don't tell me about wayward sons. I've got one who can't bear even to talk to me," Nell divulged between drinking down the remains of the bottle and ordering another.

"Looks like we understand each other," she told Connie. By the time they had had several glasses of wine each, the two women were ready to survey the landscape.

"Look to your right," Connie instructed. "I don't fancy yours!" and she laughed raucously.

The two men were smiling at them and beginning to move in their direction.

"I'll have the one in the white shirt. Ooh, look at his rippling muscles." Nell smiled at him invitingly.

Waking up the next morning with the rippling muscles next to her turned out to be more like lying next to rolls of blubber. Nell felt violently sick and grabbed the waste bin so as not to throw up on her bedroom carpet. As she staggered to the bathroom, she heard voices coming from her guest room.

"Well, I didn't have to ask you twice if you fancied a bit of slap and tickle," the woman said.

"I must have had a few," the man replied. "God knows what the wife will say when I arrive home."

"Oh, just tell her you stayed at Jimmy's... that's your mate's name, isn't it?" the woman's voice continued. "I won't tell. Your secret's safe with me so long as you pay up."

"What? I'm not paying for what you offered me without having to ask, you cheeky mare." The man was outraged.

"Well, cough up, or I'll follow you home and tell yer wife myself." The woman's voice was raised now, almost at screaming pitch.

Nell stood motionless on her landing with her waste bin still in her hand. Her head was banging and she could not believe what she had just heard. *Who* are *these people?* she silently asked herself.

Creeping down the stairs and into the kitchen, she put on the kettle and waited for her uninvited guests to appear. When they did make an appearance, she eyed them incredulously. She vaguely recognised the woman. Struggling to remember the night before, she managed a smile and said, "Good morning," and as the three people entered, she recalled the woman's name. "Oh Connie, isn't it?"

"Sure is, dear. Thanks for the bed. Lovely room, too," Connie offered.

The two men looked uncomfortable. "I don't know you, I've never seen you, I will deny all of this if I ever see you again," the man who had been arguing with Connie said defiantly. "I'm off. Come on, Jimmy. We'll have a lot of explaining to do when we get home."

As the door banged shut, Connie grinned at Nell and waved two five-pound notes in the air. "Good night," she said. "Bloody good night. Thanks, dear. We'll have to do it again sometime." She left without another word.

Nell's head hurt, but somehow she was unravelling the snippets of information that intermittently filtered into her confused mind. *Connie Mason*, she remembered. "Oh my... Ben's mother, the reason I wouldn't allow Joel to bring Ben into this house." She shuddered at the thought that a woman like that had spent the night with a strange man in her guest room. "Oh my..." she said again, "and she took money from him. Oh my God, I need a drink."

Nell didn't turn up for work on Monday morning, nor did she call in sick. Jackie rang at nine-fifteen, but could get no reply. She called again at lunchtime and a groggy Nell tentatively picked up the receiver. Holding it as far away from her ear as possible, she struggled to hear what was being said. "Nell? It's Jackie."

Nell replaced the receiver with a grimace that said she couldn't talk. The phone rang again. "Oh, go away," she groaned. "I can't talk just now." But the phone rang out and she picked it up, intending to place the receiver off the hook without saying anything.

"Nell? Don't hang up. I'm worried about you. Are you all right?" Jackie said, almost pleading with Nell to speak.

"I'm not well," she slurred. "What time is it? I'm going to throw up. Call back later," she told Jackie.

Jackie looked questioningly at the phone in her hand, knowing that something would have to be done if Nell wanted to keep her job. She had been instructed to report her findings to her employer.

When the letter arrived, Nell hadn't been to work for a week. She had not been out of her house. She had vomited every morning into the bucket she kept by her bed and then had struggled to crawl down the stairs to open a bottle of wine that made her feel better. Some days, she didn't get dressed at all. She didn't eat and only when she had downed a few drinks did she begin to feel what she decided was normal.

"What's this now?" she asked herself as the mail dropped through the letterbox. "Another bill, I suppose." She opened the envelope roughly and peered through her alcoholic haze at its contents. It was very official looking and she hunted round for her reading glasses so that she might find out what it said. "Maybe I've won the Pools," she said out loud. "Could be true if I did the Pools." She laughed at herself for being so silly. The letter was from the surgery.

Dear Mrs. Winston,

It is with regret that I have to inform you that this letter constitutes a written warning. Your non-attendance at work of late has been noted. Since we have not been provided with the required medical evidence of your indisposition, we are duty bound to warn you of impending dismissal should your attendance not improve.

I look forward to hearing from you as soon as possible to clarify the situation.

Yours sincerely,
George P Ogilvie MB ChB
Senior Medical Practitioner

Nell stared at the piece of paper in her hand. "Well, Doctor Ogilvie," she said, "you can stick your job. Who needs it anyway? I'll resign before giving you the pleasure of sacking me. So there, Mr. Senior Medical Practitioner. You are all the same... bloody doctors..." Hot tears stung her eyes. "Oh Sean," she cried, "I miss you so much." And she opened another bottle from her stash of Burgundy.

Eighteen

The news of the death of his grandmother stunned Joel. His mother had called early on Sunday morning. She had been staying with her mother for a few days as Margaret had complained of being unwell. "She must have been sick without telling me," Nell informed Joel. "By the time I arrived last Tuesday, she was already bed-ridden and couldn't talk. Her neighbour had found her sitting dazed on the doorstep. She'd had a stroke, poor thing." Nell chose not to tell Joel that she herself had had to spend a couple of days sobering up after her mother's cry for help before she was able to drive over to the Wirral. She was well-practised. She had always made sure she was sober when Joel visited each month and she was confident she'd covered her tracks. Right now, she was desperate for a drink, but somehow, common sense had prevailed and she'd kept off the wine while she had been at her mother's house.

"Are you okay, Mum? You sound very shaken," Joel observed. "Do you want me to come over to help organise things?"

"No, I'm all right," she lied. "It's all done. The vicar has been very helpful. Just be here on Wednesday for the funeral. And please make sure you are clean and tidy. I know you students—all long, greasy hair and torn jeans."

Joel sighed. "Still the same old mother, I see," he remarked. "I'll be there, don't worry and for your information, DP won't allow me out of the house if I'm not dressed appropriately. He's done a pretty good job."

"Better than I did? Is that what you're saying, Joel?" Nell asked caustically.

"No, Mother, that's not what I'm saying, but if the cap fits..." He was past caring about what his mother chose to misconstrue. "I'll see you on Wednesday."

With the funeral over, Joel stayed around while Nell played dutiful daughter and hosted the wake. Granny's house was almost cleared and the 'For Sale' sign was in place by the front gate.

"Wouldn't you like to come back to live over here?" the vicar asked Nell as the few remaining guests took their leave.

"I don't think so," Nell told him. "I have my house in Bolton and that's where my life is now."

"I just thought with Joel being in Liverpool, it would be more convenient for both of you," the vicar reasoned.

"Joel won't always be in Liverpool, Vicar," Nell said amicably. "He has designs on being a pop star."

"Oh, I see," the kindly cleric said, "I see," and he bid her goodbye.

Joel had bided his time. He wanted to get Nell alone before he imparted his news. As the last person had taken his leave, he noticed that his mother visibly paled and grabbed hold of the doorpost to steady herself. "Are you okay, Mum? You are shaking," he said, genuinely concerned that his mother might be ill.

"I'll be fine," she said, her voice quivering. "Can you just see if there's a bottle of brandy in Granny's cabinet?" She knew there was, but she had used every scrap of willpower she had not to drink it before the funeral. "I'll just have a tot to take away this sickly feeling."

Joel obliged and it was remarkable to see how quickly his mother recovered.

"Blimey! It must be good stuff! I don't know how you drink it, though. It stinks to high heaven. It makes me feel sick just to smell it," he told his now brighter mother.

"Makes you, or breaks you," Nell quipped. "Now it's time we were off. See you next month. Will you come to Bolton?"

"There's something I need to tell you before I leave," Joel announced. "I know it may be the wrong time, but I don't know if there will ever be a right time. I've got a job with Pacific Cruise Ships. I'm part of the entertainment crew on their world cruises."

"Oh." Nell didn't say anything more.

"I'm very excited about it. They've given me a free rein to organise my own backing group from their musicians and my own programme. The money is excellent and it includes accommodation and food during each trip. I couldn't ask for a better start. Loads of musicians begin their careers on cruise liners."

"Well, I hope you'll be very happy," Nell said as she found herself growing more and more eager to get away. "When do you leave?" she asked as she moved towards the door.

"In a couple of weeks, so my visit will have to be early. Is that all right?"

"Whatever, Joel, whatever. Just give me a couple of days notice before you arrive in Bolton," Nell instructed. "Now I have to go. See you later." With the obligatory kiss on the cheek, they parted company without ceremony.

Joel knew he had people to see before he left the country. The rift between him and Gerry Connolly had weighed heavily on his mind. He kept a discreet silence after Gerry asked him to leave. Admittedly, he had concentrated on getting his life in order since then and with the help of DP and Mrs. DP, he had become a happier, more fulfilled person. *I ought to have written to Maggie Connolly when she returned from her trip*, he often told himself, *but it's difficult to find the words and I'm not sure I have the confidence to admit to my misdemeanours, especially since she was the person who showed me what a happy home was all about.* His guilt was a burden on him. Gerry had not been anywhere near Casa Bellissimo in the past three years. The more the time passed, the harder it was to build bridges.

Then there was Belinda. What had happened between them was a huge mistake and he had handled it badly. He had no idea if she'd had the baby, or if she had chosen not to continue with the pregnancy. He wouldn't blame her if that was the road she had taken. And Ben? He was so in love with Bel, Joel hoped he had managed to find happiness with her.

He stood outside the shop. His thoughts were running riot. *What if they refuse to see me? I couldn't blame them. The worst scenario would be for them to tell me to get lost and never show my face in Princes Park again. Well, I can handle that, I think. I wouldn't like it, but at least I would have tried to put things right.* With fear and trepidation, he opened the shop door.

Maggie was behind the counter sorting out the cigarettes on the shelves. "My goodness, is it really you, Joel? I must say you look well, lad."

"Hello, Maggie," he said sheepishly. "I really don't know what to say. It's been so long."

"Come on upstairs, lad. I'll get Josie to take over here. She's my new assistant. Our Chrissie's married now and due to give birth anytime so I've had to get help with the shop."

"Wow! You a grandma! It's hard to believe," Joel said, delighted that Maggie hadn't asked him to leave as soon as he had shown his face in the shop.

"I'll put the kettle on and then you can tell me what's been happening. How's your Gran, by the way?"

Joel decided that honesty was the best policy. "She passed away last week, Maggie, but I must tell you that I wasn't living with her. I never went to live with her. That story was Gerry's way of protecting you from the truth."

Maggie smiled. "I knew it wasn't the truth, but God bless 'im, he never strayed from the story. I could see the hurt in 'is eyes every time your name cropped up, so eventually we stopped wondering how you were going on."

"I don't blame you for that. I suppose you know that Belinda was pregnant?" Joel said.

"Oh yes. Ben's little girl! She's a little beauty, I believe. They went to live in Bolton as soon as they were married. Apparently, Ben had a flat there so they didn't have to find somewhere to live," Maggie told him. "What a lovely couple they make. Ben worships the two of them, Gerry says."

Joel hoped he'd hidden his shock. "Oh yes, I can imagine that they'd be very happy together. And what about Gerry and Penny?"

"They're as 'appy as pigs in muck. They're engaged and saving up to get married. Maybe next year when Gerry's got 'is diploma. He went to tech to qualify as an electrician. He was top student last year when he got 'is ONC. He wants to get 'is HNC before he can settle down. I'm very proud of 'im."

"And so you should be," Joel told her. "I let you all down, I know that and I shall regret that for as long I live."

He explained to Maggie that he had been hoodwinked by Ray Greenwood and had briefly dabbled with the drug culture that was rife in the world of entertainment. "Gerry found out what I was doing and asked me to leave before you returned from your trip. I don't blame him. I would have done the same if the tables had been turned." He left out the details of his dalliance with Belinda. He decided it would merely shatter her illusions and would further interfere with the lives of those he wished all the luck in the world.

"Well, so long as you're okay now, lad," Maggie said affectionately, "no harm done."

"Thanks, Maggie. I appreciate that. Do you think Gerry will see me?" he asked tentatively.

"I'll tell 'im you've been and I'll leave it up to 'im. I can't do more than that, lad," Maggie informed him gently.

"I leave on the sixth—Thursday week. I'll give you my number, well, DP's number. He's my tutor and he took me in when I was pretty well as far down as I could go." Joel scribbled the number on a cruise line card he had in his pocket. "That's the ship I'll be on, *The Queen of the Pacific*."

"Looks great," Maggie said and she gave him a motherly hug as he left. "Thanks for coming to see us, Joel, and good luck. I hope it goes well for you."

Joel wondered whether or not he should call on Ben and Belinda when he went to visit his mother. The fact that he was the father of a little girl made him feel guilty, but he knew Ben would be a good daddy. He could decide what to do once he was in Bolton and, in the meantime, he had a lot to organise.

He called his mother early on the Saturday morning before he was due to leave on the following Thursday. "I thought I'd come over tomorrow," he suggested.

"What?" Nell croaked. Saturday mornings never found her at her best.

"I said I would like to come tomorrow. We can go to lunch at The Swan. It will be the last time for a few months," Joel reminded her.

"I asked you to give me a couple of days notice, Joel," she complained. Her head was aching, her mouth was dry and the mere mention of food made her want to retch.

"I thought I'd call in on Ben too," he informed her.

Nell felt instantly agitated. "Oh, I wouldn't do that. You haven't seen him for years and that awful mother of his might be there. I wouldn't like you to come into contact with her…"

"Mother!" Joel exclaimed. "What's up with you? Ben doesn't have anything to do with his mother. He never did, so I can't see how that will have changed."

"But it might have changed, you never know," Nell stated emphatically.

"Why would you be so concerned about it now? You always hated the woman. Anyway, I'm a big boy now and if she did happen to be there, which I very much doubt, I can handle it. If you're bothered about her being a prostitute, then don't be. I knew about all that when I was at school. It didn't worry me then and it doesn't worry me now."

"I just think you ought not to be around such women. It isn't healthy." She needed to convince Joel that he should not be where Connie Mason might be. The woman was capable of divulging information that Nell didn't want to become common knowledge.

"Well, I'll meet you at The Swan at one o'clock. Please call to book a table. They'll be busy at Sunday lunchtime," he instructed.

When she replaced the receiver, Nell had sobered up considerably. The very idea of Joel finding out about such nights as the one when Connie Mason had plied her wares in Nell's home was a very sobering thought. She had to stay off the wine and prepare to meet her son the next day.

Mrs. DP lent Joel her Mini Minor to drive to Bolton so he didn't have to worry about Sunday train services. When he arrived at The Swan, his mother was already there. Nell had made a special effort with her appearance before she met Joel for lunch.

"You're looking better, Mum, better than when I last saw you. I think Granny's funeral must have taken more out of you than you wanted to admit," he told her.

"Maybe," Nell conceded, allowing her son to presume that time was healing wounds. "It's surprising what a bit of time and Max Factor can do for a woman."

Small talk had never been easy between them, but today they each determined they would keep the conversation sociable. "How's work?" Joel asked. "And what happened to that Doctor Flynn?"

Nell shivered. "He left," she said as calmly as possible.

"I thought you liked him." Joel vaguely recalled the telephone conversation when his mother had sounded as high as a kite.

"I did," she said, trying desperately to keep in control of her emotions. "But these things happen. You know all about broken romances, don't you?"

Joel grinned. "Well, I guess so. Who's your boss now?"

Nell breathed in deeply. "I don't work there anymore. They changed the whole system and I hated it. I'll find something else. I have money in the bank and Granny's will still hasn't been read. I'll be all right until I find another job."

"That's good then," Joel agreed and Nell visibly gave a sigh of relief. At least she need not admit she had been fired.

"Did you think about going to see Ben?" she enquired, keeping her voice as light as she was able.

"Yes, I thought about it, but we had words when we last saw each other. Did I tell you he worked in Liverpool for a while? However, we didn't part on good terms. I think if I went to see him now, it would only open up old wounds, so I've decided not to bother. Maybe when I've done this trip, I'll think about it then."

Nell sighed again. Whatever had caused the rift between Joel and Ben didn't interest her. She was happy to know that Connie Mason would not have the opportunity to tell her secrets.

The visit to see Nell had gone more smoothly than he could have imagined and when they said their goodbyes, he felt he might now embark on his new career with a light heart.

Maybe she has changed after all, he thought as he drove back to West Derby. *And about time, too.*

When Thursday came, the Powell household was full of excitement. Joel had stacked his luggage in the hall the night before and they had a very early breakfast since he had to be at Queen's Dock by seven-thirty. DP and Joel loaded the cases into the car and returned to the kitchen where Mrs. DP was clearing away the breakfast things.

"You don't mind if I don't come to the docks?" she asked Joel for the umpteenth time.

"Of course not," Joel reassured her. "Saying goodbye isn't easy, even though I'm leaving for the best possible reason." He gave her a hug. "Thank you for putting up with me. I could never have survived without you and DP."

Mrs. DP sniffed loudly. "Oh, look what you've done now," she cried, wiping away her tears with her apron. "That's exactly why I don't want to be waving you off on the dockside. Off you go now before I flood the kitchen."

Joel held her closely and momentarily thought he hadn't done the same when he left his mother. "I'll write," he called as the car drew away.

With his luggage safely stored in his cabin and his fond farewells imparted to DP, Joel leaned on the rail looking down as his tutor cum guardian waved enthusiastically.

"Break a leg!" DP called in true theatrical fashion and Joel nodded animatedly. The ship's siren sounded loud and long and the big engines of *The Queen of the Pacific* shuddered into life. Shouts and cheers echoed from the quayside and almost in the slow motion of dreamlike action, Joel heard a voice from his past.

"G-o-o-d l-u-c-k, P-o-s-h-m-a-n!" Then more urgently, "Send us a postcard, you young scally."

Joel jumped up and down in delight. He'd have leapt over the rail if he could, but he shouted at the top of his voice, "Thanks, Wacker! Thanks!" and tears prevented him from saying more. He waved until Gerry, Penny, Maggie and Chrissie, together with his beloved DP, were tiny dots in the distance.

Nineteen

Nell drove home after her lunch with Joel her mind in confusion. She and her son had not talked like that for a long time and Sean had been included briefly in the conversation. Covering her innermost feelings had been difficult, but her efforts to conceal what was underneath her make-up had paid off. When she pulled on to her drive, she noticed that tears were trickling down her cheeks.

I'd better go to the shop, she thought and brushing away the tears, she reversed on to the road again. The ten-minute drive to Hanbury's gave her time to recover her composure. The recent legislation for shops to open on Sundays was a godsend.

"I wouldn't normally shop on a Sunday," she told the middle-aged woman on the till, "but I'm glad you're open." The woman smiled, but didn't engage in conversation. She noticed Nell's tearstained face and a number of bottles of wine in her trolley and she smiled deprecatingly at the clearly agitated woman.

With her larder replenished and her drinks cabinet filled, she wandered into the lounge and settled comfortably in her chair. She closed her eyes and drifted into an uneasy sleep. "Sean? Is that you?" She could see him in the distance beckoning, but no matter how she tried, she could not make her legs move.

"I love you, Nell," he called, "I love you."

"Sean? Is that you?" she cried again. "I can't reach you, I can't move."

"Can't or won't?" Sean yelled back.

"Joel's gone," she told him. "Joel's gone, Dad's gone, Mum's gone, Sean's gone, Tom's gone. I'm all alone, alone, alone..." Her words floated off into oblivion and she found herself climbing big, stone steps. Her legs were heavy and every step became a mountain to climb. She couldn't see the top of the hill. Her eyes misted over and she felt herself fall, making her wake suddenly and breathe very heavily. She jumped up quickly and ran to the window so as not to miss him. "Sean?" she called out, but she knew then that it had been just a dream, a frustrating, frightening and fleeting figment of her troubled mind.

Finding a half empty bottle in the kitchen, she poured herself a glass of her favourite Burgundy. "Here's to the lot of you," she announced raising her glass towards the ceiling. "Here's to the bloody lot of you." She gulped down the entire contents of the glass, emptied the remains of the bottle and found another one to keep her company for the rest of the evening.

~ * ~

The next months were long and hard. She didn't leave the house apart from walking to the off-licence shop to replenish her stock of drinks, always after dark. When she found that Burgundy no longer gave her the buzz she desired, she graduated to gin and when the sweet scented kick of the juniper failed to titillate her taste buds, whisky provided the power she needed. Food was spurned in favour of something that was more appetising than dry, tasteless fare that she couldn't be bothered to prepare. She drank alone. Nobody called and she called nobody. Mail piled up behind the door and she didn't care.

~ * ~

Joel was in Los Angeles. *The Queen of the Pacific* had sailed across the Atlantic to New York and then south to Florida before journeying to LA via the Panama Canal. She would be docked in LA for four days to allow passengers to go sightseeing and sample life on dry land for a short while. Joel's involvement in the entertainment industry was off to a wonderful start.

"You have done well, young Winston," the captain told him at the weekly conference. "The passengers are singing your praises..." He laughed heartily. "...singing your praises," he continued, enjoying his little joke, "and love your programme. You seem to have a good balance." He looked across the table at the Entertainments Officer. "Keep an eye on him, Leading Officer."

"I will, sir," LO Cuthbertson answered. "Are we still planning more shows on the next leg?"

"We are and make sure young Winston gets a stint in first class. I think they'll appreciate his style."

Joel grinned at the Leading Officer. Tim Cuthbertson wasn't much older than Joel, but he was an experienced sailor and a top class entertainer. He was a stand-up comedian, a brilliant baritone and an excellent ballroom dancer to boot.

The passengers love his dance classes,' Joel told DP in his monthly letter. *'He has the knack of teaching while he's performing. I have joined his class a couple of times and now I can cha-cha-cha with the best of them! I've never been short of a partner. You'd be surprised what the tropical white uniform does for a guy! You'd be very proud of me, DP, and I know I couldn't have done all this without you.*

We're in LA at the moment. What a brilliant place and the captain has instructed my Leading Officer to give me some gigs in first class when we set sail across the Pacific. It will be a long voyage and I'm looking forward to sailing into Sydney. Australia has been on my wish list for a long time...'

He had sent postcards from every port to his mother and to Maggie and Co. After six months away from home, Joel's first trip had been a huge success and he signed up for another as soon as he landed in Southampton. The crew hadn't been given time to explore Sydney, but Joel felt he would have other opportunities if and when he did a similar trip again. *The Queen of the Pacific* was going in for refit in Southampton and so it would be a few days before Joel would be assigned to another cruise liner. The company flew him up to Liverpool to start his short leave.

"Don't meet me at the airport," he told DP on the phone. "It'll be your dinner time and I can get a taxi from Speke."

"Okay, if that's what you prefer," DP agreed. *Perfect*, he thought. *It will give me time to sort everything before he gets here.*

As the taxi pulled up outside DP's house in West Derby, everything was quiet. The British late summer evening was cool, cold even, by comparison with the weather he had experienced during the past three months. The house was in darkness and Joel wondered if DP had confused the dates with some other appointment. He fumbled to find his front door key and struggled to locate the keyhole in the dark. After what appeared to be longer than necessary, he managed to open the door. *I'll sneak in and surprise them*, he thought mischievously and so put down his kitbag as quietly as possible. He couldn't see the light shining under the lounge door as he crept forward, so he presumed they were watching TV in the dark.

He found the handle on the door and gently pressed it down so as not to make any noise. *If they're watching television*, he thought, *they won't hear me and I can catch them unawares.* He pushed open the door and suddenly all hell broke loose as the light was switched on.

"Surprise! Surprise!" they all shouted. "Welcome home, Joel! Welcome home!" Before him was a sea of faces: DP, Mrs. DP, Janice, his drama tutor, Theodore Pendennis, Maria Morenzi herself and a number of students from Joel's tutor group. In addition to these people and as a wonderful gesture on DP's part, he had invited Maggie and Paddy, Gerry and Penny, Chrissie and her husband, Ronnie, all of whom were smiling ear to ear and rushing forward to greet him.

"This is much more than I could ever have imagined," he told the assembled group after he had had time to circulate. "Thank you all for coming and although I appreciate each and every one of you, I have to specially thank the Connolly family." His eyes filled with tears. "They have reasons not to..."

"Hey, Poshman," Gerry interjected, "none of yer soft stuff. That's all in the past. We're glad to be 'ere, so stop yer grizzlin'!" He grinned broadly, the old Gerry gloriously shining through. Joel nodded appreciatively and grinned back.

"I tried to contact your mum, Joel, but I couldn't get a reply," DP informed him when the others had left. "I didn't have time to go over to Bolton, seeing that you only gave me forty-eight hours notice."

"Don't worry about it, DP. I have written to her several times while I've been away and she hasn't even sent me one reply. I always gave her the advanced address like I did with you, but I didn't hear a thing," Joel explained, the weariness of the situation clear in his voice. "I give up with her and I was stupid enough to think we were getting somewhere before I left."

"Will you have time to go to see her before you leave again?' DP asked, concerned that Joel's resigned attitude suggested he'd washed his hands of her.

"I have to go to Cruise Line headquarters tomorrow to find out which ship I've been assigned to and then I'll only have twenty four hours before I sail," he explained. "It's a fast turnover, because the cruise lines are booked up to capacity at this time of year."

"You can try to call her tomorrow. Maybe you'll have more luck than I did," DP advised.

The following morning, Joel was up early and ready to go to HQ for nine o'clock. "Junior Entertainments Officer Joel Winston reporting for duty," he announced as he approached the desk.

"You're nice and early, Winston," a voice said from the back of the office.

"Hi, LO Cuthbertson. I didn't expect to see you here."

"Hello, Joel, and it's Tim when we're out of uniform. You didn't think you'd get rid of me that easily, did you?" Tim rejoined.

"I didn't think I'd be that lucky as to be assigned to the same crew as you twice," Joel told him. "Where are we off to this trip and on which ship?"

The officer behind the desk took over. "When you two have stopped socialising, I'll tell you what you need to know. You are assigned to *The Golden Phoenix* with Captain Alexander Jackson and you're sailing into Fremantle, Western Australia."

"Wow!" Joel enthused. "My dream trip. This may sound a bit far-fetched and corny, but I've often wondered what it would be like to sail into Fremantle since I learned about the convicts and the European settlers. I believe the harbour is something else."

The desk officer continued. "Well, I'll tell you, young Winston, it'll not be exactly like the pioneers, because you'll be doing the Med/Suez route, but it'll be quite an experience, I can guarantee that. You need to be on board at o-four-hundred hours on Wednesday. Early start for crew. You'll set sail at ten hundred hours."

Joel tried to call his mother without success. The phone was just ringing out and the short leave was not long enough for Joel to make the necessary visit. "Don't worry, Joel," DP reassured him. "I'll keep trying and if I don't make contact, I'll drive over to Bolton myself. One way or another, we'll find out what's going on."

"Thanks, DP, but I don't want you to put yourself out. She'll be fine. It's typical of her to be totally absorbed in herself, so just leave it for the time being. If she wanted me, she'd find a way of getting in touch. I'm absolutely sure about that." Joel appeared to be unconcerned, but he was curious. He decided to leave it until he returned from his next trip.

The voyage was indeed an experience of a lifetime. "I can't believe I'm getting paid for going on holiday," Joel told Tim Cuthbertson as they prepared for the first show of the trip.

"This is no holiday, young man. You are here to work," the officer stated adamantly, "and don't you forget it."

"I know that, sir, but I'm doing what I love and getting paid for it, not to mention all the wonderful places we visit. I don't think I would have had the chance to travel if I hadn't been given this job."

With two shows each night except Sundays when there was just one, Joel's programme was extensive and his experience was providing him with the tools to become the complete performer. It was towards the completion of the outbound voyage that a first class passenger asked the captain for permission to approach Joel with a proposition. Joel met the gentleman for coffee in the cafeteria on Sunday morning.

"How do you do, sir?" Joel greeted him.

"I'm good, young man, and very pleased to meet you. Congratulations on your performances. I have been very impressed," the passenger informed him. He was Australian and on his way home to Melbourne after a trip to London in search of new talent. "To be honest, I was beginning to think I had made a wasted trip until I saw you. All the young Poms are into rock 'n' roll these days and I need an all-round performer—like you, Joel Winston... good name, by the way."

Joel laughed at that, but he was confused and it showed. "Thank you very much, but ..."

"Jeez! I'm a real goose," the man said. "Sorry. I'm Shane Obertelli. I work for the TV network operating out of Melbourne, but we're setting up a station in Perth. We need a young, vibrant presenter for a talent show and you fit the bill perfectly, young man. What d'yer say?"

"I say what an offer!" Joel enthused. "How could I refuse that?"

Obertelli was delighted. "It'll take a while to organise. You'll need an obligatory audition, but I guess in six months we'll be ready to go. We'll set the ball rolling as soon I'm back in Melbourne."

Joel spoke to his Leading Officer and found that he could be released from his contract at the end of the trip. "This crew is going to be flown home after we dock in Fremantle," Tim Cuthbertson informed him. "We have a few days leave before that happens, so you will have time to explore Perth. If you are going to be based there, you'll need to get a feel for the place. Living in Australia will be a big culture shock after England, I'm sure."

Taking Tim's advice, Joel hired a car and drove to Perth as soon as the formalities of release from duties were completed. First he drove around Fremantle Port and stopped for lunch on Cappuccino Way, a main thoroughfare where there were lots of sidewalk cafes and people eating while the rest of the world went about its business. He sat for ages just taking in the atmosphere of his surroundings. The history he read about was fascinating and the colonial feel to the place inspiring.

"It is one of the oldest European settlements in Australia and is named after the British naval officer Sir Charles Fremantle," a friendly local told him over coffee. "The buildings in the town absolutely exude colonial splendour and the port retains its historical charm in spite of modern innovations. I'm a ten-pound Pom and I don't regret coming out here one little bit."

Joel was captivated. He had four days that he could spend finding his way around and seeing what Perth had to offer. The weather was absolutely glorious. To think that it was November and he was wearing shorts and a T-shirt was incredible. His immediate reaction was that the city was beautiful, a real mixture of old and new. There was an air of vibrant development everywhere, an odd sense of history in the making. As he wandered around, his thoughts were filled with excited anticipation. *Thinking of it as old seems so out of place*, he mused, *because most of its history only began in the nineteenth century, so compared with England, Australia is actually very young. I can't wait to live here.*

His discovery of King's Park, an enormous, absolutely beautiful area of scenic parkland in the middle of the metropolis, overlooking the Swan River and the city of Perth, filled him with awe. There were driveways, walkways, cycle paths, magnificent views over the city and what he noticed more than anything, it was so clean and litter free. The whole area had a magical aura about it and in an instant, he knew that Western Australia would be his home. "I'll be back," he said out loud as he surveyed the city from a look out point in King's Park. He felt like he belonged already.

He arrived at the airport at the arranged time. Tim Cuthbertson rushed up to him, with a very worried look on his face. "Thank goodness you're here," he said. "We didn't know how to contact you."

"Of course, I'm here. I knew the time of the flight so why wouldn't I be?" Joel informed him. "What's the problem?"

"We had a wire from somebody called Dafydd Powell."

Joel paled. DP wouldn't send a wire unless it was an emergency. "What did it say?" he asked, not certain if it were something he wanted to hear.

Tim handed him a printout of the telegram. Joel silently took in its contents.

*MOTHER IN A STATE—STOP-CALL AS SOON
AS POSSIBLE—STOP—DAFYDD POWELL—STOP*

Twenty

Joel went straight to Bolton from the airport. His telephone conversation with DP had left him under no illusions that his mother was indeed in a state. DP had gone to the house as promised, but was unable to gain access. "Neighbours said they had seen your mum intermittently going to the corner shop, but she didn't appear to go out other than that. I knocked on the door for ages, but there was no answer. The curtains of all downstairs windows were closed so I had to assume she had gone away for a few days." So he returned to Liverpool still with the problem of Nell Winston unsolved. Three weeks later, DP unexpectedly received a telephone call.

"Have you been trying to call me?" she asked, "What do you want?" Her speech was slurred and her words almost indecipherable.

"Mrs. Winston, it's Dafydd Powell. Joel's tutor. Joel is overseas at the moment, but he needs to know that you are all right," DP explained.

"So?" she snapped. "He doesn't need me and yes, I'm all right..." And suddenly the tears flowed until she was a blubbering, sobbing mess.

"Mrs. Winston," DP implored, "would you like me to come over to help? I can be there in an hour."

"No! Stay away!" Nell screamed. "'I don't need you. I don't need anybody. Just get lost and leave me alone."

DP was in despair, for Joel and for the sad lady on the other end of the phone.

"Joel will be home in a couple of weeks," he gently told the distraught woman, but she merely grunted and replaced the receiver noisily.

~ * ~

Joel found his old key and opened the door. He had to push roughly against it to dislodge the pile of mail that had accumulated, seemingly for months. He inched his way in, grimacing with disgust and covering his nose to protect himself from the revolting stench that met him as he approached the lounge door.

"Get up, Mother! What a disgusting mess! How long is it since you took a shower?" Joel regarded her with nothing less than sickening repulsion. He found it difficult to accept that the unkempt, unwashed bundle of rags that was lying on the floor like a mangy dog was his mother.

Nell was curled up in the foetal position on the hearth rug and she didn't move at the sound of Joel's voice. She sobbed uncontrollably and repeated over and over again, "I'm sorry, I'm so sorry, I'm so, so sorry." Covering her swollen, tear-stained face with hands that had long been deprived of a manicure, she dared to raise her head to make sure it was indeed her son who had come home.

Joel's initial reaction subsided and he felt an enormous sense of compassion for the woman who had been nothing but a caring mother as he was growing up. That she had misguidedly manipulated his every move, he understood now. She merely wanted what she felt was best for him.

"Come on, Mum," he coaxed and he held out a supporting hand.

Tentatively, Nell reached out as Joel stooped to enclose her in his arms. She clung to him and he rocked her gently until she ceased crying and her breathing was regular again. They remained there for a while, each with personal thoughts that didn't need to be expressed.

"Go upstairs and have a shower, Mum," Joel advised her gently. "It will wash away the blues and you'll feel better, I promise."

"You won't go away again while I'm up there?" she questioned, uncertainty etched into her troubled face.

"I won't go away. We have a lot to talk about and we can't do it in five minutes. I'll stay for a few days until we decide what we are going to do," Joel reassured her. "Go on now and I'll clear up down here."

When he heard the water running upstairs, Joel set about clearing up the mess. Empty bottles were everywhere: on the floor, behind the furniture, in coat pockets, inside shoes and boots; they were in places where one would never expect to find them, even in the oven. Nell had taken great pains not to make her problem obvious to others. Had she thrown the empties in the dustbin, her clandestine affair with Burgundy would become public, so she just stashed them anywhere in the house where they weren't on show.

"Oh, Mum," Joel groaned, "did I drive you to all this?" He knew he had contributed to her spiralling out of control, but there had to be something else. When Nell reappeared, she looked refreshed, but there was still a haunted look in her eyes.

Joel made coffee. "It has to be black, I'm afraid. No milk in the fridge." They sat in the lounge, clean and tidy now, ready to sort out their problems. Nell was trembling, not through fear, but through sheer exhaustion.

"I haven't been coping very well at all," she admitted. "The only time I could summon up a clear view on the world was when I'd had a drink, but it didn't last and when I woke up each day, the demons were there again egging me on to have another drink."

"I had no idea," Joel told her. "How could I not have seen what was happening to you?"

"I drove you away, Joel, I know what I did. I can't change that now, but I hope you can forgive me," Nell said honestly. "Sean explained to me why I did it. He was so good for me."

"What happened with him, Mum? I remember thinking that you were a different person when you told me about him." He needed to know how his mother had gone from being such a vibrant woman to becoming a raving, alcoholic wreck in just couple of years.

Nell took a deep breath before she explained about her distress after Joel left, her realisation that she had made drastic mistakes with him and her decision to give him his space. Her demeanour changed when she described her time with Sean.

"He made me feel good about myself again and most of all he made me feel loved. I hadn't felt like that since your dad died." Her eyes misted over.

"So why did he leave?" Joel asked.

"I sent him away. It was my own fault, but I really want to forget him. It hurts too much to remember. I need to face my life without him. Soon after he left," she continued, "your grandpa passed away and that was a massive shock. Dad had always been there for me, hovering in the background with pearls of wisdom, and then suddenly he'd gone."

"And then Granny too—it was a lot for you to cope with. I'm sorry, Mum. I should have been there for you. I've made my mistakes, too."

"You have nothing to be sorry for. None of this would have happened if I hadn't been so self-centred," Nell told him. "God, my head aches. Will you find me a couple of aspirins, please?"

Joel gave her the tablets with a glass of water and realised that the last time she had felt sick, he had given her brandy. *Oh God*, he thought guiltily, *no wonder she recovered quickly.*

She looked at the glass and gave a wry smile. "This is the only thing I'll have in a glass from now on. It won't be easy, but I'll do it, especially if I know you'll be around."

"Let's have something to eat and then we'll make our plans together. I'll have to go to the corner shop for some food, though." Joel eyed his mother sadly. "There's nothing in the larder. It looks a lot like Mother Hubbard's cupboard," he joked.

"Sorry, Joel, but food has not been my priority recently. I'm not sure I could eat anything. I seriously need a drink right now. I can't imagine how I'm going to survive without it." Nell looked at her son with desperation in her eyes.

"You'll do it, Mum, and I'll make sure you do, but there are big decisions to be made. We'll talk later when you feel a bit better."

He went to the shop and bought newly baked bread, fresh milk and cooked meats. He also bought tinned chicken soup. Soup would not be difficult to digest and then he might persuade Nell to eat a sandwich. Slowly and painstakingly, she sipped the soup and Joel felt relieved that at least she had made the effort. The next few days would not be easy, but he determined that he would not broach the subject of Western Australia until he felt his mother could cope with it.

One week into his stay in Bolton, Joel entered the kitchen one morning to find Nell standing by the sink with a bottle of whisky in one hand and a glass in the other. He stood silently in the doorway wondering which way she would go. To speak now would be to undo what they had worked towards for the past seven days. All decisions regarding her recovery had to be her own. Placing the glass on the draining board to release her right hand, she unscrewed the top of the bottle. Slowly she raised the bottle towards her mouth. Joel stood absolutely motionless behind her. Breathing in loudly and deeply, Nell savoured the smell emanating from the neck of the bottle. Suddenly, she tipped the bottle and held it upside down until every drop drained into the sink and down the plughole. It was a momentous occasion and, as tears ran down her face, she turned to see Joel framed in the doorway, smiling proudly at her.

"I did it," she sobbed. "I did it."

Later as they sat at the kitchen table eating the first meal Nell had prepared since Joel's arrival, they were more relaxed than they'd been for years. "I need to phone DP," Joel said. "He deserves to know what's happening and he may have received some important mail for me."

Nell paled. "Do you have to go back to sea?" she asked nervously.

"No," Joel told her, "but I do have a job offer that I am going to take up and it will mean both of us relocating if you're up for it."

"Relocating?"

"Well, this might be a lot to take in, but it has to be said. I have been offered a job in Western Australia," Joel announced excitedly. "It's in television and it won't actually start until they've established a new station in Perth, but I'll need to rehearse and they'll pay me a retainer whilst all that is happening."

Nell didn't know what to say. It was a déjà vu situation and she felt her heart pounding in her chest.

Joel continued enthusiastically. "I was in Perth on the last trip and it's a magical place. You'll love it."

Nell took hold of Joel's hand. "Look," she said quietly, "I can't deny I'm shocked. It's the Sean situation all over again..."

"Mum, listen to me," Joel pleaded. "It isn't like that at all. How can it be? We'll be together. You can leave him behind. Anyway, you'll be getting a lot farther away from him and that will help you to forget. It's a brand new start for us both."

She had avoided telling Joel the whole story of Sean, but now she had to inform him that Sean had indeed emigrated to, of all places, Australia.

Joel was surprised, but not shocked. He smiled at his worried mother and squeezed her hand reassuringly. "Western Australia is thousands of miles away from Sydney. You don't realise how vast the country is until you've been. I met some Western Australians born and bred who have never been to Sydney simply because it's expensive to fly and it's too far to drive. Sean won't ever know you are there, so you've no need to worry."

"You make it sound very inviting. Have I got time to think about it?" she asked.

"If you need it, but I have to take this job, Mum. It's a dream situation and they don't come up very often," Joel explained. "I know it's a big step, but we can take it together."

Nell lay awake for hours mulling over Joel's proposition. Her mind was not tormented this time and that gave her hope. By the time she drifted off to sleep, she had made her decision.

"That's brilliant, Mum," Joel said. "You won't regret it. You'll love Perth and we'll make a good life for ourselves. Who knows, there might be an Aussie millionaire just waiting for a woman like you!"

"I don't think so, darling. For the time being, just let's concentrate on making it work for you and me."

Twenty-one

The house in Bolton was put up for sale as soon as Nell told Joel she agreed to a new start even though it all seemed way beyond her wildest dreams. Between them, mother and son had spruced up the house and garden ready for prospective buyers and there was a steady stream of viewings each day for a week.

"The agent called. We have another viewing tomorrow morning," Nell told Joel. "Do you think you'll be able to be here? I have a hair appointment at ten o'clock and the viewing is arranged for ten-fifteen."

"No problem," Joel confirmed. "I have no need to go to see DP this weekend. He has managed to get references from all my tutors for me and he and Mrs. DP have packed up my belongings ready for me to collect sometime next week."

At ten-fifteen on the dot, the doorbell rang. Joel opened the door to the visitor.

"Hello, Joel. I heard you were back in town."

Joel was dumbfounded. "Ben!" he managed to say, but then he was stuck for words.

"Well, aren't you going to ask me in? I'm interested in buying your house," Ben said confidently. "I must say you look a darn sight better than you did the last time I saw you."

Joel was embarrassed. "I don't know what to say, Ben. Sorry doesn't seem good enough. I heard you had married Belinda… congratulations. I hope you are happy."

Ben was remarkably calm. "Look, Joel, I can't forget what a complete prick you were, but a lot of good came out of it for me. I have a beautiful wife who loves me. It took a while, but I'm confident that she's happy with me now. It's ironic really since I usually had your cast-off girlfriends at school." He grinned.

"I'm pleased for you, Ben, truly," Joel told him, "but Bel was never my girlfriend."

"We have a gorgeous little girl, Kimberley, and I have to tell you that it's my name on the birth certificate. I hope you can understand that. I love her and she's mine. That's all you need to know." Ben's manner was forthright.

"I understand, Ben. I have no claim to your happiness." He didn't want to say *to your child*. The tension between them relaxed. "I feel no connection at all. I never did and I can see you are a wonderful husband and father, something I can't really envisage for me, not yet anyway. I don't want to sound condescending, but thanks."

"Well, can we shake on it for old time's sake?" Ben asked.

Joel willingly shook his hand. "Thanks, Ben. Thank you very much."

"How come you're selling this house? I always liked it even though I wasn't always made welcome."

Joel squirmed, but explained what was happening without too much detail about how his mother had turned over a new leaf. "It's been a long, hard road, but we're getting there," he said. "The new start in Australia is what we both need. I'm very excited about it. The job is what I could only dream about before. Now it's really happening, it's hard to get my head around it."

"I'm very happy for you and I know Bel will be pleased for you, too. She's expecting again in a couple of months. That's why we need a new house."

"Dare I ask about your mother?" Joel inquired.

"She died from liver failure last year, but I'd given up on her years ago. I hate to say it, but I couldn't mourn for her after how she treated us when we were growing up. Michael is moving into my flat permanently as soon as Bel and I find what we want. I'm really proud of him. He's training to be a social worker. Ironic, eh? He's been crashing with a mate, but I guess he'll be able to move in permanently very soon. I think I've found what we need."

Nell was delighted with the news that the house had sold quickly. It held good and bad memories for her, but latterly, she felt she needed the fresh start Joel had offered. She had no idea what the future had in store, but she began to look forward with an enthusiasm that forced to her leave the past behind.

"You'll never guess who's buying our house," Joel announced as she returned from the hairdresser's.

"Then tell me if I'll never guess," she begged.

Joel looked thrilled. "Ben Mason!"

Nell was shocked. "Oh, my goodness," she cried.

"Well, that's not the response I expected. I thought you'd be pleased that it's somebody we know," Joel said.

"I am, I think," she replied, "but my conscience is pricking me. I wasn't very nice to him all those years ago."

"He's not the kind to bear a grudge and I can say that with the utmost confidence, I assure you. He's married now with a little girl and another baby on the way. He loves the house and I know he'll be happy here."

"So his mother has a granddaughter," Nell commented, her mind in turmoil at the thought of her past coming back to haunt her almost as soon as she'd left it behind. *I need a drink*, she thought and furtively looked around to see if there was a bottle Joel had missed.

"Technically speaking, yes," Joel said, "but she never knew. Apparently, she died last year. To be honest, Ben didn't seem particularly concerned. He was never in contact with her and I understand he just wants to get on with his own life."

"It's still sad, though, that she died so young. She must only have been in her forties," Nell declared. She couldn't help thinking, *There, but for the grace of God...* but she felt an enormous sense of relief that her secret was safe, confined to the grave and that's where it should stay. The mere thought of Joel regarding her with such contempt after her death filled her with horror.

"First of all, we'll have to organise your passport. If we take your documents to the Passport Office in Liverpool, we'll get it quicker than waiting for the mail. We'll apply for our visas at the same time. Let's have a coffee and then start packing," Joel suggested. "We have a lifetime of possessions to sort out."

Twenty-two

Joel and Nell arrived at Ringway airport in the early hours of a very wet, typically British winter day at the end of January. On behalf of the television company, Shane Obertelli had sent their tickets and given Joel a letter of introduction to the College of Performing Arts in Perth.

"Carry your bags, sir?" a voice asked.

Surprised that porters were available at that time in the morning, Joel turned to see who was offering the service and to tell him that he had a trolley so the luggage wasn't causing a problem.

"DP! What are you doing here? And Mrs. DP!"

The Powells had driven from West Derby the day before and stayed at the airport hotel so they might give the travellers a good send-off. "We thought we'd surprise you. Leaving the country and not having anybody to see you off would have been sad for you," DP told them. "Hello, Mrs. Winston. I'm Dafydd Powell and this is my wife, Megan. You and I have spoken on the phone, but I'm pleased to meet you in person."

Nell felt embarrassed. She forced herself to look DP in the eye. "Thank you for all you have done for Joel," she said. "We owe you both a debt of gratitude."

"No problem, Mrs. Winston. There's method in our madness in coming to see you off." He winked at Joel. "Hopefully when you are settled in Australia, we might come to visit you. We have never travelled so far away, but knowing somebody who lives there puts a whole new complexion on it."

Joel offered his hand to his tutor and mentor of the past few years. "That would be brilliant, DP. We'll keep in touch all the time. Thanks for coming. Thanks for..." He struggled to find the right words. "Well... for everything."

The intercom announced that passengers on their flight were ready to go to passport control. Joel turned and waved to the Powells until he could no longer see them. Nell hung on to her son's hand. She was very nervous. Passing the duty free shop was an ordeal. She hadn't realised that alcoholic drinks were so readily available. Joel became aware of her grip tightening on his hand and hurried past the shop to find a seat where temptation would not become too much of a problem.

"Shall we have a coffee while we wait?" he asked. "It's still only half past six and we don't board until eight. I think they'll serve breakfast as soon as we take off."

The British Airways flight to London was uneventful and with a speedy transfer at London Heathrow to a Qantas flight, they were settled into their seats and ready to face the long trip to Singapore. The airline was excellent and they did serve breakfast and then lunch in what seemed a very short space of time. Nell was tense. When lunch was being served, she looked at Joel, her eyes pleading. "Do you think I might have a glass of wine with my meal?" she asked as the hostesses began to offer drinks.

Joel paled at the thought. "Mum, I can't tell you what you can, or can't do, but I think you'd be mad to undo all the hard work you've put in during the past few months."

Nell looked like a rabbit caught in the headlights of an on-coming car as the hostess approached her.

"What would you like to drink, madam?"

Wide-eyed, she looked at Joel and then at the hostess, her whole body crying out in distress. "I'd like a glass of red wine ..."

Joel gasped.

"...but I'll just have a glass of orange juice, please." She smiled at the hostess. "I mustn't drink," she explained. "It isn't good for me."

"Well done, Mum!" Joel exclaimed quietly as the hostess moved on to the next row of passengers. "I'm proud of you."

"Thank you," Nell answered, smiling, and she turned to Joel. "I genuinely believe I shall conquer the demons with you by my side, darling."

Joel smiled and took her hand. The gentle squeeze confirmed that he'd be there for her.

When they arrived in Singapore, it was three o'clock in the morning the following day local time. The loss of eight hours made them feel very strange, and tiredness hadn't yet begun to set in. The experience of worldwide travel showed up their inexperience, especially Nell.

"It's only seven o'clock at night for us and last night if you can understand that concept," Joel remarked. "We'll be in Perth at about eleven o'clock local time so I think we might be a bit jaded by then. Our bodies will be telling us it's three in the morning."

"Will we be able to go to bed when we get there?" Nell asked. Travelling such a long distance was very new to her.

"We will," Joel explained, "but it might be better to try to keep going as long as we can so that we're not sleeping during the day and being awake all night. Our bodies will adjust in a couple of days."

The flight from Singapore to Perth was, to both Nell and Joel, out of this world. Although Joel had been to Western Australia previously, he had not experienced seeing it from the air. His flight home then had taken off at night and it was impossible to see what was below them.

"Look at that," Nell said. "It all looks barren and lifeless. Are you sure we are going to the right place?"

The terrain did indeed look barren, dry and lifeless, but there were thin wavy lines that were actually roads, or tracks at least, and so the distinct lack of buildings was not at all off-putting for Joel. "That's the outback, Mum. We'll get to know about that once we live here," he told the diffident Nell.

"Why do I suddenly feel in fear and trepidation?" she asked.

Joel took her hand. "Don't worry, Mum. It'll be fine. Trust me. And look..." He pointed to the left. "Wow! Fantastic!"

"What?" Nell asked eagerly.

"That's Ayers Rock. You must have heard of that," he declared. "Some day, we'll go there, I promise."

"It is quite something, isn't it?" Nell conceded. "You know, there's something magical about it even from up here." She settled back in her seat and she visibly relaxed as she felt a warm feeling of anticipation seeping through her veins.

The next few weeks were hectic. Rooms had been booked in a hotel until they managed to find a place of their own. They looked around the beautiful city of Perth and Nell was enthralled.

"I see what you mean now about this being a wonderful place," she told Joel, "and I understand now why you told me to give away most of my winter clothes. Here we are in February and it's summer."

Joel could hardly believe what had happened in just over a year since he was last in Perth. "I know," he agreed. "I felt like that, too, when I came here last time. Just think, Mum. This is our home now. Can you believe it?"

The audition with the television company took place at the College of Performing Arts a week after they had landed. Joel thought back to the last audition in Liverpool and smiled. He'd come a long way since then, literally and metaphorically. This time, nobody told him he'd got a posh name and he didn't have to memorise a speech from *Billy Liar*. As Obertelli had advised him, it was an obligatory audition and they had given him a programme to prepare before he arrived. He sang, he danced, he played guitar, he acted out a comedy sketch and when he had finished, his producer and director of programmes applauded with gusto.

"Well done, young man! Well done!" they said. "In the next few weeks, we'll do some rehearsals on set and some camera work and then we'll be ready to go."

Whilst Joel was rehearsing, Nell explored the city, trawled through real estate offices and found several houses she would like to view when Joel had the time. Weekends they spent together, sometimes just the two of them, sometimes with friends Joel brought from the new studio to meet Nell. There were occasions when Nell felt obliged to remain in the background, allowing the younger people to do what they wanted to do. When they were living in the hotel, it wasn't easy for her.

She sat in the bar reading her book. "Would you like a drink?" a gentleman asked.

Nell looked up. He was middle aged, bronzed, dressed in shorts and a very colourful shirt. *Why not?* she thought. She could do with some company. *One drink can do no harm.* She smiled at the gentleman. "Red wine, please," she said, "and thank you." The words came easily and without guilt.

"My pleasure," he told her as he called over the waiter. "You're English?"

"Yes. My accent sticks out like a sore thumb, doesn't it?"

"Well, it's different, but there's a lot of Poms in WA so you're not alone. I'm Ted, and you are?"

"Nell, Nell Winston. I'm pleased to meet you," she told him. "I much prefer company than being alone all evening."

The conversation was light and easy. Nell sipped her wine and savoured every mouthful. It was good, smooth and rich. She hadn't forgotten how much she enjoyed a glass of good wine. She and Ted talked for a while and she had another glass.

"Will you allow me to buy you a drink?" she asked him. "It's only fair when you have bought one for me."

"Thanks, darl, I'll have a beer with you. Very kind of you and very English if I may say so," he said grinning.

By ten o'clock, her head was spinning. She looked around the bar and through glazed eyes she saw Joel return from his evening with his co-presenter, Alice.

"Mother!" he called in dismay.

"Joel!" she called back. "How lovely to see you. Ted, this is my son, Joel."

Joel was incensed. "What the hell do you think you're doing—"

"Hold on, mate," Ted intervened.

"No, you hold on and I'm not your mate, mate," he said bitterly. "My mother has just undone months of rehabilitation with your help and it might now take a long time to put it right again."

"Oh Joel," Nell simpered. "Don't be such a stick in the mud. I'm just being sociable. There's nothing wrong with that."

"Sorry, mate. I had no idea. She just looked lonely and I kept her company, that's all," Ted told him.

"Thanks," Joel said, "but I need to get her to her room. Sorry, Alice. Can we call it a night? If you'll excuse us ..."

Alice smiled sympathetically. "No probs, Joel. See you later."

Nell rocked unsteadily as she stood up and grabbed hold of Ted's arm for support.

"Sorry, lady. I have to go. Thanks for the beer. See you around."

Not if we see you first, Joel thought ungraciously. "Come on, Mother," he instructed. "Let's see what we can do with you." He took her arm to lead her away.

Nell giggled all the way up to her room. Joel kept quiet, not trusting himself to speak with decorum should he start to blast his mother with what he was feeling inside. He removed her sandals, lifted her onto the bed and covered her with the fine linen sheet. He intended to sit with her until morning. He'd sleep in the chair. He was so angry. The sooner they were settled in their own house, the better.

Nell woke with the mother of all headaches. "Oh, my lord," she complained, "What did I do?"

"You may well ask," Joel grumbled. "I can't believe you sat in the bar all night and drank with a stranger."

"Oh, Joel. Don't be angry. I know I made a mistake. I slipped up. I succumbed to temptation and I'm suffering the consequences," she whimpered.

"Don't expect any sympathy from me," he chided. He was in no mood for pleasantries.

"I won't, but I'm sorry. I won't do it again," Nell said. "I've learned my lesson and promise to keep myself focussed on my goals. I know it'll be easier said than done, but I am determined to try."

By lunchtime that day, Nell had recovered enough to show Joel the properties she'd picked out. All three were in South Perth and one had a perfect view of the river. Joel was impressed and when they had viewed each one, they agreed that the only place they wanted to live was in the house overlooking the Swan. Within two weeks, all monies had been transferred, their furniture and personal effects had arrived by container ship from England and they were moving into what could only be described as their dream home.

The house was unusually built of sandstone and stood out from the other wooden properties in the neighbourhood. It was two storeys and stood on a large block at the end of a road running parallel to the river. An impressive balcony ran round three sides and large French windows opened onto an outside entertaining area with a barbecue and outdoor furniture all included in the sale. It was quite like nothing Nell had ever seen and she had fallen in love with it as soon as she saw it. Joel, too, was impressed and, remarkably, the furniture from the Bolton house didn't look out of place. It was comforting to be surrounded by familiar things. Nell was excited. "It's so good to be among familiar things, Joel. It's just what I need."

"Be sure to watch me tonight," Joel reminded her as he left for work.

"As if I'd be doing anything else," she told him. "My son a TV star! Break a leg, darl," she said in true Aussie fashion.

The show was going out live. It was called *Have You Got What It Takes?*, and together with Alice Churchill, chosen because of the significance of her name as well as her talent, Joel presented the first of a series of ten weekly shows. It soon became known as the "Winston Churchill Show" within the inner sanctum of the studio and the success of the first series led to another to follow and several spinoff variety shows with up and coming television personalities.

Nell became friendly with her neighbours and so was never alone when watching the show. She often had a barbecue and the men would cook while the women put the world to rights. Donnie from next door usually took on the cooking duties for Nell.

"It's sacrilege to let a woman near a barbie," he told her. "I'll make a deal. I'll do the cooking, if you'll clean up afterwards." He grinned mischievously. "Oh, and I need a few stubbies as well."

"Deal," Nell agreed, "but I have to tell you, no drinks for me. Drinking and I are sworn enemies." From then on, there was a tacit understanding that Nell did not touch a drop and the neighbours all kindly watched out for her.

Jean, Donnie's wife, became Nell's best friend. They went shopping together, they regularly had coffee at the café on the river esplanade and Nell confided that she had never been sociable like that before.

"Didn't you have a friend in England you could go out with?" Jean asked her. "I don't think the Australian way of life would be the same without having a mate to meet up with on a regular basis."

"I had friends, if I might be so bold as to call them friends," Nell divulged, "but I had so many hang-ups about Joel and being a widow that I never felt the need to socialise. That's what caused me to become a wreck." Jean had listened to Nell's abridged version of her story and sympathised with her.

"Didn't you ever want to meet somebody else after your husband died?" she asked.

"I'd be lying if I said no, but it's out of the question now. I'm happy as I am and coming here has shown me a different way of life that I have adjusted to and love, thanks to you, Jean," Nell said. "I'm thinking of finding a job."

"Really?" Jean said, surprised that Nell would want to go out to work again. "What does Joel say?"

"Joel doesn't know yet, but I don't think he'll mind. He's at the studio all day and very often late into the evening, so he'll be glad I'm finding something to occupy myself." Nell was feeling very positive.

"What sort of job will you look for?" Jean asked. She, herself, worked at home for her husband. He was a builder and she did the books as well as planning schedules and ordering supplies. "I'm a general factotum really that some would call a dogsbody," she joked.

"I did social sciences at uni, but then I became a personal secretary when I got married. When Tom died and Joel was in school, I was a doctor's receptionist. I enjoyed it then, but ..." She paused as the lump in her throat was threatening to choke her.

"Nell? What's wrong?" Jean asked, worried that her friend was becoming quite distressed.

Nell breathed in deeply. "I'm fine. I'd rather not go down that road at the moment. But as far as a job's concerned, I think I might look at real estate. There are courses I can take."

"Good on yer, Nell!" Jean declared. "Let me know if I can do anything to help."

Joel was delighted that his mother had taken the initiative to find a job. "That's great, Mum, and it will get you out and about meeting new people. You'll soon be more popular than I am!" He was joking, of course, but his job depended on popularity and since the second series of *Have You Got What It Takes?* he was finding that privacy was proving elusive.

Nell found a TAFE course very near to where she lived and immersed herself in studying real estate with a view to becoming an agent. She found that Bonnington and Rimmer Real Estate Agents were prepared to give her hands-on experience part-time while she continued her studies at evening classes. After three terms of cramming, she passed her exams and gained the necessary qualification to be employed full time. She loved the job. It was a new challenge and she revelled in the freedom it allowed her out of the office. She delighted in showing prospective buyers round properties and loved the social gatherings her employers organised when launching brand new builds. She was always careful not to drink champagne and she generally drove herself home from the meetings.

"These houses will go like hot cakes," Bruce Bonnington told her as they stood watching

Graham Rimmer delivering his well-rehearsed spiel to the assembled company.

"Well, they are something special, aren't they?" Nell commented as she took her second glass of orange juice from the tray offered by specially employed waitresses. "I might even be tempted to buy one myself."

"In your dreams, Nell." Her boss laughed. "If you can afford one of these, I must be paying you too much."

"You could always offer me a substantial discount," she joked and she walked over to her desk where she expected to be working full out all evening.

Talking was thirsty work. The waitresses had been primed to make sure that customers and employees were provided with tea, coffee, orange juice or champagne whenever they requested it and Nell kept a steady supply of orange juice as she worked. By the end of the evening, she had secured three definite sales and another two prospective buyers. She felt good and was very pleased with herself.

"See you in the office tomorrow," she called to her employers as she finished her last glass of orange juice and collected her briefcase from her desk.

"Nine o'clock on the dot," Bruce called back, knowing full well that Nell didn't start until ten.

"What did you say to me earlier, Bruce? 'In your dreams!' I think," she yelled as the door swung shut behind her.

She was smiling as she reached her car. The cool night air felt good on her flushed cheeks and she strangely felt as though she were floating. *Must be all the excitement*, she thought. She threw her briefcase and her handbag onto the passenger seat and started the engine. As she manoeuvred out of the parking lot, she blinked deliberately to clear her vision.

"Stupid, Nell," she chastised herself. "Put your lights on, idiot," and she more easily found her way to the exit once her headlights were switched on.

The road was very quiet. She was very aware of her driving for some reason and found herself concentrating on every move. The short drive home would only take ten minutes and Joel would be home, too. He'd said he would spend time with her, a rare occurrence these days with them both having busy schedules. Everything happened in slow motion, and yet there was no time to move out of the way. The bright lights were coming straight for her...

Twenty-three

Joel arrived home about eight o'clock. He'd had a hectic day and he was ready to put up his feet and relax with his mum. He knew she'd be home within half an hour so he took a quick shower and put on his robe and slippers before he started to prepare supper. When the telephone rang, he cursed. "Not now, whoever you are. This is my time." But perhaps his mum had been delayed. "Hello. This is Joel Winston," he said.

"Mr. Winston, this is South Perth Police."

"Oh no, what's happened now?" Joel asked resignedly, his first thoughts being that his mother had got drunk again and was making a nuisance of herself.

"Your mother—"

"Oh no, not again...."

"What do you mean, sir? Not again? Has she been in an accident before?"

"An accident? Oh, my God! Is she all right? Where is she? What happened?" Joel was beside himself and was instantly ashamed that he had thought his mother had been drinking. He should have been more aware that she had been working and drink would not be available. Even if it were, he had begun to trust her in those situations.

"Calm down, Joel." A kindly female voice took over. "There has been an accident. Your mother was involved in a collision with another vehicle and she has been taken to Royal Perth. Are you able to get there?"

"Of course. I'll go right away. Thank you." He quickly threw on a pair of shorts and a thin sweater before running out to his parked car on the driveway of their home. He had never been so aware of his driving ability as he was then. His mother had been involved in a road accident. He had to drive carefully.

He arrived at the hospital and rushed to find the ED. "I'm Joel Winston," he told the first nurse he found, "You have my mother here. How is she?"

The student nurse smiled. "I know who you are." She beamed. "How are you? I'm so pleased to meet you."

"Please," Joel implored. "I'm just me and I need to see my mother..."

"I'll speak with Mr. Winston, nurse." The doctor, identified by his nametag as Doctor Bertram intervened.

"Thank you, sir," Joel said as he was ushered into the doctor's office. "You're English?"

The doctor nodded. "Can't hide the accent, can I? Not that I'd want to. Are you okay?" he asked, observing that the young man before him was becoming increasingly distraught.

"Please," Joel appealed earnestly, "this is not about me. How is my mother? I must see her."

"She is in x-ray at the moment. We can't assess the extent of her injuries until we see the results."

"She's alive then? Oh, thank god." Joel breathed a sigh of relief. "Is she conscious? Has she said what happened? I saw a police car outside. Do they know what happened?"

Doctor Bertram looked seriously at Joel. "She hasn't regained consciousness since the accident. The Fire Department had to cut her free, but the ambulance officers had detected a pulse throughout the procedure. She has lacerations to her face and arms and possibly a number of broken ribs. Her right leg is definitely broken in several places. Like I said, we'll know for sure once we see the x-rays."

"Doctor..." the senior nurse called from the doorway.

"Excuse me, Joel ...you don't mind if I call you Joel?"

"That's my name," Joel said with a smile.

The nurse spoke in whispers and Doctor Bertram nodded slowly. Returning to his desk, he asked, "Does your mother drink?"

Joel paled and slunk forward, elbows on knees, head in hands. He ran his fingers through his hair several times before he could ask, "Was she drunk?"

"Blood tests have revealed that she had consumed a large amount of alcohol," the doctor informed him, "and at this point it has to be considered the reason for the accident. The other driver was conscious when he was brought in. The police are questioning him now."

Joel's mind was in overdrive. "She used to like a drink," he divulged, "but she had been at work and there is no way she would drink while she was working. Her job is too important to her. This is all very confusing."

The doctor showed Joel into a nearby waiting room and advised him to have a cup of coffee while he waited for the results of the test. He had been there for perhaps fifteen minutes when a traffic policeman came in. He shook Joel's hand and congratulated him on a good show.

"Thanks," Joel replied. "How can I help you?"

"Well, we have to go back to the scene and check everything out, but it doesn't look like it was your mother's fault. The other driver admitted to driving too fast and he came round the bend on the wrong side of the road. He's lucky to be alive. He's got away with only a few scratches. However, it seems your mother had been drinking."

"I heard that from Doctor Bertram, but it's not likely. She had been working and she wouldn't drink at work," Joel explained in an effort to divert the questioning from that line of thought.

"Where does she work?" the policeman asked. "We can check it out."

At the real estate office, Bruce Bonnington was shocked, but very amenable. "Yes, Nell Winston has been with us all evening. No, she had not been drinking. I particularly noted that she had orange juice, but I can check with the waitresses. It will have to be tomorrow, though, as they've left the office now. Please pass on our best wishes to Joel and to Nell, of course. We'll be in touch."

Joel didn't know what to think. Nell had told him those big launches were lavish occasions and there was always champagne available. *Would she have fallen off the wagon again?* he thought miserably. *It's been such a long time since her last lapse. I was so sure she'd conquered her demons. Oh, shit!*

It was almost two hours later when Joel was taken in to see his mother. She lay still and her battered face was unrecognisable with tubes seemingly everywhere. Joel cautiously approached the bed as the bleep, bleep, bleep of the machines reassuringly confirmed that she was still breathing.

"Can she hear me?" he asked the attendant nurse.

"Maybe," the nurse said gently, "but it can do no harm to talk. Sometimes familiar voices help in recovery. Talk about the things she likes."

Joel sat by the bed and took hold of Nell's hand gently. "Mum," he whispered, "it's me, Joel. First of all, I need to tell you that I love you. I always did, even though I didn't often show it. I need you to get well and we'll do all the things we planned. We'll go to Ayers Rock and to Alice Springs. I know you have longed to go there ever since you read *A Town Like Alice*. We'll go to the gold mining town of Kalgoorlie and to Bunbury, not the one in Cheshire, but the one here in WA. I'll never forget your surprise that there was actually a place called Bunbury when you thought Oscar Wilde had made it up…"

Doctor Bertram came in and gently touched Joel's shoulder. "Can I have a word?" he asked.

"Of course," Joel said. "Not more bad news, is there?"

"Your mother's right leg is very badly broken. Unfortunately, we don't have the personnel at this hospital capable of carrying out the required work. There is a doctor in Sydney who specialises in this procedure, but he will be very expensive…"

"What are the alternatives, Doctor?" Joel asked.

"We can set the leg, but it will never be straight and it is unlikely that she'll be able to walk properly again. In the worst case scenario, she might lose the leg altogether." Doctor Bertram was necessarily blunt.

"How can we be sure this other doctor can do the job if you're so adamant about the adverse effects that might result from your treatment? You understand that I need to know the facts?"

"He's world-renowned for his work. His reputation is second to none and I am prepared to personally guarantee that he'll save the leg," Doctor Bertram reassured Joel. "But I must repeat, he won't come cheap."

"Call him," Joel instructed. "Whatever it costs, just call him."

Joel left the hospital in the early hours of the morning on the advice of the doctor, who assured him Nell was unlikely to wake up for a while. "We are keeping her sedated until Doctor Flynn arrives. We'll let you know as soon as we hear from him."

"Doctor Flynn? Doctor Sean Flynn?" Joel asked incredulously.

"That's him. How did you know? He's a very quiet man and doesn't seek publicity, not even when his work is so newsworthy. He's very well known in medical circles."

"It's a long story," Joel said, "but I know he'll do a good job on Mum. I just know it."

Twenty-four

Joel called DP as soon as he arrived home from the hospital. It was seven o'clock on Friday evening when DP's phone rang. "Joel, my boy! How are you?"

"Me? I'm good, DP, but it's Mum." Joel's voice was sad.

"What on earth has happened?" DP asked, wondering, as Joel had initially, if Nell had succumbed to her demons again.

Joel told him all the details of the accident: the doctor's report, the police report and the suggestion that she had been drinking. "Her boss seemed sure she had stuck to orange juice all evening, so there has to be some mistake," Joel told his best friend and confidante. "I had just begun to trust her again and she has been doing so well with her job. I'll keep you informed, but you'll never guess who's going to do the operation."

"How could I guess? I don't know any doctors in Australia," DP said light-heartedly.

"Yes, you do," Joel reminded him.

"No, you're joking!" DP cried out with complete dismay. "You have to be joking."

Joel recounted the whole story. "I haven't told them at the hospital that Mum and he were lovers. I don't think he'd be allowed to do the operation if they knew, but I need to get him over here from Sydney and then decisions can be made."

When he replaced the receiver, Joel felt much more relaxed. He fell onto his bed and slept until the sun shone through his window. He had a quick shower, grabbed a piece of toast and a cup of coffee and called the hospital. News that his mother had opened her eyes was exactly what he needed to hear. "I'll be right there," he excitedly told the ward nurse.

"Drive carefully," she told him, but he didn't need that advice.

~ * ~

Sean Flynn was taking a welcome break from his job at the hospital. The last five years had been hectic. His departure from Bolton had been painful, but when he arrived in Sydney, a whole new world opened up to him. He instantly fell in love with the place and when he had settled into his new apartment overlooking the harbour, he sent tickets to his parents to come out to visit him. They were similarly impressed and had visited each year since then.

Sean's training had been challenging and very rewarding. His specialty in orthopaedics at university had been invaluable to the ongoing fellowship at the Sydney hospital. He had thrown himself into his work to forget Nell and he had excelled in every branch of learning. He was quietly proud of his achievements and was thrilled that he had been invited to speak about the way ahead in orthopaedic surgery at the University of California. He had returned from the States only three weeks before.

His love of golf had been his saving grace and there was no better place to play than the Royal Sydney. When he needed to hit out his frustrations, he could always find a golf-loving colleague. "I'll putt you through your paces, Flynny, if you'll pardon the pun," one had said and he enjoyed the camaraderie when time allowed. He had embarked on a couple of relationships, but nothing heavy and had chosen to remain living alone for the time being.

His telephone rang that Friday night just as he was about to sit down to dinner. He'd played golf all morning and spent the afternoon pottering around the garden. He enjoyed the tranquillity of his little secluded plot. He appreciated how lucky he was to find an apartment with a garden and he treasured his time spent tending his native plants. They attracted the birds and such birds he had never seen in the wild until he came to Australia. When the phone rang, he sighed. "I'm on holiday, for goodness sake," he said out loud. He snatched up the receiver. "Yes?" he snapped.

"Doctor Flynn?" When the answer was positive, the caller continued. "This is Doctor John Bertram from the Royal Perth Hospital. We have a serious leg injury from a road traffic accident and the son of the victim has requested that we call you to ask for your help. We don't have the expertise here and we told him so."

"Are you aware that I'm on holiday, Doctor Bertram?" Sean informed him tersely.

"I'm so sorry, sir, but no, I wasn't aware of that. The hospital passed on your number and just said you weren't there today." John Bertram was embarrassed. "But the victim's son seems to know you."

"Oh I see, so who might he be?" Sean asked, suddenly made interested by this surprising piece of information. "I hadn't realised I knew anybody in WA."

"His name is Joel Winston, the TV star of the moment in these parts," Doctor Bertram informed him. "His mother, Nell, has been involved in a horrendous accident. Her right leg is shattered and we fear she may lose it without the necessary corrective surgery."

Sean was dumbfounded. Confused thoughts invaded his brain. *Nell? In Perth? How come?* It didn't make sense.

"Doctor Flynn? Are you still there?" John Bertram asked. Sean pulled himself together immediately. "I'll get the next flight out and come straight to the hospital. I'll phone when I know what time I land. Please have a car waiting for me." He slammed down the receiver, not in temper, but in the unimaginable intensity of the moment.

John Bertram looked at the receiver in his hand and wondered what he had said to provoke such a rapid positive response.

~ * ~

When Joel arrived at his mother's bedside, she had drifted off to sleep again and he was disappointed. "Don't worry," the nurse told him, "she'll do that for a while. The pain relief is very strong and once Doctor Flynn arrives, we'll be able to do what's necessary."

"Doctor Flynn is coming then? That was quick," Joel commented. "How long before he gets here?"

"He called Doctor Bertram to say his flight lands at ten o'clock. The two hour time difference is to our advantage, but he'll have been travelling all night, so he's bound to be tired."

The nurse gently bathed Nell's wounds and made sure her stitches were clean. Joel sat by her bed, stood up, paced the floor like an expectant father and looked at the clock on the wall a dozen times in five minutes. He checked his watch to see if the clock had stopped and kept his eyes on the door in eager anticipation. He had no idea what Sean Flynn looked like, but he felt a strange sort of closeness to him.

Nell opened her eyes and could just make out her son's face through the mists that seemed to be shrouding her vision. "Joel?" she whispered.

Joel turned quickly and moved to her side. "Mum," he cried, "yes, it's me. Lie still."

"Where am I? What's happened to me?" Nell asked weakly, confused that she was unable to move and was hooked up to all manner of medical contraption.

"You've been in an accident, but you're in safe hands," he told her. "A very special orthopaedic surgeon is flying from Sydney to mend your leg..." But Nell had drifted off again and Joel had not been able to tell her about Sean. The shock might be too much for her to take at the moment.

At ten-thirty, two white-coated men appeared at Nell's bedside. One was Doctor Bertram and the other, Joel found out when introduced, was Doctor Gilfoyle, the resident consultant at Royal Perth. As he examined Nell's injuries, Sean Flynn approached the bed quietly. He nodded to Joel without saying anything and was visibly shaken to see Nell in such a mess. Sean shook hands with the two medics and asked, "May I see the records," before he made an assessment. Silently, he examined Nell more gently than he had ever examined a patient. His heart was beating fast and he instructed the staff to have a theatre ready immediately.

"I need to speak to Joel Winston," he said. "Is there a private office where I might talk to him?"

The two men were led into the anteroom at the side of the main ward. Sean closed the door quietly, but urgently. He offered his hand to Joel, who took it with immense gratitude.

"I have waited a long time to meet you, young man," Sean told him, "but never in my wildest dreams would I have thought it might be in circumstances such as these."

"I'm pleased to meet you, sir," Joel said, his emotions taking over as tears coursed down his face, tears that were a mixture of fear and of relief that his mother was going to get the best treatment available.

"I can't operate," Sean said, his voice devoid of emotion.

"What?" Joel was stunned. "Why have you come then? You have to operate. Mum might lose her leg. Please don't do this to her."

Sean walked to Joel and placed his hands on his shoulders. "Joel, I don't know what you're doing here, or what brought your mum to these shores, but I have to say that my heart is racing knowing that she's in Australia. I love your mum. I never stopped loving her even though she sent me away. A doctor cannot treat his loved ones. It would be ethically wrong for me to do it."

"Can't you just do it? I won't tell. Please, Doctor Flynn, please," Joel begged.

"I can't, but I will assist with the operation while Doctor Gilfoyle works to my instruction. I have known Declan Gilfoyle for years and I trust him. Will you give your permission?" Sean was beginning to feel desperate, too.

"Anything," Joel said. "If that's the best I can hope for, just give me the papers and I'll sign."

The seven hours that Nell was in the operating theatre seemed endless. Joel tried to sleep, but it was impossible. He attempted to read and that was even more difficult. He thought he'd write a new song. The studio was showcasing a test EP record in the next few months and had asked him to come up with some lyrics. He found the process cathartic and words came easily. By the time he had strummed out a tune in his head, Sean Flynn was at the door, still in his green theatre clothes, but smiling.

"The operation was a success," he said. "There'll be a long period of rehabilitation, but she'll be fine." He felt his own tears of joy trickle down his cheeks.

Joel ran to the man who had once made his mother happy and hugged him tightly. "Thank you very much," he said. "Will you stay at our house while you're in Perth? There's plenty of room and I know that Mum won't mind."

"I'd like that and anyway, I think we have a lot of time to catch up." *I don't know how this young man could have caused so much angst when he was growing up, but I find myself really drawn to him now.* "Go up and see your mum now. She'll be very groggy, but she'll be able to understand you. I think you need to explain that I'm here. Take it very gently. It's sure to be a shock."

With a final hug and several pats on the back in the process as men do, they parted and Joel left to see his mum, a mum who would soon be whole again.

Twenty-five

Joel sat by Nell's bed until she stirred. "Hi, Mum," he whispered, the two words filled with emotion.

"Hello, darl." Her voice was very quiet, mouse-like, timid and wary.

Joel smiled affectionately. "Proper little Aussie you're becoming," he said. "How do you feel?"

Nell shifted very gingerly on the mountain of pillows that propped her up. "Sore," she told him. "I feel like I've been hit by a bus."

"Not quite a bus, but certainly a big car. Do you know what happened?" Joel was testing the water. He knew the police would eventually be in to interview Nell.

"I don't really remember much, but I keep seeing headlights coming straight at me," Nell explained. "It's like a bad dream, but when you wake up, everything is all right."

"Do you remember being at the launch?" Joel asked quietly.

Nell closed her eyes. "I remember selling three houses and lining up a couple of prospective buyers." She smiled. "Good bit of commission coming my way."

"Did you have a drink? Sorry, but I have to ask." He was reading her reaction warily and didn't want to upset her by showing his mistrust.

"I didn't drink at all. I had several orange juices as all that talking made me thirsty," she said as proudly as was possible whilst lying in a hospital bed. "I won't let you down again, Joel..." She paused.

Joel noted the strained look in her eyes. "Don't stress about it, Mum. Just concentrate on getting better."

"...but I vaguely remember feeling strange when I was walking to my car," she divulged. She sighed deeply. "I'm tired now, darling. I think I'll take a nap."

"That's okay, I'll come back tomorrow," he whispered, but Nell was already asleep.

Sean met Joel in the family room next to the ward. "How did she take it?" he asked eagerly.

Joel looked at him questioningly.

"Have you told her I'm here?" Sean asked earnestly. "I'm desperate to talk to her."

Joel slowly shook his head and grinned at the man who had worked miracles to be there for his mother, but he couldn't resist the jibe. "You're the doctor, Sean Flynn. I shouldn't be telling you that she can't have too many shocks in one day. I really didn't have time to tell her before she dozed off again, but I will when the time is right. You'll just have to be patient." He grinned again at his little pun.

Sean knew he was right. "Being a doctor has nothing to do with how your heart rules your head when you're in love, young Winston," he admitted. "And age has nothing to do with how your heart does somersaults at the thought of..."

"Whoa there!" Joel cried. "I don't need that information, but I have to tell you, she doesn't like talking about you. I've asked her about you on a couple of occasions in the past and she's always changed the subject. That's something you'll have to sort out between yourselves. In the meantime, let's go home. We can come back first thing in the morning."

Bruce Bonnington and Graham Rimmer were waiting at the house when Joel and Sean arrived in South Perth.

"Good to see you, young man," Mr. Rimmer said. "We've just given our statement to the police."

"Should I be worried?" Joel asked. "My priority at the moment is making sure Mum gets well."

"I don't think you need worry," Bruce Bonnington told him. "The catering company called us to say that they have sacked one of their waitresses. One of their more reliable employees reported that the orange juices had been spiked by a woman who thought it was a bit of fun. The newspaper report of the accident in this morning's paper prompted her to do the right thing."

"We're sorry, Joel. Nell is a model employee for us and we wish her well," Graham Rimmer continued. "Oh and by the way, the police said we could tell you that the other driver admitted to causing the accident. It seems there are decent folks on the roads after all, although you'd never think so when the young hoons are driving past at a hundred miles an hour. Still, according to the police investigations, Nell did nothing wrong."

"Thank you very much for that and thanks for coming to tell me the news. I appreciate it. I'll keep you informed as to Mum's condition," Joel said as the two men left and he turned to Sean, who had waited at a discreet distance while Joel spoke to the visitors. "Do come in, Doctor Flynn. We need to eat."

There were a million questions to ask and Sean thought he would never find answers to them all, not immediately anyway. Joel was aware that Sean would be eager to hear what had happened since he left Bolton, but he needed to think carefully about how much he should reveal. Some things had to be left for Nell to choose whether or not she would divulge her personal information. Joel and Nell had had a tacit understanding that some things were better left unsaid. Both realised they had skeletons in the cupboard that needed to be left there. "We have smoked salmon in the fridge…"

"And green salad," Sean concluded with a grin.

"How did you know that?" Joel asked him. "Are you psychic as well as being the best orthopaedic surgeon in Australia?"

"Some things don't change," he acknowledged. "Do we have a bottle of Burgundy to go with it?" he enquired breezily.

Joel was taken aback. "We don't keep wine in the house," he said cautiously.

Sean's mind was going back to the last couple of times Nell had spoken to him on the phone. "I think I understand that."

"Mum doesn't drink at all now and I only have a beer when I'm out with friends. I can go to the bottle shop if you like."

"No, I'm fine. It's been a long day and perhaps we both need an early night. We'll demolish the smoke salmon and salad while you tell me about your fame and fortune. From what I hear, you are *the* face of television in these parts." Sean was impressed and said so.

Joel enjoyed recounting his time at the Maria Morenzi Theatre School as well as telling Sean about the Casa Bellissimo in Liverpool and his first job on the cruise liners. He told him that DP had become his mentor at college, but not the reasons why. He left the Connollys out of the equation as he did Ben and Belinda, yet all the time thinking of them with mixed and confused emotions. "As for this job in Perth, it's an absolute dream. I think I might just wake up one morning and find myself back in Bolton!"

"You have done very well for yourself, I see, and please excuse me for mentioning this, but that's what you set out to do, isn't it, to stand on your own two feet? Your mum and I once talked about it. She was very determined to let you find your own way at that time." Sean sounded almost fatherly in disclosing these details.

"Determined—yes that describes Mum very well. Her determination and our joint stubbornness almost ruined our relationship for a while, but we're back on track now. Australia has given us a brand new start," Joel said, knowing that he hadn't spoken out of turn.

Sharp knocking on the door interrupted their conversation. Joel opened it to find Donnie and a very distraught Jean from next door. She grabbed hold of Joel and hugged him tightly.

"I've only just found out," she cried wildly. "We were in Mandurah for a few days, but when I opened the paper just now…"

"Come in," Joel invited. "This is Doctor Sean Flynn from Sydney. He's an old friend of Mum's." General nodding and shaking of hands got over the formalities and Joel continued, "Mum's not fine, but she will be. The accident wasn't her fault and she must have found the only driver in WA who is prepared to admit he was driving too fast and on the wrong side of the road. In that respect, she's one very lucky lady!"

"Thank God for that at least," Jean sighed. "When can I see her?"

"Sean?" Joel threw the question to the doctor.

"Leave it for a couple of days," he advised. "She's got a lot to contend with at the moment, so peace and quiet are a must."

"All right, but, Joel, let me know if you need anything—groceries, laundry, cleaning …" Jean was fussing and Donnie grabbed her arm.

"Come on, Auntie Jean," he quipped and then said to Joel, "She'll be moving in if you give her half a chance."

"Thanks, Jean, but I'm fine. Sean will be here for a few days and I think the two of us can manage to make beans on toast at least," Joel reassured her.

He went to see them out and Jean caught hold of his arm. "He's some doctor!" she whispered in awe. "No wonder your mum kept quiet about him. What a spunk!"

"Jean!" Donnie chastised. "Trust a woman to say that," he said to Joel and winked as they bid each other goodnight.

The following morning they were up early and went for a jog along the river. Once showered and changed, they drove to the hospital early. Sean went in officially to see Dec Gilfoyle and Joel made his way to the ward. Remarkably, Nell looked a lot brighter. Her cuts appeared to be healing quickly and the bruising was now displaying a hint of brownish yellow around the darker blue areas.

"How are you today?" Joel enthused. "You look heaps brighter." He kissed her on her cheek and went to hug her.

"Oh, don't hug me, sweetheart. My ribs are sore, but I'm feeling more like me today. At least I've got rid of some of the tubes and wires," she told him. "The nurse has left the oxygen in case my breathing gets difficult." Her voice was very soft, but she sounded mildly confident.

"How does your leg feel?" Joel asked.

"Like lead!" she joked feebly. "Actually, I can't feel much pain now and the cast keeps it pretty rigid. I have to try to walk on crutches later and I'm a bit scared of that."

Joel reassured her to allay her fears. He related how Jean had come panicking and banging on the door, adding exaggerated detail to entertain Nell as he imitated her friend with a very impressive impersonation, and Nell laughed. "Please don't make me laugh," she whined, "my ribs..." She held herself gently until she recovered her calm.

Joel wasn't expecting what he heard next. "The nurse told me a famous consultant from Sydney came to operate on my leg," she announced. "I wonder if he knows Sean Flynn. There can't be that many hospitals in Sydney."

"He'll probably be in to see you later. You can ask him then," Joel said. "Are you sure you want to know about Sean Flynn?"

"Well, it would be nice to know how he's going on. He's probably married by now and I can accept that. I've become quite philosophical over the past few years. You know, what will be, will be and all that." Nell smiled at Joel who smiled back knowingly.

The two uniformed policemen appeared at the entrance to the ward and asked permission to speak with Nell. Joel stood by her bed, confident now that she would not be charged.

"Good morning," she greeted them, her voice still weak. "I know you have to ask me questions, so I hope I have the answers." Joel had said nothing to her regarding the information Bonnington and Rimmer had revealed. Telling her that her orange juice had been spiked would only add to her confusion.

"We'll keep this as brief as possible, Mrs. Winston," the most senior of the two stated officiously. "First of all, it has been brought to our attention that you had been drinking before you drove home."

"Oh no, officer." Nell spoke quietly, but with confidence. "Not alcoholic drinks anyway. I drank orange juice all evening. I never drink while I'm working, in fact, I don't drink at all."

"Your blood alcohol level was high, but—"

Nell looked afraid. "But I didn't drink," she reiterated.

"—we know now that somebody had spiked the orange juice and you weren't aware of that at the time. We also know you were not responsible for the accident. Your speedo recorded that you did not exceed the speed limit and you were driving on the left side of the road as required."

"That's good news, but who would be so vindictive as to spike my drinks?" she asked, very afraid of what was in store.

"One of the waitresses thought it was funny, but not only did she lose her job, she is facing charges as well. However, you have been very lucky this time, Mrs. Winston. We will not be charging you with being drunk in charge of a vehicle because we don't know if you were, or you were not, but..." The officer adjusted his hat and stood to attention before he delivered his final words. "Let this be a warning to you. It's not everyday that a driver will admit to driving recklessly, but the man who hit you, did. You must have a guardian angel." With that he left, his silent partner following in close pursuit.

Nell's mind was reeling from the revelations of drink spiking and possibly being drunk in charge of a vehicle. "I thought I felt a bit woozy in the car park," she told Joel again, "and you know what? I remember driving off without switching on my lights.

Thank goodness I noticed before I left the parking lot. It's all falling into place."

"Don't worry about all that now," Joel reassured her. "Once you've mastered those crutches, we'll get you home," he said, but he was distracted by the young staff nurse who was setting out the table for lunch.

"Well, I'm breathing a very deep sigh of relief," Nell conceded. "How many more shocks am I expected to take?"

"Just one," a voice said from behind the screen.

"Sean?"

Joel grinned. "There's somebody here who needs to see you." He discreetly joined the nurse in the anteroom to give doctor and patient time and space.

Sean appeared from behind the screen in his white coat, his black curls unruly and his green eyes shining with excitement. He stood for a moment before he ventured forward to take Nell's hand in his. "You feel good," he said, "Oh, so good."

Nell looked into his eyes. "Are you famous now?" she asked.

"I've become more qualified," was all he was prepared to say.

"Qualified enough to mend my leg?"

"Well, enough to assist Doctor Gilfoyle," he conceded.

"Sean Flynn," Nell cried, "I may be incapacitated at the moment, but my brain is functioning properly. Doctor Gilfoyle wasn't qualified to carry out the operation and they had to fly out a consultant from Sydney. Is that you? Did you operate on my leg?"

"Doctor Gilfoyle did."

"But ..."

"I directed him, Nell. I'm not allowed to treat loved ones. I love you. Please don't send me away."

Nell squeezed his hand gently, an action that said she would not send him away again. "We have a lot to talk about," she told him. "Where are you staying?"

"I have a room in a place down by the river. The young man who owns it has looked after me royally," he said.

"Joel?"

Sean nodded. "I have to go back to Sydney in a couple of days, but now that I know you are here, I'll be back. Now, it's time to get you onto your crutches..."

Twenty-six

When Nell returned home, Sean had long gone back to Sydney, but had called daily for a progress report. They had not had the opportunity to talk at length and both knew that there were issues that needed to be discussed. Nell was happy with the situation. She had time to recuperate and to familiarise herself with the fact that Sean was once again in her life. There was no urgency.

Joel returned to the studio to complete the third series of *Have You Got What It Takes?* and he worked in his newly acquired home recording studio to produce his first record. A regular visitor was staff nurse Sheralyn Nilsson, who been assigned to assist Nell in her rehabilitation. Joel invited her to listen to his songs and welcomed her comments.

"What do you think of this?" he asked, as he strummed a few chords and played around with pitch and lyrics.

She was generally forthright, but not tactless. She reminded Joel of Belinda, but she had Swedish blonde hair, more like Penny's. He had written to the Connollys regularly and sent newspaper cuttings of his reviews. Gerry and Penny were married and renovating their house in Maghull, not too far away from Penny's parents. *'They'll come in handy when the nipper's born,'* Gerry wrote, *'seeing as our Chrissie uses Mam all the time to baby-sit her little David. He's a proper little Scouser, Poshman. You should hear him shouting, 'Come on, you Reds!' God love him.*

I haven't seen Ben for a while, but Belinda phones Penny every so often. I think Ben's got promotion at one of the Bolton branches of the bank. Fancy them buying your house! I think we'll drive over to see them before Penny has her hands full with nappies and bottles and things. Did I tell you I'd bought a new Ford Capri? Now I'm a bona fide electrician, the work is pouring in and the money's bloody good.

Well done with your new show. Maybe ITV will buy it and show it over here. Let's hope the record will sell worldwide. We'll be first in the queue, Poshman.'

Joel loved Gerry's letters. They reminded him to keep his feet firmly on the ground and not to forget where he came from. One day, he would go back to the UK and see them all.

"What do you think of these, Sheralyn?" Joel asked as she peeped in the studio after her afternoon session with Nell. He had cut a demo disc and wanted to test it out. She went to sit in the armchair near the door and put on earphones as Joel sat behind the equipment fiddling with mixers until he found the right blend.

Sheralyn closed her eyes and rested her head on the back of the chair. She removed the band that tied back her hair and allowed her tresses to fall in silky strands across her shoulders. Joel held his breath. *She's beautiful,* he thought, but chose to ignore his confused emotions and continued to play his songs.

The first was his own "Flight of Fancy" that he hadn't sung since his college interview. He had forgotten how appropriate the words were to his ambition then and were still very relevant now. Next came the Simon and Garfunkel hit, "Bridge Over Troubled Waters" and while Sheralyn could have no idea of its significance, Joel realised that Australia had been his bridge over troubled waters and had helped him and his mother overcome most of their problems. He stopped the record before playing the final song.

"The Beatles were just setting out when I was at college in Liverpool," he told Sheralyn. "My tutor had their demo tape before they had hit the Liverpool scene." He grinned mischievously. "He swore me to secrecy at the time and now I've just blown it. Ah well, I guess the world already knows how successful they are."

When he restarted the record, the significance hit them both with the same intensity—Sheralyn because of a heart long ago being broken, Joel finding real love for the first time in his life. It wasn't planned. It just happened.

'I'm looking for love,
For the love of my life,
I need to feel loved and adored.
I'm looking for love,
For the romance of dreams,
Just being with you, I want more
Than a fleeting hello.
Please say those three words
I love you to me
And then I'll be perfectly sure...'

Joel had walked over to the chair where Sheralyn was sitting and gently taken her hands in his. She looked into his eyes and realised their feelings were the same. Cupping her face in his hands, he kissed her lips gently.

"Wow, Staff Nurse Nilsson, we didn't see that coming," he whispered gently as he nuzzled her hair, "but I liked it—no, correction, I loved it."

"You asked my opinion of the songs, Joel," Sheralyn reminded him. "Well, I loved them all. You could have been singing to me personally and I guess that's how you want the girls to feel when they listen."

"Yes, I guess so, but—"

"But as regards the kiss..." She looked at him as though she were about to tell him off for being so bold. "I'd like to do it again to make sure I wasn't dreaming."

Joel pulled her to her feet and took her into his arms. He kissed her more urgently, but past experiences told him to hold back. This time he intended to allow love to grow.

Nell watched as Joel's relationship developed into romance and she was delighted. Joel was twenty-seven years old and a successful entertainer in Australian theatre and television. She knew Sheralyn was devoted to him, not as a celebrity, but as a person. The young nurse had never seen his shows and made a conscious decision not to do so.

"I love you for being you, Joel, not for being famous," she told him. "I didn't even know who you were when we met, other than being my patient's son. That side of your life is alien to me. I'll listen to your music and I'll give you my honest opinion about it, but I won't interfere with your fans. They need to think you are there for them, not that I have allowed them to borrow you for a couple of hours."

"Darling Sher, you are the best thing that ever happened to me," he declared. "You don't need to hide away. The Beatles still sold records even when their relationships became public."

Sheralyn understood what he was saying. "Joel, I would like to keep on working, not being just the girlfriend of a celebrity. Nursing is important to me. I don't want to be known as Joel Winston's love interest. I want people to know me as Sheralyn Nilsson, nurse extraordinaire." She grinned broadly at him. "I'll stop working when we have babies."

Joel looked at her wide-eyed. "Whoa there, girl. I hadn't thought of babies just yet. I almost..." He stopped abruptly. Telling her about Belinda's baby must not be a part of this relationship, he decided. The child was Ben's, and he had promised to acknowledge Ben as her father.

"You almost what?" Sheralyn asked, curious why he had stopped so suddenly.

"I almost thought you were expecting a proposal," he interjected quickly.

"Maybe I am," she revealed, "but not until you are ready. I love you enough to wait until the time is right."

"I love you, Staff Nurse Nilsson," Joel reassured her. "Perhaps when I see your dad next time, I'll ask his permission to whisk you down the aisle."

Sheralyn laughed. "He'll say take her quick! We've had enough of her."

"All in good time, darl. All in good time."

~ * ~

Mr. and Mrs. DP were due to arrive in the middle of December. Their planned trip down under was carefully orchestrated by Nell, who had kept it secret from Joel. With the help of Sheralyn, she had prepared the guest room and done extra shopping in advance of their arrival. Joel had been working long hours at the studio, but was taking time off over Christmas and the New Year. Sean was due to arrive on the twentieth of December and the festive season promised to be wonderful.

"Sheralyn and I are going out early tomorrow," she informed Joel over breakfast.

"How early?" Joel asked. "I have to be at the studio by nine. Will you have left before then?"

"We thought we'd leave at about half past seven so that we'll be in the city when the shops open," she lied, but it was a necessary deception to safeguard the secret. DP's flight was due to land at eight o'clock, so by the time they'd cleared customs and immigration, she and Sheralyn would be waiting to greet them in arrivals.

"Are you driving?" Joel asked. Nell had recently replaced her car after the accident, but she hadn't driven into the city yet. "I think I'd be happier if Sheralyn came to pick you up."

"It's all arranged, darl," Nell said, "so don't worry. Sheralyn will be here in time to see you before you leave."

The following morning, it was all she could do to hide her excitement. "I don't think I've ever seen you so hyped up," Joel remarked. "If this is what an impending visit of Sean does to you, he'd best move in and fast."

"It must just be the whole Christmas thing," Nell suggested. "It doesn't feel like Christmas because of the sunshine and I don't think I'll ever get used to Christmas trees and fairy lights in summer."

"I hope we're not having a hot turkey dinner," Joel said. "Seafood, salads and a barbie will be fine. Let's dine by the river. It will be perfect."

"You leave catering to me," she advised. "Thank goodness you recorded the carol concert last week. It will be good to watch you on Christmas Eve and what a treat it will be for Sheralyn. She doesn't know what she's been missing."

"Sheralyn gets a personal performance before everybody else, so she knows what I do," Joel stated with a little irritation in his voice. "I just wish she'd be a bit more interested in the public me, but she won't get involved at all."

"Perhaps she's nervous about how to behave towards you in public," Nell suggested.

"How do you mean—behave?" Joel asked. "She doesn't have to become a different person just because people will be looking at her."

"Listen to yourself, Joel," Nell continued. "You've just talked about the public you and now you're saying that Sheralyn doesn't have a public persona. Make your mind up. Are you a different person for your public?"

Joel thought for a moment before he answered. "Externally maybe—you know, always smiling, being flirtatious, joking more than usual and certainly dressing for the part, because that's what the public want to see, but inside, I'm still me—mildly serious, sometimes over-sensitive, but always wanting to do well."

"Do you think Sheralyn would like the public Joel?" Nell pointedly enquired.

"I don't know, but she loves the real me and that's all that matters."

"Think about it, darl. She doesn't want to be made to choose," Nell informed him. "Staying out of your other life makes it easier for her to love you for being you and not for being a hot-shot TV personality."

"Wow, Mum, harsh words indeed. Am I meant to shrink back in horror?" He wasn't sure he liked the bluntness of his mother's assessment.

"No, sweetheart, I'm not being harsh. I'm just trying to see it from Sheralyn's point of view. I doubt she would ever be so blunt with you, but I can be, because I'm your mother." She smiled and gave him a hug. "Still my Joel, I see."

"Okay, point taken, Mummy!" he said sardonically, openly acknowledging his mother's reference to the Winston ego. "Now, get yourself organised, or the girl of my dreams will be here before you are ready."

The DPs arrived on time and marvelled at the December weather. They had discarded their jackets and sweaters in Singapore and stuffed them unceremoniously into hand luggage.

"Welcome to Australia," Nell greeted them and introduced Sheralyn as Joel's reason for living.

"You must be the motivation for his music sounding so good," DP told her affectionately. "Anybody who can influence my star student so beautifully is my friend for life." He gave her a hug and kissed her cheek while Mrs. DP smiled in agreement.

Joel arrived home from the studio at seven o'clock. It had been a long day and he knew Sheralyn would be home with her parents so he need not go to collect her from the hospital. They had agreed she would spend the evening with her parents for a change.

He kicked off his thongs at the door and threw his baseball cap onto the hall table. "I'm home," he called. "I'll take a shower and be right down."

"Fine, darl. See you in a few minutes," Nell called from the kitchen. She carried on as normal as DP and his wife sat quietly in the lounge room. Joel always went straight to his room, took a shower and then returned to the kitchen where he and Nell had dinner. If Sheralyn joined them, they still ate in the kitchen. Only when they had visitors did they eat in the dining room.

"I'm in the lounge room," she called as he came down the stairs.

"Are we having visitors?" he asked light-heartedly, for he knew Sean wasn't expected for a couple of days.

"Just come here. I want a word with you," she coaxed.

"Not another lecture, I hope. I haven't forgotten what you said this ..." He stopped in his tracks. His jaw dropped. "DP!" he cried and ran to the man who was his guiding light in all that he had achieved. As he hugged both Dafydd and Megan Powell enthusiastically, he caught sight of Sheralyn over DP's shoulder. "Hi, babe, I didn't expect to see you tonight. Are you in on this, too?" he asked with complete surprise.

"I wouldn't have missed this for the world. Your mum and I have been planning it for months. I think we'd have killed each other if either one of us had let slip what was going on," she said. "Mind you, we just hoped that DP's letters to you wouldn't give you a hint of their trip."

"It was very difficult," Mrs. DP told them. "We even swore Gerry to secrecy. We know how excited he gets and he just might have let the cat out of the bag."

Joel laughed. "Gerry would have revelled in keeping it from me. He'd love having the upper hand. Just wait till I write to him again."

Showing the DPs around their adopted country was wonderful for both Joel and Nell. During the four weeks the Powells were there, they sampled the whole different lifestyle and thoroughly enjoyed Christmas in the sun. Sean came and went and by the time the month was up, the Winstons were able to reflect that entertaining their first visitors from the UK had been a hugely satisfying experience.

"Time has flown,' Joel declared as he stood in departures at the airport saying his fond farewells to Dafydd and Megan. "I'll miss you, but I'll call and I'll write and you'll be the first to get a copy of my album, promise."

"Thanks for everything, Joel," DP said. "I can't tell you how good it makes me feel to see you happy and settled. We'll come again for the wedding."

"What wedding? Mum's and Sean's? I reckon they'll tie the knot before I do," Joel told him.

DP shrugged. "I hope you don't keep that little girl waiting in the wings for too long, Joel. She worships you and I mean you, not the TV personality. Keep that in mind, young Winston."

"Oh dear," Joel responded. "You always call me that when you're being serious." But he offered no hint as to his intentions towards Sheralyn Nilsson.

Twenty-seven

For her fiftieth birthday in July, Nell decided to fly to Sydney to see Sean. Since Christmas, Sean had not been able to take time off to visit Nell in Perth and although they spoke frequently on the phone, they hadn't yet found the time and privacy to broach the issues that needed to be discussed.

"I really don't want to publicise my half-century coming up," she confided. "Joel is filming all that week and Sheralyn will be here to make sure he eats properly."

Sean laughed. "Oh Nell," he declared, "Will you ever stop worrying about Joel? He's more than capable of looking after himself. I think you know that really."

"I do know, but he'll always be precious to me," she said quietly. "It's difficult for a mother to let her son go completely."

"Well, I hate to be the one to tell you this, but remember the old adage, 'a daughter's a daughter all her life, but a son is a son till he marries a wife.' Be prepared, Nell. Just be prepared."

"If that wife is Sheralyn and I'm sure it will be, then I'll find it easy to hand him over. I love that girl. She is perfect for him."

So come July, she packed her case and took the five-hour flight to Sydney. She had never flown alone, but she enjoyed the experience and Sean met her at the airport to drive her into the city to his harbour apartment. "I thought I'd give you a treat," he told her. "I don't normally drive home this way, but it will allow you to see the Harbour Bridge first hand. Driving over it is wonderful and you'll be able to see the new Opera House that was opened last year. You'll love it, Nell."

Nell did indeed feel in awe of the world-renowned landmarks. "I can't believe I'm actually here!" she exclaimed. "How I wish my dad were able to see this. He would have loved everything. Mum would too, but with Dad's interest in feats of engineering genius, all this would have fascinated him." Her eyes misted over. She had grieved for both her parents since they'd passed away, but her dad missed out on so much as he'd died in the prime of his life. Sixty-one wasn't old. He didn't even have time to enjoy his retirement.

Sean sensed her melancholy and interrupted her thoughts. "Come on, darling, chin up," he said gently. "We have years to catch up in the next few days and then we have our whole future before us."

Sean looked adoringly mischievous. "I have smoked salmon and green salad in the fridge," he announced cheekily just before dinner.

Nell couldn't help but laugh. "My, my Sean Flynn, you have remembered that after all this time. Happy days, eh?"

"How could I forget it, Nell? You brought light into my life, but then almost as soon as it was burning brightly, you snuffed it out." He had decided that, if they were to have any future at all, he would have to be honest about his feelings.

Nell had had similar thoughts. "If I could take back all my actions, knowing what I know now, I would," she confessed. "At the time, I had too much going on in my life to ..."

"Joel?"

"Well, yes, Joel, but I had no idea what I wanted from my own life. I'm not making excuses, but I seemed to be floating somewhere between fantasy and reality and I didn't like either of them." She struggled to put into words how Joel had wiped out her self-confidence and how Sean had given her some semblance of self-worth again. "When we talked—our counselling session, you remember?—I felt that a burden had been lifted. I still needed Joel to come home, so to speak, but he had to do it on his own."

"We had so much going for us, Nell. I wanted you to understand that," Sean reminded her. "I needed you to trust me and you didn't."

"I wanted to, Sean. I really wanted to, but I misjudged you. I'm so sorry for that," she cried. "You came, you saw, you conquered and then you announced that you were leaving. What was I to think?"

"But I asked you to leave with me, darling. I wanted you by my side," he emphasised, taking her hands in his.

"But it seemed to be a *fait accompli* to me. You assumed I would adhere to your will with no consideration for my circumstances, or my ties to Joel and yes, I still had those strong maternal feelings for my errant son. Rightly or wrongly, I couldn't just leave him behind and travel to the other side of the world." Nell was becoming agitated. "God, I need a drink ... but then no doubt you have gathered that I don't, correction, can't drink now."

"I knew you were drinking too much when I spoke to you on the phone before I left," Sean told her. "Poor Nell. I wish I'd known what I was doing to you." He moved closer to her and held her tightly. "I also got the hint from Joel while you were in hospital when he said that you don't keep drinks in the house. I didn't want to mention it until now. Let's face it, we never got the chance to talk, I mean really talk and ..." He grinned impishly. "...do you realise we slept in separate beds over Christmas and New Year?"

She smiled back at him, acknowledging what he said. "Every time we spoke on the phone, I was conscious that we weren't really communicating," she admitted. "Weren't you?"

"To be sure, I was," he said, the old brogue taking over unconsciously. "But we're talking now, my darling, and it's oh, so good."

"To cut a very long story short," she divulged, "the drink took over. You'd be ashamed of knowing the Nell Winston that evolved out of all that mess. Truly, Sean, you would be appalled."

"I don't think you would have liked me either, if you knew the truth," he confessed.

Nell related all the gory details, Stan the Man and rippling blubber included. "And then there was Connie Mason."

"Who's Connie Mason?" Sean asked.

"She was Ben's mother, a known prostitute, and I allowed her to ply her trade in my guest room!" Nell confessed blushing profusely. "Not only that. I felt sure that somehow she would find a way to tell Joel what I had done and I was paranoid about that for a while."

"How much of this does Joel know?" Sean asked. "I love that you are sharing all this information with me, but I get the feeling it's the first time you've spoken of it."

Nell looked sheepish. "He knows about the drink problem, but nothing of the rest," she revealed. "I'm not sure what purpose it would serve to tell him."

"Is it wise to have secrets, Nell?"

"No, but I really can't see that upsetting Joel again will help our relationship. It happened, I can't change that, but I can try to forget." Nell felt she was being forced to justify herself. "I'm not proud of any of it and I would prefer to forget that it ever happened."

"But you told *me*, Nell." Sean tried to comfort her. "I'm pleased about that. I can't say I like to think of you in those situations, but..."

"Please, Sean," she pleaded, "don't make me humiliate myself anymore. I wouldn't blame you if you put me on the next plane back to Perth and told me it's over between us. I've made some massive mistakes that I'll regret for the rest of my life, but I don't want Joel to know about them. End of discussion."

Sean moved closer to her and took her into his arms. "Not quite the end of the discussion, I'm afraid," he said. "I can't tell you how much I appreciate your honesty and I think I should return the compliment."

"I don't believe you've been as irresponsible as I've been, Doctor Flynn," she declared.

Sean looked straight at her, his green eyes sparkling in the soft lights of the room. "I was pretty cut up about your rejection. I threw myself into planning the trip out here and went to a farewell party at the golf club the night before I left."

"That's nothing to be ashamed of," Nell reassured him.

"Ah, but it doesn't end there," he revealed. "There were people at that party whom I'd never seen previously. I'll swear there must have been gate-crashers, but some woman took me to her bed that night."

Nell gasped.

"I have no idea who she was. I didn't even ask her name. I could blame the wine, but I won't. She wasn't English. She was Dutch, I think, but she was very forward," he explained, his embarrassment evident. "She asked for a lift home and then very bluntly asked me if I wanted sex."

Nell put her head on his chest and whispered, "Poor darling. It would have been too difficult to say no when only a short time before, I had more or less told you that *I* didn't want you."

"It was weird," he said almost light-heartedly, "We did it and then I left. No questions asked. I still have no idea who she was and she made it pretty clear she wasn't bothered about me. I think we just filled a need in each other at the particular time and that was that."

"Have there been others?" she asked. "Five years is a long time for a man to remain celibate."

"I've had a couple of relationships, but nothing serious. Australia is the perfect country for socialising. You must have realised that by now," he said.

"So where do we go from here?" Nell asked with some trepidation.

"We go to bed," he said and scooped her into his arms, carrying her into his bedroom where the moon shone through open windows and the harbour lights twinkled on the water below.

Afterwards he held her gently. "Nell Winston, will you marry me?"

"Are you sure you know what you're doing?" she asked.

"I have never been so sure of anything in my life."

"Then my answer is ..." She paused dramatically and grinned. "Yes!"

"You won't regret it, Nell," he assured her. "I love you so much."

"I know," she told him, "and I love you, too."

Twenty-eight

Joel relished the freedom of the house while his mother was in Sydney. He knew he ought to be mapping out his future, but there was always something that prevented him from making the final decision. Having the house to himself for the long weekend gave him space to do what blokes do and he didn't intend to reflect upon his future for a while, certainly not this weekend.

Sheralyn called on Friday night when he returned from the studio. "I thought we might spend the weekend together at your place," she suggested. "We've never had the chance to be on our own for a whole weekend."

"Oh, I'm not sure, Sher," he mumbled almost inaudibly. "I thought I might hang out with the crew this weekend."

"You thought what?" she cried, unbelieving. "I have the whole weekend off and you decide to hang out with the crew?"

Joel cringed. "I planned it weeks ago, Sher. I didn't know you'd have time off and with Mum being away, it seemed the ideal opportunity to spend a bit of leisure time with my mates from work. It isn't often we get to meet up socially. You understand, don't you, babe?"

"I'll tell you what I understand, Joel Winston," she declared angrily. "I understand that you kiss me, you hug me, you tell me that you love me, but you never want to go that step further. This weekend would have helped us to bond, if that's the right word, because at this moment in time, I don't know what the right words would be to make *you* understand." She sobbed uncontrollably.

Joel knew he had stuffed up and stuffed up royally. "Please don't cry, Sher," he said in an effort to calm her. "I have to be with the crew this weekend. Too much arranging has gone on to cancel at this point. I'll see you on Wednesday and we'll go out for dinner."

"Stuff your dinner, Joel. I've had enough. If you love me, you'll do the right thing." She slammed the phone down hard and left Joel to think about what she had said.

He locked himself in his studio and immersed himself in making music. He always found it creatively cathartic, and some of his best music had been written in times of stress. When his workmates arrived on Saturday afternoon, he was ready to snap out of his reflective mood and up the gear to party mode.

The camera crew were a lively lot and soon the beer was flowing and the barbecue heating up ready for "The feeding of the five thousand," as Joel put it. Alice brought along her partner, Myrna, and they were the only two girls there. With loud music, flowing beer and steak, snags, prawns and burgers cooked to perfection, they were soon swinging along to Elton John, David Bowie and Marvin Gaye.

"What d'you reckon, Joel? Do you think you'll ever get to the UK and US charts?" Danny the props guy asked him.

"I don't know, do I?" Joel said, his enunciation not clear because of the beer he'd consumed in the last few hours.

Alice began to laugh heartily. She had kept on a par with the guys and she was well oiled. Myrna produced a little packet from her pocket and waved it around.

"Anybody want a spliff?" she asked.

Several of the crew jumped at the offer and Joel actually didn't discourage them.

"What about you, Joel? Ever tried pot?" Alice asked.

"Truthfully?" He wasn't sure he wanted to go down that road again, but he was relaxed, his mates were here, they were having a good time and... "Well, yes I have, actually."

"Oooooh!" Alice called excitedly across the room. "So our little Pommie friend is not the innocent goody two shoes we thought he was. Come and join us, Winston, and show us what you're made of."

Joel had forgotten how good it made him feel and he drifted off into oblivion for a while. Time stands still when your brain is addled with beer and cannabis. *No Mum, no Sheralyn, no worries*, he thought. He shifted on the floor to make himself comfortable...

Sheralyn surveyed the deck and the lounge room with horror. Joel was propped up against the couch and his guests had long left.

"Several taxis had rolled up at the house about midnight," Jean had informed her as she arrived on the drive, "so no doubt they'd booked them in advance. They were all pickled, I can tell you that," she told the bewildered Sheralyn.

"Thanks, Jean. I'll just go and see what state the place is in," she said giving no hint of the turmoil she was feeling inside her head.

"Do you want me to come with you, darl?" Jean offered.

"No thanks. I'll be right," she replied as she climbed the steps to the front door.

The tongue loosening that goes with marijuana was well in place even a number of hours later. "I smoked pot in Liverpool when I was eighteen," he divulged, laughing at the thought of that old green shed behind the Cabin Club. "I got a girl pregnant," he told whoever was listening. "I'm a dad, but nobody knows. I don't even know myself. My mate's her dad now and good luck to him. I nearly got busted, too, but lady luck smiled on me that day…" He laughed raucously. His head was spinning and he felt ravenously hungry. "Will somebody get me a burger? I'm starving…"

"I don't think you want a burger for breakfast," a voice in the distance told him.

"It's supper, not breakfast," he informed the mysterious person who seemed to have appeared out of the mists that surrounded his head. He squinted through bloodshot eyes. His throat was dry and his head hurt. For a moment he was back in his attic room over the Connollys' shop, and in the space of a few seconds, he again regretted everything untoward he had done in his life.

"Do you realise you talk in your sleep?" the voice enquired less than amicably.

Joel tried to focus in the right direction. "Oh God," he groaned. "Sheralyn? How long have you been here?"

"Long enough," she spat at him. "Do you know you talk in your sleep?" she repeated.

She gave him a glass of water and a couple of paracetamol. "Take those," she instructed. "I don't know why I should help you, but I guess my profession won't allow me to let you suffer, though God knows, I'd like you to suffer all the agonies of hell."

"What have I done to make you so angry?" he asked naively.

Sheralyn breathed in deeply and almost retched. "My God, Joel, this place reeks of dope and you ask why I'm angry?"

Slowly the light dawned. Myrna!

"I could blame somebody else, you know. I didn't bring the pot into my house," he said with bristling swagger.

"And I suppose somebody held you down while they stuffed a spliff in your mouth and told you to draw on it." Sheralyn sneered. "Do me a favour, Joel and grow up."

He felt himself growing angry and he didn't want her telling him what he could and couldn't do. "Get off your high horse, Sher.

I've been down that road with my mother and it wasn't pretty. She ostracised herself from me trying to rule my every move. I'm certainly not going to allow you to run my life for me."

Sheralyn stood back and calmly walked towards the door. "I'm glad I saw you as you really are, Joel. The fact that you have left a girl pregnant somewhere in the UK and allowed some other dude to bring up your child speaks volumes about your character. Your one saving grace, if I can call it that, is that you didn't trust yourself with me. At least I should be grateful you didn't even try to get me pregnant." She felt a very odd sense of rejection mixed with relief. "It's a pity you didn't love me enough to trust me, too. I'm out of here." She managed to hold back the tears. "There's no way I'll allow you to see that you've made me cry again, Mr. arrogant and self-centred Winston," she said quietly as she closed the door behind her.

Joel wondered for a long time how Sheralyn had found out about Belinda and then, piecing together the snippets of their conversation as his memory returned, he realised she'd said that he'd talked in his sleep. The pot had really messed up his life this time. He managed to clean up the house before Nell returned with the news of her forthcoming marriage.

"Congratulations, Mum. I'm very happy for you."

Twenty-nine

"But why doesn't she want to see you anymore?" Nell asked. "You were so good together."

Joel was in no mood to discuss what had happened. He had unwittingly opened up his cupboard full of skeletons to Sheralyn, even though he'd intended to keep it well and truly shut. He'd promised Ben.

"She has decided she doesn't love me anymore, simple as that," he explained and hoped his non-committal answer would suffice. He shut himself away again and immersed himself in his music. He knew he could produce his best work without the interference of outside influences.

Some weeks later, Nell picked up the phone and dialled Sheralyn's number. "Will you meet me for coffee?" she requested earnestly. "Sean and I are getting married in a few weeks and I have things to discuss with you."

They met at London Court in the city, a typically British arcade that was most pleasant and very relaxing. Sheralyn looked sad.

"Hello, Nell, how are you?" she asked timidly as they found their way to a table away from the main body of the café.

"All the better for seeing you," Nell said gently. "I have so wanted to call, but Joel asked me not to interfere and I have to do as he asks. If you knew our history, you'd understand. I cannot allow my once over-zealous need to control his life ever to surface again."

"So why are you here?' Sheralyn asked, easily recognising that Nell was contradicting herself.

"I'm here for me, not for Joel, although I feel very underhanded in not telling him I was meeting you," Nell confessed. "I really don't know what went wrong with you two and I'm not asking you to tell me, but I've missed you."

"I've missed you, too," Sheralyn admitted, "and I'd still like to be your friend, but I'm not ready to face Joel yet and I don't know if I ever will be."

"Oh dear," Nell cried, "and I wanted you to be my witness at my wedding."

Sheralyn began to cry, obviously overcome with all manner of conflicting emotions and she didn't know how to deal with them. "I'm overwhelmed with all of this, truly, but I can't deal with Joel right now."

"Can't you tell me what went wrong with you two, dear?" Nell urged. "It would be easier to know what to say to you if I knew what was going on."

"You'll have to ask Joel if you really want to know. He has issues that he needs to deal with himself before he can commit to any relationship," Sheralyn revealed tentatively.

"What sort of issues?" Nell asked, her mind running riot with all sorts of sexuality problems. "He's not..."

Sheralyn needed to smile wryly at Nell's suggestion. "Oh no, he's certainly not that," she vowed.

Nell was growing more and more curious. "Well, what then?"

"Nell, he's your son. Ask him if it's important to you. If not, then just let it lie," Sheralyn told her adamantly. "He knows where he stands with me and if he is the person I think he is under all this façade, then he'll sort it out and get on with his life." She recovered enough to order coffee and say, "Now tell me about the wedding. Where will it be and what are you going to wear?"

Nell returned home in a very pensive mood and it showed in her quiet demeanour over dinner.

"Is there something wrong, Mum?" Joel asked. "You've hardly said a word since you came back from the city."

"I have a lot to think about," she conceded. "I'm worried about you."

"Why? You have no need to worry about me," he assured her light-heartedly.

"I saw Sheralyn today..."

"You did what? Oh Mum, please don't tell me you are trying to run my life again," he cried. "Sheralyn has made it quite clear she doesn't want anything to do with me. What am I supposed to say? I'm trying to stay calm, but you have to know this really upsets me, not only that Sheralyn doesn't want me, but the fact that you are interfering again. Why are you doing this?"

"I want her to be my witness at my wedding, but she says she can't face you just yet, if ever." She needed to tread warily. "What's it all about, Joel?"

"I'm not sure I want the answer to this question, but what else did she say?" Joel asked.

"That's just it. She wouldn't say anything. She thought there were issues you needed to sort out for yourself and told me to ask you if I wanted to know what those issues were," Nell explained.

"What sort of issues?" Joel asked, deliberately skirting round the subject.

"You must know what she's talking about, Joel. Whatever it is has caused two people in love to separate. I know you still love her.

I can see it in your eyes and she certainly still loves you with all her heart," Nell revealed. "It's tragic if you can't sort out your differences and get on with spending your lives together."

Joel sat in silence. His mind was in turmoil. He thought he had solved his problems before they left the UK, but now they had suddenly resurfaced, seemingly out of the blue. He didn't know what he should do. The main issue was his child, whose existence ought not to have been public knowledge. The other issue was the dope. Sheralyn had become party to that knowledge and that of the child because of his own stupidity and irresponsibility. Should he tell his mother what happened nine years ago? He sighed deeply. "There are things that happened a long time ago that have had some bearing on how Sheralyn regards me," he told Nell.

"What sort of things?"

"I'm not sure that telling you now will help."

Nell paled. A few weeks ago she had a similar conversation with Sean and decided that Joel should never be told the real truth about her life as a drunk. Now, it was obvious that Joel had secrets, too, that he didn't want to disclose.

"If Sheralyn knows, then what could be so wrong in telling me?" she asked plaintively.

Joel's expression was full of pain and pathos. "I made a promise to a friend that I would never divulge the information, but when you were in Sydney, I smoked dope and in my dazed ramblings, I broke that promise. Sheralyn heard me."

Nell was stunned. "You smoked pot in my home? How could you be so stupid? Was Sheralyn here to see it?"

"No, she wasn't invited. I organised a party for the crew and she didn't come, but she arrived the following morning when the others had gone home. I was totally spaced out and was apparently rambling in my sleep." He felt that revealing this would perhaps relieve some of the guilt he was feeling.

"I don't know what to say," Nell admitted.

"You can't say much really, can you, Mum? It would be rather like the pan calling the kettle..." he said.

"That's pretty much below the belt, Joel, and you know it," Nell chastised him. "It would be pointless to lose our tempers just now, but, face it, Joel, we haven't been honest about all the tensions between us for years."

"If you want honesty, you can have it, but you have to remember that truth hurts and we have protected each other from the more brutal truth during the past few years. It doesn't need a super-brain to work that out," he declared.

"Does tact have any bearing on this conversation?" Nell asked.

"I would hope so, Mum. We don't have to be deliberately hurtful, but some of this soul-searching might be upsetting for both of us." Joel's voice was very gentle. He was feeling very vulnerable and was sure his mother was too. "I don't want to hurt you, Mum. I'll go first if you like..."

Nell sat in silence as he related his days in Liverpool, the Connollys, The Cabin including the green door and the Powells. He left his dalliance with Belinda until last.

"I didn't love her. We just got carried away on the wave of excitement, but she liked me and I didn't feel inclined to reciprocate, if you know what I mean..."

"Oh, Joel," Nell whispered, "I did so try to get you to treat girls nicely..."

"But I didn't treat her badly other than rejecting her..." He paused, not for effect, but to gather his thoughts. "And how many times had I been dumped? It didn't seem like a big deal to me at the time. I was honest with her about how I felt."

"So why is it bothering you now? Have you realised that you love her after all? I'm trying to make sense of all of this."

"She got pregnant."

"Oh, my God!" Nell cried. "You're a father?"

"Well, yes and no," he confessed. "I got her pregnant, but Ben's the father."

Nell was confused. "I don't understand. You fathered a child, but Ben's the father? It doesn't make sense."

"Ben loved Belinda all along and he picked up the pieces when I did a runner. He told me to stay out of their lives and he put his name on the birth certificate. It sound's futile now, but it's the truth."

"And now you would like to claim your child? Oh, Joel, what a bloody mess!" Nell declared.

"No, I don't want to claim the child. I never did and Ben is the perfect father. We made our peace when he came to view the house," Joel told her.

"But..."

"I know what you're going to say, why did I talk about it when I was high? Well, I don't know. I guess it was in my subconscious. I really don't want to disrupt the child's life nine years on, nor would I ever come between Ben and Belinda. I still feel comfortable with the decision I made."

"Does Sheralyn know all this?" Nell asked.

"Of course not. She just picked up that I had a child she thinks I abandoned and in a way I guess she's right, but it's not so simple," he reasoned. "Her problem is more that I haven't slept with her. She thinks I don't love her, but I do."

"Once bitten, twice shy, Joel? But there's always the pill these days," Nell acknowledged. "You should explain to her, though. I think she'll understand. Don't have secrets between you. Sean and I exposed our innermost secrets when I was in Sydney. We both felt the need to do so before we could totally trust each other again."

"I'll see. I'll have to give it time. I would hate to bare my soul and then have her still reject me. Now, what do you have to tell me?"

Thirty

"I'll have to leave most of the planning to you, darling," Sean told Nell. "My diary is full right up to two days before the wedding and I can't delay any of the scheduled operations. But you leave the honeymoon to me. I have booked a month off from December eighteenth and my secretary will act according to my instructions."

"Just be here on the twentieth and I'll be happy," Nell said. "Joel is being very helpful and I have the catering in hand. Jean is making our cake, her gift to us. She's makes wonderful mud cake and her decorating skills are very professional."

"Sounds like you have it all in order. Now why doesn't that surprise me?" He laughed and bid her farewell.

They had gained permission to have the ceremony under a gazebo on the riverbank and the reception would be in a marquee erected in Nell's back yard. Sheralyn had been a frequent visitor to the South Perth house, but had strategically managed to avoid Joel until the day before Sean was due to arrive.

"I'll get it," Joel called when the doorbell rang. He didn't need to be at the studio until after lunch and had helped Nell with some of the necessary household chores in preparation for the onslaught of visitors. "Oh," he said as he opened the door and then for a moment it was as though time stood still.

Sheralyn bristled. "I didn't think you'd be here," she said, her tone surprisingly confident, "otherwise I wouldn't have come." She didn't sound angry, merely reconciled to what had happened between them.

Joel acted on impulse. "Come with me," he invited as he took her hand and led her across the deck and down the steps into a beautifully prepared garden, across manicured lawns towards where the marquee was being erected by skilful, tanned men in green work shorts and big bush hats to protect them from the sun. He guided her towards the bench that faced the river and indicated that she should take a seat.

"We need to talk," he said, "We've put it off for too long."

"What makes you think I want to talk to you?" she responded, not with animosity, more with unexpected calm.

"It's a risk I'm prepared to take, so I hope you'll listen." Joel moved to sit on the bench, but made sure there was distance between them. "I owe you an explanation."

Sheralyn sighed. "I'm not sure that any explanation will excuse your past, Joel..."

"Please," Joel pleaded. "Let me try at least..." He began by telling her about his strained relationship with his mother, his time at the Connolly house and the simple facts about Belinda. "We were eighteen years old and we just got carried away in the heat of the moment. I never led her to believe I was in love with her, because I wasn't."

"But you abandoned her when she fell pregnant."

"I know that's what it looks like and to a point it's true, but I didn't know about the baby until weeks later," Joel explained. "During that time, my best mate, Ben had begun a relationship with her and told me to keep the hell away. He was the one who told me about the baby. They're married now and Ben's named as the father on the birth certificate. He wants it that way. The child, a little girl called Kimberley, is officially his and he asked me to be happy for him."

"And you can live with that?" Sheralyn asked incredulously.

"I know how it must appear to you. It seems that I am a heartless, not to mention gutless, cad who had his way with a girl and ignored her when she got pregnant. I can't deny that on the surface that's what it was, but I never felt any emotional attachment to Belinda, or to the child," Joel confessed. "What is so wrong with stepping out of the square and facing facts? Sins of the flesh—pure and simple." He didn't sound like the male chauvinist Sheralyn expected; rather, she heard a sympathetic understanding that surprised her greatly.

"You make it sound so clinical," she stated. "This is a child we're talking about, your child. I'm having a hard time seeing beyond the cold, hard truth of this."

"Look, Sher, Ben loves Belinda and he loves Kimberley. I might be her father, but Ben is her daddy. We made our peace before I came out here. He and Bel bought our house in Bolton." Joel was struggling to put his feelings into words. "I was young and irresponsible. I'm not proud of what I did, but I had to stand back and decide what was best for the child. I could have made a fuss years later when I found out Belinda didn't have a termination, but I didn't. I don't want to ruin their lives now. They are a family and have had another child since I left."

"Put like that, it doesn't sound quite so bad," she told him. "I wish you'd told me at the outset of our relationship. I think I understand now why making love to me was always a big deal for you, but there are ways to avoid pregnancy these days and we should have talked about it." She paused. "And then there's the little situation with the dope..."

"I'm sorry," he said, "really sorry. No excuses, I should never have accepted the spliff. I'd been down that road before and I knew what I was doing. And while I'm baring my soul, I had smoked the remains of the joints just before you turned up that morning."

"How could I ever trust you, Joel?'

"I'll just have to earn it," he said with conviction. "I love you, Sher. I have never felt like this and I want to be with you. You were the one person who kept my feet on the ground, well, you and Gerry Connolly. He's the most grounded person I have ever met. Calls a spade a spade and is always honestly, but tactfully blunt."

"I'd like to meet him sometime," she said. "I might need to ask for his advice when you get out of line."

"Does that mean...?"

She nodded and moved closer to him. "Mates?" she asked quietly.

He took her in his arms. "More than mates, darl, much more."

~ * ~

Nell had been busy for months. Her telephone bill would be extortionate and she hoped Joel wouldn't investigate. She made sure she was first to the mailbox each morning when she thought it was due.

"My telephone bill will be colossal," she told Sean during one of their daily conversations.

"Blame me, Nell, if needs be," he reassured her. "Joel will think we've been talking too long. And don't worry. Everything will be okay."

"I promised never to interfere in his life again, though," she said guiltily, "and I've done it in a big way this time. If it all goes wrong, he'll never forgive me."

"Who else have you told?" Sean asked gently.

"Nobody. I couldn't risk telling anybody else except you although I've been tempted to tell Jean on a couple of occasions, but she's the world's worst secret keeper. I did ask her to make a rich fruit cake as well as the mud cake. I told her I'd need to send some to the UK. That should cover everything, and the caterers just need final numbers a week before," she informed him. "Now that it's getting close, I'm really nervous."

"Don't be," Sean told her. "It'll be fine."

Nell's job at the real estate agency was coming to a close. Her decision to move to Sydney after the wedding had not come as a surprise to anybody. Bonnington and Rimmer had given her glowing references and her résumé had been forwarded to their counterparts in Sydney.

"Will you help to install the camp beds in the guest rooms?" she asked Joel as they had breakfast the day before Sean was due to arrive.

"No problem," he replied. "How many of Sean's guests will need accommodation? Are they staying here, or in a hotel?"

"Some will stay here and others at The Royal." It was only a little white lie, but it was accepted.

When the doorbell rang, Joel called out to her that he would answer it and she caught sight of the young couple walking hand in hand across the garden towards the marquee. "Thank you, God," she whispered up to the heavens. "Step one accomplished."

When they returned to the house, she feigned surprise. "Well, well, you two," she cooed, "is this what I think it is?"

"Could be," Joel disclosed, "but we're going very slowly. I need to prove to this beautiful person that I'm serious about making her happy."

Sheralyn smiled shyly at Nell. "You said that love would find a way and I guess it has. No need to worry about your wedding ceremony now, Nell. We'll be the perfect guests."

"I know you will," Nell told her. "What brought you here today? I thought you said you had to work this morning."

"They changed my shift and I wanted to make sure my dress had arrived. I had my final fitting last weekend," Sheralyn said. "I thought Joel would be at the studio, but…" She paused and grinned. "…I'm glad he wasn't!"

"The dresses aren't being delivered until tomorrow and the flowers on Saturday morning. I have so much to do tomorrow, but I don't want you here until Saturday," Nell informed her. "I'm even sending Joel away to stay at The Royal with Sean and some of his family. It's really exciting that his parents and his brothers are all coming over to see him tie the knot. They're in Sydney already."

"Sounds wonderful. I'm looking forward to it much more now that Joel and I are together again." Sheralyn looked lovingly at the young man who had taken her to hell and back during the past few months. "We have a lot of time to catch up."

He blew a kiss and said, "I love you."

"Love you, too. Will you meet me at the hospital after my shift? I finish at eleven," she asked.

"I'll be there," he said. "Now come on, we have camp beds to install."

Sean arrived with his family the following day, and Nell had planned a barbecue with Jean and Donnie and now Sheralyn and Joel. At the end of the evening, she politely ushered them out of the house.

"Tomorrow is my busiest day," she told them. "Much as I would love to see you, I have to put an embargo on the lot of you, Joel included. I need the house to myself."

Sean was very supportive. "All right, darling, I'll keep them entertained all day. You and I can't see each other anyway. Bad luck and all that," he joked, "and I think we've had our share of that already."

"I'm recording all day tomorrow," Joel informed them, "but I'll go straight to The Royal from the studio. I'll have to keep an eye on my future step-father and make sure he doesn't get drunk …whoops, sorry, Mum, bad joke."

Nell looked at him pointedly. "No problem, darl. Just because I can't drink doesn't prevent Sean from having a glass of wine if he wants to. I trust him." She looked at her husband-to-be with great affection.

Friday was Nell's V-Day. Her planning of the past few months was due to come to fruition and she woke up that morning with a mixture of fear and excited anticipation. The day began well and the first part of her project went off without a hitch. Her co-conspirators were ensconced in South Perth and informed of the procedure for the following day. Their instructions had to be carried out to the letter for her plan to meet with success.

On Saturday morning, the flowers arrived early before Nell went to the hairdresser's with Sheralyn. By eleven o'clock, they were in the kitchen drinking coffee with Jean, who had placed the cakes on the plinths by the side of the bridal table. They chatted excitedly about the future and how much Nell would be missed when she moved to Sydney.

"I'll be back to visit often," she told them. "This house is Joel's now. I signed it over to him last week. He doesn't know yet, so no telling secrets, you two. I have to choose the right time to tell him."

The guests made their way to the gazebo soon after lunch. The ceremony was to take place at three o'clock, but champagne cocktails and soft drinks were being served from two-thirty. Nell and Sheralyn changed in Nell's room and her plans seemed to be working well. At two-fifty exactly, the Rolls Royce Silver Shadow arrived at the house to transport the bride and her witness to the perfect location on the river. Behind was a stretch limo following at a discreet distance.

"You look beautiful, Nell," Sheralyn whispered as they walked down the drive to the car.

"So do you," Nell said. "I'd better make sure you don't steal the show." She laughed nervously.

Sheralyn was dressed in the palest blue silk, which complimented her fair skin and enhanced the blue of her eyes. The strapless gown flowed gracefully over her slim body and her face shone with confidence.

Nell had insisted that Joel should be with Sean at the front of the congregation. She had considered that he might give her away in the traditional way, but decided she would like to walk alone along the red carpet to meet Sean before a flower-strewn altar.

"This is a journey I began on my own," she explained, "but it ends with the man of my dreams waiting to carry me off into the sunset. I want Joel to be there to support him and to remember that we are now a family."

"That's so romantic, Nell," Sheralyn commented. "You are so thoughtful and sensitive."

Sean gasped as he turned to watch Nell walk down the red carpet in a beautiful ivory silk gown that draped her still slim figure in delicate folds. The diamante-encrusted fitted bodice with shoestring straps sparkled in the sunshine and her chestnut curls flecked with tiny diamante-centred roses, framed her lovely face. To the tune of "True Love," made famous by Bing Crosby, she glided into the arms of the man she thought she had lost.

She stood between Sean and Joel, the two most important men in her life, as she said her vows and listened to Sean declaring his love to the world.

"Nell, I need you to know that I found the love of my life when I met you. Our road has been a rocky one, but everything comes to him who waits. I waited and waited until I found my everything in you. I love you and always will. Today our life together begins and will truly last forever."

The celebrant had necessarily been included in the plan earlier. As soon as the ceremony was over, Nell signalled to the musicians to play as arranged for the guests of honour to make their entrance. "When you walk through a storm, hold your head up high and don't be afraid of the dark..." It was the song made famous by Gerry Marsden and adopted by the Liverpool Football Club supporters as their anthem. "...and you'll never walk alone. You'll never walk alone."

Joel turned round to see what was happening. The significance of the Liverpool connection was not lost on him. At the far end of the red carpet were Dafydd and Megan Powell followed by Gerry and Penny Connolly with the two-year-old Robbie.

Joel was stunned and looked at his mother. "Forgive me, darling. I've taken charge again for the final time. I thought we could make this a double wedding." She beckoned to Sheralyn to come and stand with Joel.

"Are we up for it?" Joel asked the ravishingly beautiful girl by his side. He looked questioningly at Sheralyn's father, whose face was a picture of joy, and he nodded vehemently.

"Why not?" she said, smiling happily.

They turned to face the celebrant, their hands clasped tightly.

"There's just a couple more things," Nell told him, "before we can continue."

Joel took a deep breath and regarded his mother with a mixture of shock and bewilderment.

"This envelope contains the deeds of the house. As from today it belongs to you and Sheralyn, a home in which you can raise your children and secondly..."

The music started again—"It's very clear, our love is here to stay. Not for a year, forever and a day..."

Nell turned and pointed to the end of the red carpet. There was a very pretty little girl dressed in pink walking slowly in front of her parents and her little brother. She scattered rose petals before her as she moved forward. Kimberley Mason had travelled all the way from Bolton, England, to be bridesmaid at her uncle's wedding...

Meet

Vera Berry Burrows

Vera Berry-Burrows is a UK-born former teacher of English Language and Literature, living in Queensland, Australia with journalist husband, Alan. She has a son and two grandsons living in the UK. She has been writing for a number of years and has had numerous non-fiction articles published in the UK and in Australia. She was educated at Farnworth Grammar School in Lancashire, trained as a teacher at St Katharine's College, Liverpool and gained a Bachelor of Arts degree with the Open University.

Since she took early retirement in 1994 having been in the teaching profession for thirty one years, writing has become her compulsive hobby. *Tomorrow Never Comes* is her first novel, but not her last. Several other writing projects are in the pipeline including *A Life In And Out Of Order -a rivetingly interesting autobiography of a nobody.* In her own words, "Look at what life has brought your way and tell a story."

Works by Vera Berry Burrows

Tomorrow Never Comes - Marriage, a new home and a new baby, Joel Thomas, all make up a perfect life for Nell Winston until suddenly her husband is no longer there and she turns into a woman possessed of compulsion to rule her son. Her strength is drawn from her unwavering sense to control until the young Joel decides to make a stand against her. Her domineering, self-absorption, along with egotistical stubbornness, takes her into a life that becomes her worst nightmare.

Joel's apparently selfish show of independence leads him along an extremely rocky road to eventual success in the Swinging 60's and with a complete reversal of roles, he takes charge of his mother's life. Will the new start in a different country bring the fulfillment they are both seeking?

Regarding Kimberley - Show business executive Kimberley Mason always felt something was missing from her life. She forms an association with a theatrical agency in Australia and uncovers a secret kept by her parents for thirty years. Revelations about her birth shatter her world. Discovering her real father is Australian television celebrity Joel Winston, she cuts herself off from the family she had always thought to be perfect

Leaving behind her past in England, she moves to Australia to be with the man she loves, her business partner, Simon Obertelli. Will running away ensure her future happiness or will the complications of accepting her famous father only lead to heartache?

Connections - Jane O'Connell did not envisage that her early retirement would completely disrupt her life. With too much time on her hands, she finds it difficult to adjust to her new existence. In her obstinate selfishness, she alienates herself from her family and friends. Running away from all things familiar appears to be her only option, but is it? Will the connections she makes really solve the problems she encounters in her life after work?

Family Matters - For three children left without a mother in the middle of World War Two, survival was all they could hope for. Their father struggled as a single parent, but instilled into his children, determination, ambition and self-respect so that they might succeed in post-war years and achieve everything which he was denied during his life.

This is their story.

My Name is Aphrodite - Rodi Bartlett sits on a plane taking her to the land of her conception. She can't call it the land of her birth because when her mother was sixteen years old, she had flown back to England from Corfu at the end of two weeks in the sun, unaware she was pregnant. When her mother, Adele dies young, details of the father, Cory Demetriou are exposed in her will and he has never been told of his daughter's existence.

Rodi's relentless search for the father she has never known, takes her to Corfu, mainland Greece and beyond. Filled with determination, setbacks, hope and love, this is the story of a young woman's quest to fulfil her mother's dying wish, but will Cory Demetriou accept her as his daughter twenty-six years on?

Dare To Dream - Left on the doorstep of St Anthony's Catholic Orphanage in Bolton, Northern England, Anne Marie O'Shea is placed in the guiding hands of another orphan named Bella Jones. As the years pass by, Bella accepts her lot for what it is; Annie dreams of a wonderful life, that special bit of magic that everybody deserves. When Bella is killed in a road accident at the age of twenty, Annie is left to fend for herself, to make decisions about her future and combat all the fears she has about forming lasting relationships. With numerous ups and downs, nurse training and emigration to Australia, a series of unbelievable co-incidences eventually puts the magic in her life that she could previously only dream about.

Payback - Julietta's holiday becomes a nightmare when she is swept up in the frenzy of other people's abhorrent need for revenge.

A Message to Our Readers

Enjoy this book?

You can make a difference.

As an independent publisher, Wings ePress, Inc. does not have the financial clout of the large New York publishers. We can't afford large magazine spreads or subway posters to tell people about our quality books.

But we do have something much more effective and powerful than ads. We have a large base of loyal readers.

Honest reviews help bring the attention of new readers to our books.

If you enjoyed this book, we would appreciate it if you would spend a few minutes posting a review on the site where you purchased this book or on the Wings ePress, Inc. webpages at:

https://wingsepress.com/

Thank You